The New York Times

IN THE HEADLINES
Vaping
BIG BUSINESS

THE NEW YORK TIMES EDITORIAL STAFF

Published in 2020 by New York Times Educational Publishing in association with The Rosen Publishing Group, Inc.
29 East 21st Street, New York, NY 10010

Contains material from The New York Times and is reprinted by permission. Copyright © 2020 The New York Times. All rights reserved.

Rosen Publishing materials copyright © 2020 The Rosen Publishing Group, Inc. All rights reserved. Distributed exclusively by Rosen Publishing.

First Edition

The New York Times
Caroline Que: Editorial Director, Book Development
Phyllis Collazo: Photo Rights/Permissions Editor
Heidi Giovine: Administrative Manager

Rosen Publishing
Megan Kellerman: Managing Editor
Julia Bosson: Editor
Greg Tucker: Creative Director
Brian Garvey: Art Director

Cataloging-in-Publication Data
Names: New York Times Company.
Title: Vaping: big business / edited by the New York Times editorial staff.
Description: New York : The New York Times Educational Publishing, 2020. | Series: In the headlines | Includes glossary and index.
Identifiers: ISBN 9781642823691 (library bound) | ISBN 9781642823684 (pbk.) | ISBN 9781642823707 (ebook)
Subjects: LCSH: Vaping—Juvenile literature. | Electronic cigarettes—Juvenile literature. | Smoking—Health aspects—Juvenile literature. | Youth—Tobacco use—Juvenile literature.
Classification: LCC HV5748.V375 2020 | DDC 362.29'6—dc23

Manufactured in the United States of America

On the cover: After making billions of dollars and joining forces with Big Tobacco, Juul is trying to reinvent itself as a public-health crusader; Caroline Tompkins/The New York Times.

Contents

7 Introduction

CHAPTER 1

The Rise of Vaping

10 The E-Cigarette Industry, Waiting to Exhale BY MATT RICHTEL

22 Where Vapor Comes Sweeping Down the Plain BY MATT RICHTEL

33 E-Cigarette Makers Are in an Arms Race for Exotic Vapor Flavors BY MATT RICHTEL

38 'Vape' Joins Pot Lingo as Oxford's Word of the Year
BY JESSICA BENNETT

40 Feeling Let Down and Left Behind, With Little Hope for Better
BY RICHARD FAUSSET

49 A Lobbyist Wrote the Bill. Will the Tobacco Industry Win Its E-Cigarette Fight? BY ERIC LIPTON

55 From 0 to 10 Million: Vaping Takes Off in the U.S.
BY NICHOLAS BAKALAR

57 Q&A: The ABCs of E-Cigarettes BY JAN HOFFMAN

CHAPTER 2

Safe to Vape?

61 A Hot Debate Over E-Cigarettes as a Path to Tobacco, or From It BY SABRINA TAVERNISE

67 Race to Deliver Nicotine's Punch, With Less Risk BY BARRY MEIER

73 Is Vaping Worse Than Smoking? BY JOE NOCERA

76 Smoking, Vaping and Nicotine BY JOE NOCERA

79 Can E-Cigarettes Save Lives? BY JOE NOCERA

82 Smokers Urged to Switch to E-Cigarettes by British Medical Group BY SABRINA TAVERNISE

85 E-Cigarettes Are Safer, but Not Exactly Safe BY AARON E. CARROLL

88 Safer to Puff, E-Cigarettes Can't Shake Their Reputation as a Menace BY SABRINA TAVERNISE

93 Some Older Smokers Turn to Vaping. That May Not Be a Bad Idea. BY PAULA SPAN

97 She Couldn't Quit Smoking. Then She Tried Juul. BY JAN HOFFMAN

CHAPTER 3

The Risks of Vaping

103 Selling a Poison by the Barrel: Liquid Nicotine for E-Cigarettes BY MATT RICHTEL

107 Some E-Cigarettes Deliver a Puff of Carcinogens BY MATT RICHTEL

112 Dire Warnings by Big Tobacco on E-Smoking BY MATT RICHTEL

117 Vaping Can Be Addictive and May Lure Teenagers to Smoking, Science Panel Concludes BY SHEILA KAPLAN

122 This May Be a First: Exploding Vape Pen Kills a Florida Man
BY JACEY FORTIN

124 Vaping Is Big Tobacco's Bait and Switch BY JENEEN INTERLANDI

128 First Death in a Spate of Vaping Sicknesses Reported by Health Officials BY MATT RICHTEL AND SHEILA KAPLAN

CHAPTER 4

Teens Vaping

132 E-Cigarettes, by Other Names, Lure Young and Worry Experts
BY MATT RICHTEL

137 E-Cigarette Use by U.S. Teenagers Rose Last Year, Report Says
BY SABRINA TAVERNISE

140 Plain Old Vaping Gives Way to 'Dripping' Among Teenagers, Study Says BY JACEY FORTIN

143 Marijuana and Vaping Are More Popular Than Cigarettes Among Teenagers BY JAN HOFFMAN

146 'I Can't Stop': Schools Struggle With Vaping Explosion
BY KATE ZERNIKE

152 Did Juul Lure Teenagers and Get 'Customers for Life'?
BY MATT RICHTEL AND SHEILA KAPLAN

163 Addicted to Vaped Nicotine, Teenagers Have No Clear Path to Quitting BY JAN HOFFMAN

CHAPTER 5

Trying to Quit

170 F.D.A. Imposes Rules for E-Cigarettes in a Landmark Move
BY SABRINA TAVERNISE

175 New York State Bans Vaping Anywhere Cigarettes Are Prohibited
BY SARAH MASLIN NIR

177 Vaping Products That Look Like Juice Boxes and Candy Are Target of Crackdown BY KATIE THOMAS

180 San Francisco Voters Uphold Ban on Flavored Vaping Products
BY JAN HOFFMAN

184 Altria to Stop Selling Some E-Cigarette Brands That Appeal to Youths BY SHEILA KAPLAN

188 Juul Suspends Selling Most E-Cigarette Flavors in Stores
BY SHEILA KAPLAN AND JAN HOFFMAN

194 The Price of Cool: A Teenager, a Juul and Nicotine Addiction
BY JAN HOFFMAN

203 How to Help Teenagers Quit Vaping BY JAN HOFFMAN

207 F.D.A. Accuses Juul and Altria of Backing Off Plan to Stop Youth Vaping BY SHEILA KAPLAN

212 Glossary
214 Media Literacy Terms
216 Media Literacy Questions
218 Citations
222 Index

Introduction

FIFTY YEARS AGO, cigarettes were a major part of American culture. Men and women smoked on airplanes, in restaurants and in movie theaters. However, after years of warnings by researchers and public health activists on the health risks associated with tobacco use, cigarette smoking has been on the decline. As the anti-tobacco lobby has increased in prominence and the addictive qualities of cigarettes have become better understood, the question remains: What can be done to help smokers quit? E-cigarettes, which operate by vaporizing liquid nicotine (otherwise known as "vaping"), have been presented as one solution: They allow those dependent on nicotine to move away from cigarettes and to take up a habit without the health risks associated with tobacco cigarettes. They have even received the approval of the British Medical Association, which suggested that vaping may be a safer alternative to smoking.

And yet, as vaping has helped smokers quit, it has also drawn in a new generation of smokers who now find themselves addicted to e-cigarettes. This has disproportionately affected teenagers, who have taken to vaping in large numbers. E-cigarettes are easy to conceal and lack the pungency of cigarettes, making the habit easy to hide from parents. The rise in vaping among young people has led to a concern among public health advocates, who explain that nicotine can actually disrupt brain development in young people and make it harder to quit down the road.

As vaping has grown in popularity, so have questions about its safety. Originally heralded for their ability to deliver nicotine without the tar, formaldehyde and other additives that are part of tobacco cigarettes, e-cigarettes are still being studied, and the long-term

JASON HENRY FOR THE NEW YORK TIMES

James Monsees, co-founder and chief executive of Juul, holds his Juul at the company headquarters in San Francisco, May 17, 2018.

consequences of their use remains to be seen. There are dozens of substances in vaping products whose impact is still largely unknown. The fact is, e-cigarettes are vehicles for the delivery of nicotine, a highly addictive substance that comes with its own health risks. In fact, e-cigarettes can deliver an even higher concentration of nicotine than traditional cigarettes.

The rise of vaping has led to a booming e-cigarette industry. Altria, the parent company of Philip Morris, was one of the early pioneers of smokeless nicotine, working to ensure that Big Tobacco wouldn't be left out of the market. However, Altria's products were quickly surpassed by Juul, a vaping company based in San Francisco whose products have grown in popularity to the degree that "juuling" has become almost synonymous with vaping. The rise of this multibillion-dollar industry has led many to wonder about the ethics of profiting from introducing addictive products into the market.

Now, the federal government and local communities are scrambling to respond to the surge in vaping. Federal regulators have set age limits to prevent young people from obtaining vaping products. They are also considering banning flavored products that are marketed to young people. Schools and parents, struggling to stay on top of the issue, are leading vaping education workshops to highlight the potential health risks associated with frequent vaping and e-cigarette use. Some have even resorted to monitoring how many students enter the bathrooms at one time, to discourage the sharing of e-cigarettes.

Much is unknown about the future of vaping. Once the science on the health risks of vaping becomes clearer, researchers will have to decide whether e-cigarettes are helpful tools or dangers in their own right. And as one generation of smokers finds refuge from the tyranny of cigarettes and another finds its way into a new addiction, the vaping industry will continue to expand and profit.

CHAPTER 1

The Rise of Vaping

In the early 2010s, after years of battles between public health advocates and the tobacco industry, a new product began to make its presence felt across America: e-cigarettes. Using vaporized nicotine that lacked the tar or additives that made cigarettes particularly carcinogenic, e-cigarettes promised to reshape the face of the tobacco industry. The articles in this chapter follow the meteoric rise of vaping.

The E-Cigarette Industry, Waiting to Exhale

BY MATT RICHTEL | OCT. 26, 2013

GEOFF VULETA was in the crowd at a Rolling Stones concert last year when Keith Richards lit up a cigarette on stage, the arena's no-smoking policy be damned. Feeling inspired, Mr. Vuleta, a longtime smoker, reached into his pocket and pulled one out himself. People seated nearby shot him scolding glances as he inhaled. So he withdrew the cigarette from his mouth and pressed the glowing end to his cheek.

His was an electronic cigarette, a look-alike that delivers nicotine without combusting tobacco and produces a vapor, not smoke. Mr. Vuleta, 51, who has a sardonic humor, clearly relished recounting this story. He is the chief marketing officer for NJOY, an electronic cigarette company based in Scottsdale, Ariz., and it is his job to reframe how everyone, nonsmokers included, view the habit of inhaling from a thin stick and blowing out a visible cloud.

Mr. Vuleta, who told his tale in the office of Craig Weiss, the NJOY chief executive, calls this a process of "renormalizing," so that smokers can come back in from the cold. He means that literally — allowing people now exiled to the sidewalks back into buildings with e-cigarettes. But he also means it metaphorically. Early in the last century, smoking was an accepted alternative for men to chewing tobacco; for women, it was daring and transgressive. Then, in midcentury, it became the norm. As the dangers of tobacco — and the scandalous behavior of tobacco companies in concealing those dangers — became impossible to ignore, smoking took on a new identity: societal evil.

Mr. Vuleta and Mr. Weiss want to make "vaping," as e-cigarette smoking is known in the industry, acceptable. Keith Richards might still be smoking tobacco, but in Mr. Vuleta's vision, that grizzled guitarist's gesture could inspire the audience, en masse, to pull out e-cigarettes. "The moment Keith Richards does it," he said, "everyone else does, too."

Mr. Vuleta's words are more exuberant than the official company line, which is that NJOY doesn't want everyone to smoke e-cigarettes but only to convert the 40 million Americans who now smoke tobacco. The customers NJOY attracts, and how it attracts them, are at the center of a new public health debate, not to mention a rush to control the e-cigarette business.

At stake is a vaping market that has grown in a few short years to around $1.7 billion in sales in the United States. That is tiny when compared to the nation's $90 billion cigarette market. But one particularly bullish Wall Street analyst projects that consumption of e-cigarettes will outstrip regular ones in the next decade.

NJOY was one of the first companies to sell e-cigarettes; now there are 200 in the United States, most of them small. Just last year, however, Big Tobacco got into the game when Lorillard acquired Blu, an e-cigarette brand, and demonstrated its economic power. Within months, relying on Lorillard's decades-old distribution channels, Blu displaced NJOY as the market leader.

FRED R. CONRAD/THE NEW YORK TIMES

An NJOY e-cigarette. A pioneer in its industry, NJOY now has 200 rivals, including major tobacco companies.

Mr. Weiss still sees NJOY as having an advantage — in building e-cigarettes that look, feel and perform like the real thing. It's a different strategy than that of competing products that look like long silver tubes or sleek, blinking fountain pens.

"We're trying to do something very challenging: change a habit that is not only entrenched but one people are willing to take to their grave," said Mr. Weiss, who is not a smoker but has tried both regular and e-cigarettes. "To accomplish that, we have to narrow as much as possible the bridge to familiarity. We have to make it easy for smokers to cross it."

To some, though not all, in public health, that vision sounds ill-conceived, if not threatening. Among their concerns is that making smoking-like behavior O.K. again will undo decades of work demonizing smoking itself. Far from leading to more smoking cessation, they argue, e-cigarettes will ultimately revive it, and abet new cases of emphysema, heart disease and lung cancer.

"The very thing that could make them effective is also their greatest danger," said Dr. Tim McAfee, director of Office on Smoking and Health at the Centers for Disease Control and Prevention.

To achieve his ends, Mr. Weiss is building a company of strange bedfellows. He has hired former top tobacco industry executives, but also attracted a former surgeon general, Dr. Richard H. Carmona, who has joined the board. NJOY recently hired away a prominent professor of chemistry and genomics from Princeton to be the company's chief scientist. The company has attracted investment from Sean Parker, the former Facebook president, and Peter Thiel, the PayPal co-founder. There has also been a celebrity endorsement from the singer Bruno Mars.

Mr. Weiss sees his company as doing something epic. Not long after he was named its president in June 2010, he asked his psychologist if he might record his regular sessions. It was an unusual request, but he thinks that recording his thoughts might ultimately help him write a book or movie script about how he and the company made the cigarette obsolete.

"We're at this incredible inflection point in history," he said, adding that the company has a chance to "make the single most beneficial impact on society in this century."

Over dinner at Federal Pizza, a trendy place in Phoenix owned by a close friend, Mr. Weiss put a Camel Crush cigarette onto a table beside an NJOY King. "These are almost identical," he says, "but we still have a ways to go."

The two sticks on the table were roughly the same size. But NJOY's weighs around 5 grams, more than twice as much as the Camel. When squeezed, the NJOY isn't as spongy, and it lacks the Camel's fragrance (though a nimbus of tobacco bouquet emerges when you open the pack). The tip is plastic with an LED glow, not real fire, and it produces no ash.

These distinctions can mean everything to heavy smokers for whom each detail in the smoking ritual — a "moment in the day," as

Mr. Vuleta summarizes the experience of each cigarette — adds up to something exquisite.

"Smokers talk about a 'throat hit,' " Mr. Weiss explained as he sipped a strawberry wine cooler over pizza, referring to a tickle or slight burn at the back of the throat, a part of the overall Pavlovian experience that comes before the nicotine rush. It's something, he said, that the company's products are becoming better at imitating, along with changing the chemistry inside the e-cigarette so that nicotine is absorbed more quickly by the body, more like the real thing. But it is not there yet.

The NJOY King, which sells for $7.99, is disposable and tries to deliver as much nicotine as a pack of 20 cigarettes; other kinds of e-cigarettes are rechargeable, their nicotine fluid refills costing around $3 or $4.

If the NJOY and a regular cigarette look similar on the outside, the inside is another story. Inside the e-cigarette's polycarbonate tube casing is an integrated circuit, a small computer chip. Then comes a lithium-ion battery and a wick wrapped in cotton soaked in a mixture of nicotine and a carrier liquid of glycerol and propylene glycol. The battery is turned on when the user drags on the stick, heating the gadget's inside to around 180 degrees and turning the nicotine into vapor. When inhaled, it leaves the throat with an "ambient feel," Mr. Weiss calls it — a caress, not the desired throat hit.

Not all e-cigarette companies embrace experiential authenticity the way NJOY does, and some make a deliberate effort at difference. NJOY executives like to mock the more exotic efforts. "An e-cigarette that doesn't look like a cigarette, but looks like a silver tube with a white light at the end, is anything but an exquisite experience," said Roy Anise, NJOY's executive vice president in charge of sales, who came to the company from Philip Morris, the tobacco company whose parent is Altria. Mr. Anise worked in the tobacco industry for 24 years, eventually in the division that sold smokeless products.

FRED R. CONRAD/THE NEW YORK TIMES

Geoff Vuleta, chief marketing officer, sampled an NJOY King.

Blu eCigs, NJOY's biggest competition, are slender black tubes, with tips that glow blue, not ember-red. Murray S. Kessler, the C.E.O. of Lorillard, which sells Blu, described the look as "edgy" and "cool" and said that, with such a look, there is a better chance to make it a "complete replacement" to the cigarette. "I don't want to emulate a cigarette," Mr. Kessler said. "The big idea isn't to try to keep people in cigarettes, but to normalize smoking e-cigarettes and vaping as the next generation."

E-cigarettes that look different, he said, could "solve the social stigma issue" and erase the tension of smoking in public places.

Doesn't that cannibalize his tobacco business? Yes, he said, it might, but he added that his shareholders "don't care whether we sell cigarettes or e-cigarettes" so long as the company maintains profits. Right now, though, real cigarettes are much more profitable, as Mr. Kessler conceded, but he said he thought that e-cigarette profit margins could grow.

Bonnie Herzog, a tobacco industry analyst at Wells Fargo who is particularly bullish on e-cigarettes, said that there was room for different e-cigarette styles. But tobacco companies have a decided edge over small companies like NJOY, she said, because of their entrenched distribution, deep pockets and databases of contact information for millions of customers.

Her assertion seems to be borne out by the success of Blu. Since being acquired by Lorillard, Blu has a convenience-store market share that has climbed to 39 percent from 12 percent in a little more than a year, while NJOY's has fallen to 30 percent from 48 percent. (NJOY expects its revenue to triple over this year to more than $100 million; Mr. Weiss declined to be more specific about sales.)

Lorillard is pushing hard, saying it will spend $40 million this year on marketing — a budget that amounts to 35 percent of the $114 million in Blu sales in the first half of the year.

Two other big tobacco companies are exploring the market. The MarkTen, from Altria, can be recharged; it is being sold in Indiana in a test. The Vuse, from the R. J. Reynolds Tobacco Company, is a long, silver model that is being tried in Colorado.

If those large companies decide to go full force into the market, they could further erode NJOY's market share, adding a business reason for Mr. Weiss to vilify the tobacco giants. One selling point of NJOY may be its likeness to real cigarettes, but another could be that it was never a tobacco company. He has brought on Mr. Anise and others with tobacco experience, he said, because success depends on relationships with convenience stores that sell cigarettes. But, unlike Mr. Kessler, Mr. Weiss can still rail against the companies that "kill half their customers."

Mr. Weiss, who turned 40 in July, didn't come to NJOY as a public health advocate or even as someone whose life was touched by the hazards of smoking. "I have no personal 'my dad died of lung cancer' type of story,' " he said. Rather, his zeal seems to be equal parts outrage and inborn entrepreneurial excitement. He obtained the first of his three patents at age 15 — it was for a net to catch tennis balls — and went on to become a lawyer before starting a hedge fund.

NJOY was started by Mr. Weiss's brother, Mark Weiss, a lawyer in Scottsdale, who was inspired by a crude version of an electronic cigar at a trade show in China in 2005. In 2009, the company faced a near-death experience when a shipment from China, where the NJOY cigarettes are made, was seized at the port of Long Beach, Calif. The Food and Drug Administration charged that the e-cigarettes were an unapproved drug-delivery device.

NJOY initially argued that it had made no health claims and therefore shouldn't be regulated. But just months after the seizure, the Family Smoking Prevention and Tobacco Control Act was passed. It gave the F.D.A. the power to regulate tobacco products, but not to ban them. (At the time, Craig Weiss was a shareholder but not part of management; he did weigh in on legal matters.) After the change in federal law, NJOY updated its legal position, arguing that nicotine is derived from tobacco, and therefore that the F.D.A. had the power to regulate e-cigarettes under the new law. In a 2010 ruling, a federal district court in Washington accepted that argument, preventing an outright ban of NJOY's product as an unregulated drug delivery device and punting the specifics of how the products should be regulated over to the F.D.A.

The F.D.A. has said it plans to issue preliminary rules for public comment on e-cigarette regulations as soon as the end of this month, but the partial government shutdown appears to have delayed that process. Earlier this month, the European Parliament endorsed limits on sponsorship and advertising of e-cigarettes, and on their sale to minors, but scrapped tougher regulations favored by some in public health that would have regulated them as tightly as medical devices.

Some critics say NJOY and other e-cigarette companies are trying to have it both ways. "When it's convenient to be like tobacco, they're like tobacco," says Stanton A. Glantz, director of the Center for Tobacco Control Research and Education at the University of California, San Francisco, "and when it's not convenient, they're not."

One day in mid-August, Dr. McAfee, the tobacco expert from the C.D.C., received an e-mail with statistics about e-cigarette use among young people. The statistics compared e-cigarette experimentation in 2012 with that of 2011, the first year the C.D.C. had collected data on the phenomenon.

Alarm bells went off the instant Dr. McAfee saw the numbers: among students in grades 6 to 12, experimentation with e-cigarettes had doubled, to 6.8 percent from 3.3 percent. Not surprisingly, the numbers were higher among high school students, 10 percent of whom reported trying an e-cigarette, more than double the share in 2011.

Within hours, Dr. McAfee called Mitch Zeller, the director of the Center for Tobacco Products of the F.D.A. As Dr. McAfee recounted his conversation, he told Mr. Zeller: "This is not business as usual."

One of the strongest predictors of whether someone becomes a lifelong smoker is how early he or she starts experimenting, and Dr. McAfee saw experimentation with e-cigarettes as a gateway to tobacco. Three weeks later, the C.D.C. issued an "emergency note from the field," a communication typically reserved for acute disease outbreaks.

From a public health perspective, e-cigarettes raise two questions: How harmful are they? And, regardless, will they lead to smoking cessation or, perversely, reinforce the tobacco smoking habit?

Most public health officials seem to agree that the levels of toxins in e-cigarettes are far lower than those in traditional cigarettes. But they also say that far too little is known, not just about potentially harmful aspects of particular brands of e-cigarettes, but also about whether there is harm from "secondhand vapor." Dr. Glantz of U.C.S.F. says that in the absence of data, indoor smoking bans should also cover e-cigarettes.

Mr. Weiss asserted that such indoor bans would eliminate a competitive advantage for e-cigarettes and thus harm the effort to normalize this alternative behavior. More broadly, he said, public policy should err on the side of giving e-cigarettes a chance, even if everything about the health effects isn't known. "This idea of saying we don't have data — that 'in the absence of data we're going to act' — is potentially condemning people to a painful and early death," he said. Public health officials who want more research before accepting vaping, he said, are "suffering from P.T.S.D. from the lies they were told by tobacco companies."

The public health officials don't disagree; in fact, they say they blew it with cigarettes by ignoring warning signs, waiting years to mount ironclad scientific proof and thus allowing a deadly habit to take hold. They are trying to learn from the past. "We can't allow e-cigarettes to establish themselves the way cigarettes did and, five years from now when all the scientific questions are answered, try to stuff the genie back in the bottle," said Dr. Glantz, who advocates tighter regulation.

Another area of sharp disagreement is the question of whether e-cigarettes really help people quit smoking. Given that electronic cigarettes aren't considered as satisfying a nicotine rush, skeptics worry further that if the e-cigarette takes hold, it will lead people to using the tobacco version.

There is no data to validate that concern, just as there is little data on cessation. Surveys suggest that e-cigarette users are quitting or cutting down on cigarettes. But one scientific study, published in September in The Lancet, a British medical journal, found that six months into smoking e-cigarettes, 7.3 percent of users had quit smoking tobacco. That was the statistical equivalent to the modestly effective patch (a quit rate of 5.8 percent).

"We were hoping for the magic bullet," said Natalie Walker, director of addiction research at the National Institute for Health Innovation in New Zealand, and one of the study's authors. "We were surprised by the low quit rate." Still, she says she thinks e-cigarettes have potential as "another tool" and notes that they have a crucial advantage over other nicotine replacement strategies: "E-cigs have a large and dedicated fan club."

Dr. Carmona, the former surgeon general who has joined NJOY's board, is not willing to accept defeat. As surgeon general, he emphasized the dangers of secondhand smoke, and e-cigarettes seem to him the best bet for a cessation device. "We don't have all the answers" he said, "but we see there is potential for this to be a very disruptive force in cessation."

Mr. Weiss favors regulation that would require companies to disclose ingredients, set manufacturing standards and prohibit sales to minors, but he objects to restrictions on marketing. At the moment, absent F.D.A. regulations, e-cigarette companies, unlike tobacco companies, can sponsor sports and entertainment events, or advertise on television.

What they can't do is make health claims; if they did, they would face regulation as a drug company. So the ads tend to be implicit, as in one that ran during the Super Bowl last year. In it, a handsome man smoked an NJOY with a voice-over that said: "You know what the most amazing thing about this cigarette is? It isn't one," and then continued, "The first electronic cigarette with the look, feel and flavor of the real thing."

Reynolds, the maker of Vuse, has a commercial that sounds much like old TV ads for cigarettes, promising "a perfect puff, first time, every time." A commercial for Blu features Jenny McCarthy complaining she doesn't like a kiss "that tastes like an ashtray."

Mr. Weiss said NJoy's Super Bowl ad prompted a 40 percent uptick in sales in the five markets where it ran. That kind of impact is why he doesn't want the F.D.A. to forbid television advertising. "Any ad restrictions that limit our ability to let smokers know they have an alternative only serves the interest of Big Tobacco," he said, because tobacco companies have such an edge on the traditional channels of distribution. He does agree, however, that there should be no advertising during children's TV shows. He declined to say how much the company spends on marketing.

The push for regulation is coming from many quarters, including a majority of the state attorneys general. Forty of them wrote a letter in September to the F.D.A., seeking "immediate regulatory oversight of e-cigarettes, an increasingly widespread, addictive product." The letter said that the nicotine in e-cigarettes "has immediate biochemical effects on the brain and body at any dosage, and is toxic in high doses."

Then, last week, the group sent a second letter reiterating its position, urging rules that would "ensure that companies do not continue to sell or advertise to our nation's youth."

In the first letter, the state attorneys general singled out NJOY's Super Bowl ad, not in its appeal to youth but the way it looked just like the thing it seeks to replace: "The advertisement depicted an attractive man smoking an e-cigarette that looked just like a real cigarette."

Mr. Weiss doesn't see a problem with this. "We want it to look exactly like a cigarette because that's how we're going to get smokers to change behavior," he said. For decades, he noted, there have been smoking alternatives, like patches and pills and gum, that were nothing like cigarettes. Going down that road, he said, is "Einstein's definition of insanity — doing the same thing over and over again and expecting a different result."

At the same time, he conceded that his strategy "creates some confusion" that "is not irrational to me, and just requires education."

"People say, if it looks like a duck, and quacks like a duck, it must be a duck."

Mr. Weiss's challenge, if he's to reach what he envisions as a place in history, will be to prove that looks can be deceiving.

Where Vapor Comes Sweeping Down the Plain

BY MATT RICHTEL | APRIL 26, 2014

NICK WHITSON, who is 32 and covered with enigmatic tattoos — the number 13, an upside-down cross — stood in front of a table scattered with dozens of bottles of colorful liquids and a handful of syringes, preparing to mix Trevor Curren his usual.

Mr. Whitson manages a small shop called Vaporlicious in an Oklahoma City strip mall. He sells flavored nicotine liquids for devices known variously as e-cigarettes, vape pens, tank systems and e-hookahs. In the last 18 months, the number of vaping shops in the state jumped from a handful to 300, with names like Vapor Haven, the Vape Hut, Vapor World, Creative Vapor and Patriotic Vapes.

In the back room of Vaporlicious, Mr. Whitson took a syringe, drew several milliliters of pomegranate-flavored liquid from a plastic container and squirted it into a small bottle. Then he injected a mixture of nicotine and two additives into the red liquid. He capped and shook the bottle, wiped his hands on his jeans and walked to the front counter. He handed the concoction to Mr. Curren, who held the e-liquid up to the light, appreciating its vivid color.

Mr. Curren, 47, took up chewing tobacco at age 10 and switched to cigarettes in seventh grade. When he discovered e-cigarettes in 2011, he quit smoking — and within six months, he said, was able to taste his food and started jogging again. He also regained self-respect and now holds his head high at the Harvest Church in Norman.

"I feel like I'm one step closer to God," he said. So precious is his e-cigarette that he wears it on a lanyard around his neck: "This takes the crime out of smoking."

Around the country, there are an estimated 5,000 vape shops. But Oklahoma, with 6 percent of those shops and a little more than 1 percent of the United States population, has a disproportionate share.

NICK OXFORD FOR THE NEW YORK TIMES

Justin Mustain, right, demonstrates an e-cigarette for Becky Parton at OKC Vapes in Oklahoma City. In 18 months, the number of such shops in Oklahoma has risen to 300 from just a handful.

Business is booming. "You can't even get commercial retail space in Tulsa right now in that 1,200- or 1,500-foot range because everyone is opening a vapor store — it's crazy," said Chip Paul, who owns two of the nearly 50 stores in Tulsa, and who estimates that a typical store can bring in $400,000 a year after start-up costs of less than $50,000.

What has made Oklahoma a vaping hub is a heavy concentration of smokers, many desperate to quit, who are creating both demand and supply. Converts to e-cigarettes are taking advantage of the relatively low cost of starting a business to become zealous sellers.

"The trend moves from the coasts inward and from Oklahoma outward," said Daniel Walsh, the chief executive of Purebacco USA, a company in Michigan that ships e-liquid to retailers nationwide and tracks the retail trends. "It's somewhat anomalous," he said of Oklahoma. Or it could be, he said, that "Oklahoma is simply ahead of the trend."

Last week, the Food and Drug Administration for the first time proposed rules for regulating e-cigarettes, including prohibiting sales to minors and requiring producers to register with the agency and disclose manufacturing processes.

But many crucial questions still fall to the states. Should there be indoor vaping bans, for example, or excise taxes? The F.D.A., in its release on Thursday, didn't address marketing or whether to ban flavorings, which some critics say appeal to children. State-imposed limits played a big role in reducing traditional cigarette use, and health officials said states could play a similar role this time, pulling back the reins on e-cigarettes until more is known about their potential hazards.

For instance, some studies show carcinogens in the vapor, particularly in a new generation of more powerful e-cigarettes. Liquid nicotine is toxic and it can be absorbed into the skin. Public health officials shudder when they hear about people like Mr. Whitson, who mixes the e-juice without gloves — and just a few feet from a crib where his 4-month-old daughter sometimes sleeps. (He says that he's careful and that the company uses only "food-grade products that are kosher.")

Oklahoma has already taken a few steps. Gov. Mary Fallin has prohibited vaping on state property, and last week signed a law prohibiting sales to minors. Some 18 percent of Oklahoma high-school students have experimented with vaping, nearly double the national average. While the F.D.A. rules would also prevent those teenagers from buying e-cigarettes, they are now just proposals.

The prospect of further regulation troubles many small-business people here, including Sean Gore, a former rodeo cowboy and recovered meth addict turned consultant to the oil and gas industry, who has become a leader in the state's vaping industry. On May 1, he plans to open his third vape shop in the Oklahoma City area, and he also serves as chairman of the state industry lobbying group, the Oklahoma Vapor Advocacy League. He welcomes regulations like outlawing sales to minors. But others worry him, like product regulation, which he fears could subject even small vape shops that make their own products and mix their own liquids to federal oversight. That might be costly to the shops, which he views as the right-spirited pioneers of the e-cigarette boom.

He also opposes state action to raise taxes, limit marketing or ban vaping indoors. More rules, he fears, would work only to benefit deep-pocketed tobacco companies that have also entered the $2 billion e-cigarette industry. Regulation, he said, will take "a product that has the potential to save thousands of lives and give it back to the industry that's killing people."

Most galling to him are rules that prohibit e-cigarette makers from claiming, without providing scientific evidence, that their products are safer than cigarettes. "It doesn't take a rocket scientist to figure out these products are much safer than cancer sticks," he said. While health officials drag their feet, Mr. Gore asked, "How many more people have to die?"

PINEAPPLE OR CARIBBEAN PEACH?

Mr. Gore has dull blue eyes, a bull rider's thrice-broken jaw and a painfully apt last name. "Once, I got a horn in my eye," he said as he steered his Ford 150 pickup north on Interstate 235.

At arm's reach in the truck's center console were his three regular vaping devices, which he described as a Kanger Pro II with a 2.4-ohm coil atomizer and 2,900-milliamp battery and Caribbean-peach flavored nicotine; a Copper Nemesis; and the LA Edition Sentinel, with a 22-millimeter drip tip.

"It's the Lamborghini," he said.

Mr. Gore decided to try e-cigarettes about a year and a half ago, after judging a bull-riding event. "I had a patch on my back, a dip in my lip, a chew in my cheek," he said. "I was smoking a cigarette and chewing nicotine gum, and I said: 'Something's not working.' " He grew up on a ranch and had been chewing tobacco since he was 5 years old.

Oklahoma is big smoking country. Two years ago, 23.3 percent of the adults were smokers, one of the higher rates in the nation — only 11 states were worse. Nonetheless, that's a sharp improvement from 2011, when smokers accounted for 26.1 percent of the adult population and only three states had higher percentages.

Current and former state health officials say smoking rates have been moving lower since 2001, when the figure was 28.7 percent. They say it reflects education efforts, increases in cigarette taxes and indoor smoking bans. The per capita annual consumption of cigarettes in the state has fallen to 67.2 packs in 2013 from 108 in 2001.

But Mr. Gore asserted that state officials simply won't acknowledge what he sees as the clear reason behind Oklahoma's improvement relative to other states.

"All of a sudden it just happens in one quick swoop about the time e-cigarettes come into the market," he said. "This is the largest step forward in tobacco harm reduction in last 50 years." He added: "It's hard to ignore."

Given the short history of e-cigarettes, it's not clear how well they work as a way to quit smoking in the long term. But there is anecdotal evidence. A novel study of 215 vape shop customers in Oklahoma found that 64 percent of them had completely quit cigarettes, something verified through Breathalyzer tests that measured carbon monoxide, which is present in smokers.

"It's incorrect to say it hasn't been a cessation tool," said the study's lead researcher, Theodore L. Wagener, a psychologist who is co-director of the Oklahoma Tobacco Research Center and an assistant professor at the University of Oklahoma Health Sciences Center. "It's working for some people."

But he doesn't know if his sample was representative of the population. "We don't know if those are just the cream of the crop," he said.

What makes Dr. Wagener hopeful is how impassioned people can become about vaping. People actually like e-cigarettes — especially compared with, say, nicotine gum or other nicotine replacement therapies. "You don't see a lot of N.R.T. stores opening up," Dr. Wagener said.

He views Mr. Gore as a growing force in spreading the word. "Sean is the de facto leader," Dr. Wagener said, one with a strong personality. When Mr. Gore gave him permission to do research at his stores, Dr. Wagener said, he received a call warning that Mr. Gore had a troubled past, including methamphetamine addiction, which led to several convictions for drug possession, as well as a conviction for second-degree burglary. Still, Dr. Wagener said, "I actually like Sean."

Mr. Gore said he put that ugly part of his life behind him after a near-fatal car accident when he was high. He has since found religion, he said, and a sense of mission. "God needs experienced workers," he said of his e-cigarette advocacy. "If I can help one person come out of that hole, then it's all been worth it."

He pulled his Ford into a strip mall in Edmond, a suburb of Oklahoma City. Get Vaped, his shop, is in a corner spot, next to a parcel-shipping store. It replaced a gold-buying business.

Inside are display cases with the latest vaping gear. On the wall are menus of dozens of flavors, organized into categories: Tobacco (cigar, Pall Mall, Marlboro); Fruit Pantry (pineapple, dragon fruit); Sweet Tooth (cinnamon coffee cake); Novelty (bacon). In the back of Get Vaped, an employee — wearing gloves — mixes the flavoring with solvents and the desired concentration of nicotine, ranging from zero to 3.6 percent. A 10-milliliter bottle goes for $6.99 and 30 milliliters for $13.99.

"I really like orange," said Laura Petersen, 42, one of a handful of customers on a slow Monday morning in March. She described her happiness at giving up a two-decade, two-pack-a-day habit and being able to vape at her desk, in the car, in restaurants. It's convenient, she said, not having to go outside and brave the elements.

She has cut back to just a few irresistible cigarettes when she first wakes up.

Mr. Gore sympathized and offered counsel. "Here's what I did: I put it on my night stand," he said, referring to his e-cigarette. "Do that.

If you take two or three puffs when you first get up, I promise you: The urge will go away."

As Mr. Gore rang up her orange-flavored e-juice, he suggested that she get involved politically to help vapers shape policy and prevent a state tax on the devices. His group includes 17 stores and has hired a lobbyist to push an agenda to protect the industry from cigarette-like regulations. He doesn't want indoor smoking bans. "What's the point?" he asked. "If there was risk to human health, I could see it, but since there's not, there's really no need for it." Trouble is, health officials warn that e-cigarette vapor could be harmful to children and developing fetuses. Mr. Gore also objects to an excise tax, which he said would raise prices and hurt demand.

"You wouldn't put a tax on Weight Watchers health food," he said to Ms. Petersen. She agreed that the idea seemed nuts.

A DEFINITION AND A HOT DEBATE

In early April, at a hearing of the Appropriations and Budget Committee of the Oklahoma House of Representatives, a Republican member named Pat Ownbey was close to losing his temper. The hearing was about legislation that, at least on its face, would forbid the state tax commission from levying an excise tax on e-cigarettes.

But Mr. Ownbey, 60, a businessman who owns rental properties, saw the legislation as a stealth method for legally defining e-cigarettes as "vapor products" and not "tobacco products."

That difference in wording is significant. A "tobacco product" suggests the possibility of government regulation, because tobacco products are already regulated. A "vapor product" is a whole new category.

Exasperation creeping into his voice, Mr. Ownbey argued to his fellow committee members that nicotine is derived from tobacco and is thus, quite obviously, a tobacco product. (This is, in fact, what gives the F.D.A. its authority.) He said he had been incredulous to hear supporters of "vapor product" language argue that nicotine isn't a tobacco product because it can be derived from eggplants.

It's ridiculous, Mr. Ownbey argued, given that it takes "something like 20 eggplants" to make enough nicotine for a single cigarette.

Legislators are having similar discussions. Already, 33 state legislatures have passed laws prohibiting e-cigarette sale to minors, according to the National Conference of State Legislatures. The new F.D.A. regulations would extend that ban to all 50 states. But the rules are not yet approved and would not, as of yet, override state laws, according to the conference. In the meantime, those state laws include other provisions — including varying definitions of e-cigarettes, according to an analysis by Doug Matheny, retired chief of the Tobacco Use Prevention Service in Oklahoma, who now tracks tobacco industry lobbying at tobaccomoney.com.

In state laws preventing youth access, his analysis shows, five states — Alaska, Kentucky, Vermont, Wisconsin and Virginia — say explicitly that e-cigarettes are not tobacco products, at least 18 states define e-cigarettes as belonging to a nontobacco category without explicitly saying that they aren't tobacco-related, and 10 states have deemed them tobacco products.

States can be expected to wrestle with questions about where e-cigarettes can be consumed, how they will be marketed and taxed, said Terry L. Cline, Oklahoma's commissioner of health. "It's the same debate we had with tobacco, but this one is complicated by not yet having the science, both about the benefits and risks," he said. He added that he "would be ecstatic if this product ends up being proven to be a tobacco-cessation product," but the evidence isn't here yet.

Dr. Cline praised the F.D.A. for proposing disclosure of ingredients in products and requiring manufacturing standards. "What could not be allowed to continue is the risk of unregulated products being mixed in kitchens and back rooms without any oversight," he said. "It's a disaster waiting to happen."

On the question of how to categorize e-cigarettes, Mr. Ownbey said he would explore deeming them "smoking cessation" therapies, like nicotine gum. E-cigarette companies strongly resist this idea because it would mean conducting expensive research to prove that the product does what they imply it does. So e-cigarette companies avoid using the term "cessation" and instead say e-cigarettes are great for "harm reduction."

The logic infuriates Mr. Ownbey. "They don't want it to be a cessation product, but that's all I hear," he said.

For his part, Mr. Gore noted that language could have a surprising emotional force. The question of what to call these products — vapor, tobacco, cessation therapies — means something beyond the words themselves. "The categorization is a huge thing for us," he said. "We consider ourselves nonsmokers and nontobacco users. That's huge for us. We've made a huge step."

In the end, Mr. Ownbey carried the day. But the bill to ban an excise tax was just a skirmish. Shortly after, both houses of the Oklahoma Legislature passed by wide margins another bill, which prohibited sales of e-cigarettes to minors. The legislation defined e-cigarettes as "vapor products." (But it stopped short of saying they weren't tobacco products.)

Still, this troubled several major health groups, including the local chapters of the American Lung Association and the American Heart Association, which urged Governor Fallin to veto the bill. The American Cancer Society wrote: "A separate definition can create a risk of e-cigarettes being exempted from other tobacco control laws, including smoke-free laws."

In the end, Governor Fallin signed the law; better to have something in place that protects youth, Dr. Cline said, even if it is imperfect.

AN UNEASY ALLIANCE

Mr. Gore doesn't have the full support of the vaping world. In fact, some shop owners take issue with his views and what they characterize as his bulldog style.

Among his detractors are John and Stephanie Durst, whose OKC Vapes is one of the most popular vape shops in Oklahoma City.

The Dursts have come a long way since 2011, when Ms. Durst was working at Panera Bread and started vaping in place of smoking. She was saving a lot of money — she and her husband had been spending as much as $225 a month on cigarettes — but she was carrying around a handful of cruder, early e-cigarette devices and thought that there had to be a better way.

She started contacting flavor and nicotine manufacturers in China, ordering online, mixing her own e-juice — green apple, blueberry, strawberry — and selling it.

By June 2011, Ms. Durst was handing out business cards at bars and advertising e-cigarettes on Craigslist. Five to eight cars a night would come by their house. "It got to the point we had tell our neighbors: 'We know it looks like we're dealers but we're trying to run a business out of our home,' " Mr. Durst said.

The Dursts now own four vaping stores and expect total sales this year to exceed $4 million.

The Dursts want vaping to succeed, and they think it can, even with regulation. Unlike Mr. Gore, they're fine with vaping bans in public parks and even in restaurants. They also favor licensing and health inspections of people making e-liquids.

"I can't preach that enough," Mr. Durst said in a phone interview.

"Tobacco self-regulated themselves into rich bank accounts and killed a lot of people," Mr. Durst continued. "Let's not screw up with e-cigs."

A year ago, tobacco companies, which own several e-cigarette brands, supported state legislation that would have required e-cigarettes to be sold through licensed and regulated wholesale systems. They are systems that Big Tobacco already has in place, so the rule would have given those companies a huge advantage over upstarts, according to Mr. Matheny of tobaccomoney.com.

"For all intents and purposes, it would've put the mom-and-pop vape shops out of business," Mr. Matheny said, because they didn't have those expensive systems. A groundswell from vape shop owners, including Mr. Gore, helped kill the legislation.

Now, however, Mr. Gore's group has formed an alliance with Big Tobacco, which was involved in crafting the bill prohibiting youth access to e-cigarettes and the one on excise taxes that Mr. Ownbey opposed. Several lobbyists for the tobacco industry declined to comment for this article.

Mr. Gore finds his loose alliance with Big Tobacco to be useful for now, but also unnerving, given the companies' financial muscle — and the threat they could pose to vape shops.

"They're getting into the e-cig industry," he said. "We can't stop them."

He contends that they are profiteers who don't care about people's health. He sees Oklahoma's mom-and-pop shops differently. They are run by the victims of cigarette companies, he said, who have found an antidote to the ill effects of tobacco — and who just might see their own payday in the process.

"We're in it to make a buck and raise our families as well," he said. "Who's not?" But he said he had a different long-term aim: getting people to quit cigarettes, then to reduce their nicotine levels on e-cigarettes until they are free forever of addiction.

"If we work our way out of a job," he said, "I don't have a problem with that."

E-Cigarette Makers Are in an Arms Race for Exotic Vapor Flavors

BY MATT RICHTEL | JULY 15, 2014

TWISTA LIME, Kauai Kolada, Caribbean Chill, Mintrigue. Exotic cigarette flavors like those were banned in 2009 out of concern they might tempt young people.

But the flavors tobacco companies once sold look like plain vanilla compared with the flavor buffet now on offer — legally — by the fast-growing electronic cigarette industry.

News on Tuesday that Reynolds American had agreed to buy Lorillard, uniting two of the nation's biggest tobacco companies, highlighted how important e-cigarettes have become to the declining tobacco industry. Both Reynolds and Lorillard have pushed hard into e-cigarettes, which offer a new way of delivering a puff of nicotine.

For now, those companies' flavors are relatively modest, though they may feel pressure to expand into the explosion of competition for the consumer palate, with e-cigarette flavors such as banana cream pie and cotton candy.

Across the e-cigarette industry, more than 7,000 flavors are now available and, by one estimate, nearly 250 more are being introduced every month. The array of tastes goes far beyond anything cigarette companies ever tried.

Flavors have become central to the conversation because e-cigarette makers say that the rainbow of tastes differentiates them from deadly cigarettes.

But the claim that e-cigarette flavors won't attract children has prompted an outcry from some policy makers, who say consumers have been down this road before with tobacco. Federal health authorities have outlawed most cigarette flavorings except menthol, arguing that they lure the young into nicotine addiction. While the Food and Drug Administration has proposed regulations for e-cigarettes, it has not limited marketing or flavors, which the agency is studying.

At a Senate committee hearing in late June, lawmakers denounced manufacturers for marketing practices that they said appealed to children, including the embrace of flavors that are forbidden in ordinary cigarettes. "I'm ashamed of you," Senator Jay Rockefeller, Democrat of West Virginia, told several executives. "You're what's wrong with this country."

Jason Healy, the president of Blu eCigs, told the Senate Committee on Commerce, Science and Transportation that the average age of people using cherry flavored e-cigarettes, for example, was 40. Such flavors "decrease the ability or possibility of adult users who use e-cigs switching back" to cigarettes, he said. Blu eCigs, a subsidiary of Lorillard, is being sold to the British company Imperial as part of the deal announced on Tuesday. Lorillard and Reynolds said they would focus their e-cigarette efforts on Reynolds' product Vuse, which in June was introduced in 15,000 stores nationwide.

For now, Vuse has only two flavors, original cigarette flavor and menthol, but the market is changing quickly as evidenced by the experience of other leading e-cigarette companies. Most notable is the experience of NJOY, which has turned to flavors to help stanch plummeting market share.

Ten months ago, NJOY's chief executive, Craig Weiss, said in an interview that other manufacturers used flavorings "to attract children." NJOY, he said then, was avoiding candy- and fruit-like flavorings, in part because "they drive regulators crazy."

NJOY's investors include Sean Parker, the Napster co-founder and former president of Facebook, and Bruno Mars, the pop star.

But NJOY's share of the convenience store market has gone into free fall, dropping more than half in the last year to less than 10 percent, according to Wells Fargo Securities. Consumer surveys suggest that most people who use e-cigarettes — including those who have smoked — tend to prefer flavors other than tobacco. In the next few weeks, NJOY plans to expand into flavors like "Butter Crumble" and "Black and Blue Berry." Mr. Weiss said in an interview that the company had little choice after focus groups showed that flavors were "critical."

"Flavor is essential to vapers' satisfaction," Mr. Weiss said. He added that research funded by his company showed that flavors "provide no additional appeal to youth."

The e-cigarette market is rapidly shifting, and flavors are central to that. Viking Vapor, one of hundreds of websites selling e-cigarettes, offers 13 pages of alphabetized flavors, from Apple to Watermelon Menthol. But the market for disposable e-cigarettes, commonly found in convenience stores and sold by the likes of NJOY, Vuse and Blu eCigs, appears to be slowing — consumers seemed to be switching to more powerful devices, analysts said. According to Wells Fargo, consumer sales of e-cigarettes at convenience stores fell 17 percent in the month that ended June 7, after falling 10 percent the month earlier — the first time since e-cigarettes came onto the market that consumers spent less at convenience stores. Wells Fargo hypothesized that sales were gravitating to the Internet and "vape" stores, where figures are harder to measure.

Some in public health circles see the debate over flavorings as a sideshow. The central question, they say, is whether e-cigarettes are effective tools to get people to stop smoking tobacco. Others say the issue of flavors crystallizes the debate about the risks and benefits of these products, which many consider far safer than conventional cigarettes. At the same time, there is widespread concern that use of e-cigarettes will renormalize the act of smoking and invite in a new generation of participants, particularly through the lure of flavors.

"It defies logic to think that such flavors would not make e-cigarette use more appealing and even normal for children," said James Pankow, a chemistry professor at Portland State University in Oregon, who has studied cancer risk from cigarettes.

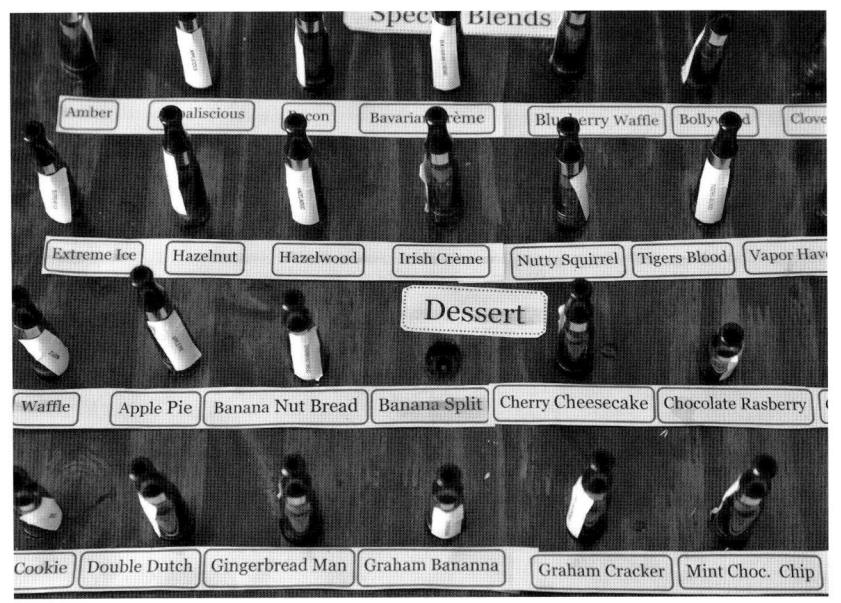

NICK OXFORD FOR THE NEW YORK TIMES

More than 120 e-cigarette flavors are available at Vapor Haven in Oklahoma City. By one estimate, makers create nearly 250 flavors each month.

Mr. Weiss of NJOY, hoping to address personal concerns about flavors, funded a study this year to see if the company's new flavors would appeal to young nonsmokers. The study, an online survey conducted by Saul Shiffman, a pharmaceutical industry consultant and psychology professor at the University of Pittsburgh, found that young people were not particularly attracted to the flavors. Flavors did make e-cigarettes more attractive to adult smokers, Professor Shiffman concluded.

Senator Richard J. Durbin, an Illinois Democrat who has called for e-cigarettes to be regulated like conventional cigarettes, said that those results came as no surprise given that NJOY paid for the research.

"Let me be as dismissive as possible: When they start talking about their own research, I say 'been there, done that,' " Mr. Durbin said in an interview. "We listened to those tobacco companies for decades while their so-called experts tried to divert our attention from the obvious."

Mr. Weiss said NJOY did not influence the findings. "I get the appearance of a — 'quote-un-quote' — industry funded study," he said. "But we didn't have time to get it funded by a third party."

In reality, the study took only a few weeks, Mr. Shiffman said, allowing for the possibility that other studies could be done quickly by independent sources. Asked about that prospect, Mr. Weiss said: "What's the magic number of studies? Two studies? Four studies?"

About a year ago, NJOY, based in Scottsdale, Ariz., named to its board Dr. Richard H. Carmona, the former surgeon general who had been an ardent foe of tobacco companies. Before joining the NJOY board, Dr. Carmona said he asked the company about the use of flavors and was told it "was not on the table at that time."

Dr. Carmona, who also works at a nonprofit health organization, the Canyon Ranch Institute, said that NJOY's research was a good start but that it was critical that independent researchers validate the findings. Like Mr. Weiss, Dr. Carmona said he was willing to take the chance and go forward, given that e-cigarettes have the potential to get people to stop smoking conventional cigarettes.

"Research like that could take months or years," Dr. Carmona said. "So we go with a theory, we go with a hypothesis. It's no different than any other market."

'Vape' Joins Pot Lingo as Oxford's Word of the Year

BY JESSICA BENNETT | NOV. 21, 2014

"BACK IN MY DAY, it was just weed; it was just getting high," said Joel Schneider, 55, sipping a cup of coffee. "Vaping? No. We'd never heard of vaping."

Mr. Schneider, the owner of a pot-friendly bed-and-breakfast in Denver (it brands itself a "bud-and-breakfast"), had just learned that "vape" was chosen as the Oxford Dictionaries 2014 Word of the Year. That is, a group of lexicographers got together and measured the word's use, determining that the term — used to describe the process of inhaling and exhaling the vapor produced by an electronic cigarette (or "vape pen") — had proliferated, along with the habit. (Last year's word of the year was "selfie.")

"The growing popularity of e-cigarettes, combined with the legal cannabis industry, created a perfect storm," said Katherine Martin, a lexicographer involved in the selection.

Yet "vape" is only the tip of the linguistic iceberg, at least when it comes to marijuana. Spend a few days in Colorado, where retail sales of pot have been legal since January, and you stand to end up tongue-tied more than once. Weed? Nope. It's now "cannabis," a subtler term. "Smoking" has become "consuming," or, if it's with a vaporizer, "vaping." Pot itself is often referred to as "product," and the industry is referred to as the "cannabusiness."

"There is definitely a new vernacular that comes with the dawn of mainstream cannabis," said Andy Juett, a Denver comedian who runs a pot-themed show. "There, I just did it: I wouldn't have even used the word 'cannabis' two years ago."

Call it cannaslang. Linguists say its evolution is not particularly surprising: Drugs have long produced a casual lexicon. There are at least 200 synonyms for the word "drunk," as chronicled as early as 1737 in something called The Drinkers Dictionary.

Yet when it comes to pot, the new terminology goes beyond describing the high (though, indeed, "green out" is the new "black out"). There are now terms for the business (pot entrepreneurs are "ganjapreneurs") and its sociology (bias against stoners is "cannabigotry"). The act of disliking a person who vapes is called "vape vitriol"; "cannasseur" refers to a pot connoisseur.

Some of the words are silly, but others are strategic: a way to give pot some class. "We work very hard to mature the messaging and vernacular of this industry," said David Kochman, a lawyer for OpenVape, a Denver-based company that manufactures vaporizers. He notes that "buds" are now referred to as "flowers," and "trim" (the leftover parts of a marijuana plant once the flowers are removed) is "raw material."

As for vaping, the word itself appears to date back to 1983, according to Oxford, when it was used in a scholarly article to describe "an inhaler or 'noncombustible' cigarette" that looked "much like the real thing" but delivered nicotine through a vapor. It would be a decade before it would catch on, appearing in online forums amid the jargon of marijuana. Yet even a few years ago, if you heard the word, you might have been more likely to think "Star Trek" than e-cigarette, said Axie Blundon, OpenVape's social media director. "You imagined vaporizing somebody into thin air," he said, "like a stun gun."

These days, vape beat out "slacktivism" (lazy activism) and "normcore" (grandpa fashion worn as a statement) — as well as another pot term, "budtender" — for the grand word title.

"I feel like vape is a more refined term," said Chandler Davis, a 24-year-old budtender in Denver. "Here and there, we're making smoking a little classier."

Feeling Let Down and Left Behind, With Little Hope for Better

BY RICHARD FAUSSET | MAY 25, 2016

NORTH WILKESBORO, N.C. — Kody Foster had finished his Wednesday afternoon shift at the warehouse where he earns $12.50 per hour. Normally, he would be packing himself into his Ford Focus, with its Bernie Sanders sticker and plaque with the number 48, in honor of the stock-car racer Jimmie Johnson.

But this week, Mr. Foster, 26, couldn't get the Ford's check engine light to turn off, and the dealership told him that fixing it would cost $1,000, which he didn't have. So instead, he borrowed his sister's ancient red minivan, with its sliding door that doesn't shut right.

He drove along River Road, the hillsides lush and tangled with kudzu, then up Main Street in this faltering Appalachian town, the largest in a county that has seen its factory jobs wither, its Nascar track shutter and its homegrown business — Lowe's, the home-improvement chain — move its headquarters to a Charlotte suburb in 2003.

Mr. Foster's destination, wedged between a pizza parlor and the opioid addiction clinic, was the Tapering Vapor, a bare-bones e-cigarette shop and makeshift lounge that serves as his modest oasis, a place to catch a mild nicotine buzz and let a world of worry float away on banks of big, cloying, candy-flavored clouds.

In an America riddled with anxieties, the worries that Mr. Foster and his neighbors bring through the doors of the Tapering Vapor are common and potent: Fear that an honest, 40-hour working-class job can no longer pay the bills. Fear of a fraying social fabric. Fear that the country's future might pale in comparison with its past.

Wilkes County, with a population of nearly 69,000, has felt those stings more than many other places. The textile and furniture industries have been struggling here for years, and the recession and the

GEORGE ETHEREDGE FOR THE NEW YORK TIMES

Andrew Taylor, the general manager of the Tapering Vapor, an e-cigarette store, blowing a big cloud against a countertop.

loss of the Lowe's headquarters have helped drive down the median household income. That figure fell by more than 30 percent between 2000 and 2014 when adjusted for inflation, the second-steepest decrease in the nation, according to an analysis of census data by the Pew Charitable Trusts.

Still, the regulars at the Tapering Vapor — overwhelmingly white, mostly working class and ranging from their 20s to middle age — provide a haze-shrouded snapshot of an anxious nation navigating an election year fueled by disquiet and malaise.

Mr. Foster drove past the old Key City furniture plant; the original business was killed off by cheap imports and the Great Recession. The new tenant, a legal moonshine maker called the Copper Barrel Distillery, was proudly hawking bottles of the product that had once been the not-so-secret shame of this place — as well as $19.99 ball caps, made in Bangladesh, emblazoned with the distillery's logo.

He parked next to the addiction clinic, with a discreet sign that read, "Mountain Health Solutions." Just a few hours earlier, it had been the busiest business on the block.

The Tapering Vapor was almost empty save for Andrew Taylor, the manager. He stood behind the counter under a Guy Fawkes mask, the universal symbol of protest and disaffection, and near the dry-erase board listing dozens of flavors for sale. The names suggested fantasia and abundance: Summer Melon, Broken Neon, Caramel Latte, Unlimited Power.

The two friends greeted each other with a joke borrowed from a popular Vine video. Mr. Taylor, 22, blew out a cloud that smelled like orange cheesecake

Moments later, another customer, Karen Chapman, came in carrying an oversize handbag. She ordered a bottle of nicotine-laced liquid flavored like dark chocolate and tobacco.

She said she had quit smoking cigarettes in March, soon after her favorite character on the reality television show "Mob Wives," Angela Raiola, died of cancer. Ms. Chapman, 47, said she had two master's degrees and was currently holding six part-time jobs — a mix of clerical, academic and online work, none of which provided health insurance.

"This is not the life I saw for myself," she said.

Now Mr. Foster was at work at the counter, his eyes locked in concentration under his ball cap. He was building a custom heating coil for the kind of powerful vapor-delivery device he and his friends prefer: a walkie-talkie-size gadget called a vaporizer, or a mod. It was a complicated procedure, involving an electric drill and a spool of 36-gauge alloy wire.

Mr. Foster has always had a knack for building. Before the recession, his father built fancy mountain retirement homes here. Now retirees were nosing around the North Carolina mountains again, and his father was building again. Sometimes Mr. Foster pitches in.

But this afternoon, as he sucked on a mod loaded with a banana-strawberry concoction, he was trying not to think about the trouble he was in. About how he messed up by buying the little white Ford off the showroom floor in 2012; the $265 monthly payments were killing him.

How his Verizon bill inched close to $300 the month before because he lost track of how much video he had streamed.

How he, his wife and their 4-year-old son were living at his mother-in-law's place after the landlord sold the house they had been renting for $400 per month. How even a two-bedroom trailer in a crummy neighborhood around here was going for $600 per month. "More than I can handle," he said.

And how his second child was due in July.

"It's not just me. There are other people in similar boats," Mr. Foster said. He acknowledged that maybe he was to blame for some if it. Maybe he should have stayed in college. Maybe he should have kept better track of his cellphone's data plan.

But in his America, he said, it seemed that just a few bad choices could doom anybody who wasn't born with Donald Trump money. "If you make just one poor decision," he said, "then you're screwed."

Mr. Foster's social life is the Tapering Vapor. And it is his online chatter with friends and strangers while he is immersed in the virtual worlds of games like Battlefield and Grand Theft Auto V on his PlayStation. The Internet means that few ideas are exotic anymore, even in a place like this, and Mr. Foster has been evangelizing to friends and co-workers lately on behalf of the documentary "Zeitgeist: Addendum." Mr. Foster had watched it online and was intrigued by its critique of international capitalism and its banking and monetary systems.

Mr. Foster likes Mr. Sanders's promise of universal health care, and his pledge to make tuition free at public colleges and universities. His dream, which seems distant now, is to one day return to school and study marine biology.

His support for Mr. Sanders makes him an outlier in largely conservative Wilkes County. Mr. Trump won the March 15 Republican primary here with 47 percent of the vote, garnering more than twice the votes of Hillary Clinton, who won the Democratic primary.

Among those who chose Mr. Trump was Mr. Taylor, a native of western North Carolina who never knew the world before the North American Free Trade Agreement or the Internet. He is a gamer and amateur musician. He attends Baptist Bible study and owns a throwback "Legend of Zelda" T-shirt. He plays bluegrass and the White Stripes.

And though globalization provides him with his preferred instruments of leisure — a foreign-made Xbox and a cheap, sturdy Japanese acoustic guitar — he is also one of globalization's discontents.

On the whole, Mr. Taylor agrees with Mr. Trump that the United States, particularly places like Wilkes County, received raw deals from the trade pacts that began with the passage of Nafta. Some of the textile and furniture industry remains here. But it is not like it was. Or at least the way people tell him it was.

He has long been skeptical of big government, and the way government works generally. It did not help that the Food and Drug Administration announced greater regulation of the e-cigarette industry this month. He figured it would soon put little shops like this one out of business.

"I don't think he's going to be worse than anybody else up there," Mr. Taylor said of Mr. Trump. If nothing else, he said, "He'd be somewhat more interesting to watch things unfold under."

Like many others here, both successful and not, Mr. Taylor and Mr. Foster are united in their belief that they are living among the ruins of a lapsed golden age.

The post-World War II success story that people once told about themselves here was captured in a 1948 promotional film, uploaded to YouTube by the State Archives of North Carolina, called "This is Progressive Wilkes County." It shows the locals of that era bustling on now-sleepy downtown thoroughfares here and in Wilkesboro, the smaller sister city across the Yadkin River, as shopkeepers offered pies and pastries, men's suits and prescription drugs.

GEORGE ETHEREDGE FOR THE NEW YORK TIMES

Kody Foster and his 4-year-old son, Noah, at the Tapering Vapor.

"Every day is Saturday in these thriving mountain towns," a narrator says.

Today, Michael A. Cooper, Jr., 30, a lawyer who grew up in North Wilkesboro, compares the county to a Jenga tower whose pieces scattered when the old industries pulled out. The methamphetamine phenomenon crested here two or three years ago, but the labs continue to flourish among its 754 square miles of hollows and low mountains. Perhaps even more prevalent are prescription drugs — particularly opioids like Oxycodone and Opana.

Mr. Cooper is a rare young white-collar professional who stayed in town. Many of his clients are people he went to high school with and are now in trouble over drugs or caught in the tangle of family court and dead-end jobs. It doesn't surprise him that Mr. Trump's message resonates.

"If there were winners or losers in America in this century, they were the losers," he said. "You're talking to people who haven't won in 30 years, and now somebody is telling them they're going to win again."

Mr. Trump is popular here for a number of reasons. The county is 93 percent white, but from 1990 to 2014, the Hispanic population there grew from 360 people to 4,154, according to census figures. On a Wednesday in March, Brona Wood, 58, a maintenance worker at the county courthouse, came in to the Tapering Vapor for a bottle of liquid called Fruity Juice. If Mr. Trump is elected, she said, "The Mexicans is going to stop coming in here and taking everybody's jobs."

Eddie Settle, the chairman of the County Commission, was giving a driving tour of the county a few days before the March primaries when a pickup truck adorned with a Confederate flag passed by. It is a common sight here, Mr. Settle said, though he argued that the Confederate symbol has less to do with racism than an ingrained suspicion of those in power. He said the same dynamic explained Mr. Trump's appeal: "It's not because he's Donald Trump. It's because he's anti-establishment."

As part of his tour, Mr. Settle drove by the large chicken processing plant in Wilkesboro, operated by Tyson Foods. Pay on the production line ranges from $10 to just under $14 per hour. It employs about 2,800 people.

Out on Route 421, near the bustling Wilkesboro Walmart, the highway is lined with common American chains — Sonic, Chik-fil-A, Dollar Tree, Hardee's, Taco Bell, Sally Beauty Supply — a sign of the area's low-wage jobs. The county's unemployment rate was almost 15 percent in February 2010. In April, it was 5.4 percent, about the same as the national rate.

"We don't have an unemployment problem here," said Jim Smoak, the chairman of the Wilkes Economic Development Corporation. "We have a wage problem."

Even before Mr. Trump's rise, government and business leaders here had concocted a plan for making Wilkes County great again. They introduced advanced engineering and computer training in high schools, and at the community college, they added computer controlled lathes and mills and a programmable practice production line — all to train future workers for the Kia or Hyundai plant or other big manufacturing facility the county hopes to lure. So far, no luck.

Some of the clientele at the Tapering Vapor have made their own luck, working hard and earning a measure of economic security. Others are just getting by.

Billy Williams, 30, walked in wearing an oversize football jersey, with a front tooth conspicuously missing, and asked for a strawberry-raspberry liquid called Beetlejuice. He said he had been working a few hours a week at a restaurant across the river. It was not as many hours as he'd like, but he said it was the best work he could find, given his felony cocaine conviction from many years ago.

Kim Shumate, 58, walked in, looking for a replacement part for her mod. She quit smoking cigarettes after her house went into foreclosure in 2012. That was after Lowe's, at the height of the recession, stopped contracting with her husband's company, which had built the interiors of new stores.

Ms. Shumate cries when she thinks about her old house, with its big porch and its trails through the woods. So she tries not to think about it at all.

Lonnie Ramsay, 45, walked in looking for help. He described a nasty falling-out with his girlfriend and said he just wanted to get home to a nearby city. But he only had $25 to his name. He said he had been making $10 an hour at a factory.

One Friday afternoon someone brought a pair of virtual reality goggles hooked up to a laptop to the shop. Mr. Foster exhaled a cloud that smelled like a Popsicle. He said he had been reading up on the idea, explored in the "Zeitgeist" movie, of a "resource-based economy" — a system in which, he said, "There's no money and everything is controlled by computers and resources are equally distributed and there's no ownership or anything like that."

GEORGE ETHEREDGE FOR THE NEW YORK TIMES

Shawn Anderson, left, and Terry Brown showcased plumes of vapor. Some e-cigarette users compete to see who can exhale the longest and densest clouds.

"The system we have now is going to collapse," he said. "And technology, the automation process, is going to keep taking over and over."

That, he said, would free up people to do what they wanted.

Chris Lentz, 36, a worker for a utility company in a pair of mud-caked boots, frowned and asked, "If people were just given everything they ever needed, then what's the point of going to work?"

And so it went: the thick, sweet haze; the frustrations, diversions and digital toys; and the sense, in this jagged, hyperconnected moment, that everything is possible, or nothing is.

Mr. Foster took a turn with the virtual reality goggles, and put himself on a roller coaster. His body squirmed and bounced on the sofa as he rounded and flew down the virtual tracks until he became queasy, and said he'd had enough.

A Lobbyist Wrote the Bill. Will the Tobacco Industry Win Its E-Cigarette Fight?

BY ERIC LIPTON | SEPT. 2, 2016

WASHINGTON — The e-cigarette and cigar industries have enlisted high-profile lobbyists and influential congressional allies in an attempt to stop the Food and Drug Administration from retroactively examining their products for public health risks or banning them from the market.

The campaign targets a broad new rule that extends F.D.A. jurisdiction to include cigars, e-cigarettes and pipe and hookah tobacco.

The bipartisan effort has featured a former senator who did not register as a lobbyist before going to work for the cigar companies and a former Obama administration official, now a private consultant, who is trying to undo his earlier work reviewing the rule. In addition, one member of Congress introduced industry-written legislation without changing a word of it.

The battle shows how, nearly two decades after the $200 billion settlement between tobacco companies and state attorneys general to compensate the public for health consequences of smoking, the industry still wields extraordinary clout in Washington.

With its army of more than 75 lobbyists, tobacco-aligned companies have argued that the F.D.A.'s so-called Deeming Rule could hurt public health by forcing a large share of e-cigarette companies out of business.

"The F.D.A. has blatantly ignored evidence that our products improve people's lives," said Christian Berkey, chief executive of Johnson Creek Enterprises, one of the first companies to sell the e-liquid ingredient used in e-cigarettes and vaping products.

F.D.A. officials acknowledge that e-cigarettes, made out of tobacco-derived nicotine, are potentially less harmful than cigarettes. But they insist they must examine whether the electronic cigarettes or the liquid nicotine juices might contain toxic chemicals like diethylene glycol, an ingredient also used in antifreeze, or candy-like flavors contributing to the surge in the numbers of teenagers using e-cigarettes. They also want to examine the safety of the e-cig devices themselves after reports of battery-related burns.

"In the absence of science-based regulation of all tobacco products, the marketplace has been the wild, wild West," said Mitch Zeller, the director of the F.D.A.'s Center for Tobacco Products, which is in charge of enforcing the new rule. "Companies were free to introduce any product they wanted, make any claim they wanted, and that is how we wound up with a 900 percent increase in high schoolers using e-cigarettes and as well as all these reports of exploding e-cigarette batteries and products that have caused burns and fires and disfigurement."

The lobbying effort has been led by the Altria Group, the nation's largest tobacco company, which has a growing e-cigarette unit.

Documents obtained by The New York Times show that Altria last year distributed draft legislation on Capitol Hill that would eliminate the new requirement that most e-cigarettes already on sale in the United States be evaluated retroactively to determine if they are "appropriate for the protection of public health."

The proposal was endorsed by the R.J. Reynolds Tobacco Company, which has its own e-cigarette unit, as well as the National Tobacco Company, a major seller of loose tobacco, and trade associations representing the cigar industry and convenience stores, the documents show.

Altria delivered its proposal, entitled "F.D.A. Deeming Clarification Act of 2015," to Representative Tom Cole of Oklahoma in April 2015, the documents show, even before the F.D.A. rule became final.

Just two weeks later, Mr. Cole, a Republican, introduced the bill — with the title and 245-word text pulled verbatim from the industry's draft.

"Yes, we have shared our views with many policy makers, including Congressman Cole's office," David Sutton, a spokesman for Altria, said in a written statement, after being presented with a copy of its "legislative language" draft and Mr. Cole's resulting bill, which has 71 co-sponsors and is still pending in the House.

Separately, former Senator Mary Landrieu, Democrat of Louisiana, spent part of her first year after losing re-election pressing officials from the White House, State Department and F.D.A. on behalf of the cigar industry — even though records show she had not registered as a lobbyist as required by federal law, which Ms. Landrieu said was an oversight.

"This is my fault," she said. "I'm calling my lawyer now to get it corrected."

The electronic vapor industry — representing smaller companies that sell e-cigarettes that can be refilled with vapor juice — also has a lobbying contingent, buttressed by a highly motivated community of consumers and vape shops.

Mr. Cole, and Representative Sanford D. Bishop Jr., Democrat of Georgia, who co-sponsored one of the tobacco-related measures originally drafted by Altria, said that the rule would bankrupt small businesses and curb the availability of e-cigarette options, which some use as a way to quit smoking.

"I don't like regulating in the rearview mirror," Mr. Cole said in an interview.

Mr. Bishop and Mr. Cole are also two of the top House recipients of tobacco industry campaign donations, with Mr. Bishop receiving $13,000 from Altria this election cycle and a total of at least $60,000 from the industry since 2004.

Representative Nita M. Lowey of New York, the ranking Democrat on the House Appropriations Committee, said it was embarrassing that more than 70 lawmakers had signed on as co-sponsors of legislation that lobbyists from Altria and other industry groups originally wrote.

"For Congress to consider going backward in how we regulate the public health hazard is simply mind-boggling," she said. "It wasn't that long ago that tobacco companies were telling the public that cigarettes were not addictive and denying clear evidence that they caused cancer."

Matthew L. Myers, president of the Campaign for Tobacco Free Kids, who helped negotiate the 1998 tobacco settlement, said: "It is worse than spoiled kids who don't get their way. It is bullies that don't get their way and who are holding public health hostage."

Industry executives and their allies on Capitol Hill dismiss such criticism, noting that they support provisions intended to prevent youths from buying and using e-cigarettes or cigars.

"The argument that it would make it more accessible to children is fallacious," Mr. Bishop said.

The cigar industry lobbying pitch has gained the most traction in Congress.

Arguing that premium cigars are more of a recreational product with fewer health risks than cigarettes, the industry has been separately pushing members of Congress to enact legislation that would broadly exempt "premium cigars" from the new F.D.A. oversight. A bill to do so — also written in part by industry lobbyists — was introduced by Senator Bill Nelson, Democrat of Florida. It has 20 co-sponsors, while an identical bill in the House has another 165 co-sponsors.

The industry lobbyists, in addition to Ms. Landrieu, include Paul DiNino, a former finance director of the Democratic National Committee and onetime senior aide to Senator Harry Reid of Nevada, the Democratic leader. Mr. DiNino is assigned to enlist prominent Senate Democrats.

Mr. Reid, records show, contacted the White House on the industry's behalf, with his spokeswoman explaining that cigar-oriented events are important to Las Vegas.

To target the House, the cigar industry hired former Representative James T. Walsh, Republican of New York, a former House Appropriations Committee member, who has implored lawmakers and their staffs to back the exemption for cigars.

Mr. Walsh and his lobbying partners from the firm K & L Gates drafted language that was inserted into a House Appropriations bill approved by the full committee in April that defines an exemption for a premium cigar and that would prohibit the F.D.A. from spending money in the 2017 fiscal year on enforcement provisions.

"My fingers are crossed," Mr. Walsh said, about the prospects for getting the exemption.

Another critical assist came from Andrew Perraut, who until 2014 served as a desk officer at the Office of Management and Budget division that reviews major federal regulations, including the F.D.A.'s tobacco rule.

White House records show that he helped represent the Obama administration at more than a dozen meetings with outside parties, mostly pressing the government to ease the rule, before he was hired by a cigar-industry trade organization and by NJoy, a manufacturer of e-cigarettes.

Within less than a year, records show, Mr. Perraut was back at the Office of Management and Budget on the other side of the table.

Because Mr. Perraut was not a senior official and the regulation affects numerous industry players, federal revolving door rules did not apply, an agency spokeswoman said. Mr. Perraut said he was simply trying to help stop a "train wreck" that will be caused by the F.D.A. overreach.

Richard W. Painter, who served as the White House chief ethics lawyer during the George W. Bush administration, said Mr. Perraut's quick turnabout violated the spirit of President Obama's ethics pledge, intended to prevent former aides from lobbying the executive branch.

"Even if it is not prohibited, it is just not appropriate," he said.

Interest groups attempting to shape the debate also have financial patrons with a clear stake in the outcome.

Americans for Tax Reform, a conservative group, and National Center for Public Policy Research, a pro-free market think tank, have come out against the F.D.A. rules, even as they receive funding from the e-cigarette and tobacco industry, including Altria and R.J. Reynolds, records show.

Jeff Stier, a scholar at the National Center for Public Policy Research, and Grover Norquist, from Americans for Tax Reform, both said they opposed the F.D.A. rule as bad policy.

The American Lung Association, which has spoken out in defense of the rule, accepts contributions from pharmaceutical companies like Pfizer and GlaxoSmithKline, which sell smoking-cessation products that could lose sales if e-cigarettes continue to gain market share, Mr. Stier added.

Erika Sward, an association lobbyist, while acknowledging the money her nonprofit group has received from companies that sell smoking-cessation treatments, said the criticism of her group is a diversionary tactic.

"For so many years the focus in fighting tobacco wars has been on the cigarette industry," she said. "With historic declines in cigarette use, which is wonderful, what we are seeing is a surge in use in other tobacco products. And their push on Capitol Hill reflects this new clout."

From 0 to 10 Million: Vaping Takes Off in the U.S.

BY NICHOLAS BAKALAR | AUG. 31, 2018

Since 2004, millions of American have started using e-cigarettes. More than half also smoke traditional cigarettes.

SOME EXPERTS HAVE suggested that e-cigarettes can help wean people off regular cigarettes; others believe that they reinforce the smoking habit and increase the user's exposure to nicotine.

But there's no dispute that e-cigarettes have grown popular since their introduction in 2004. Now a nationwide survey has found that 10.8 million adults in the United States are vaping.

The analysis, published in the Annals of Internal Medicine, found that 54.6 percent of e-cigarette users were also smoking cigarettes. About 15 percent of vapers had never smoked cigarettes, and 30.4 percent had quit smoking them.

The study is based on data from the Behavioral Risk Factor Surveillance System, a national survey conducted by the Centers for Disease Control and Prevention. In 2016, the researchers surveyed 486,000 people 18 and older by telephone in every state and the District of Columbia, as well as Guam, Puerto Rico and the Virgin Islands.

More than half of e-cigarette users were younger than 35, and the prevalence decreased with increasing age. It was highest among people ages 18 to 24, both occasional and daily users.

Over all, almost 6 percent of men and 3.7 percent of women were vaping. But there were sharp differences among particular demographic groups.

The prevalence was 9 percent among bisexuals, for example, and 7 percent among lesbians and gay men, compared with 4.6 percent among heterosexuals. Almost 9 percent of transgender people were vapers.

People with cardiovascular disease, cancer, asthma and depression were also more likely than others to be using e-cigarettes, and the rate was 10.2 percent among people with chronic obstructive pulmonary disease. Almost 2 percent of pregnant women were vaping.

E-cigarettes were most commonly used in Oklahoma and in the Southeast, and least often used in North Dakota and California.

"The use of e-cigarettes in the U.S. is a complicated picture," said the study's senior author, Dr. Michael J. Blaha, an associate professor of medicine and epidemiology at Johns Hopkins.

"People who try e-cigs are at risk for a variety of health conditions. But you have former smokers, daily smokers, occasional smokers — it's going to be difficult to sort out the health effects."

Dr. Blaha added, "Almost everyone would agree that the use of e-cigarettes among people who have never smoked — we're up to almost 2 million people — is something we have to watch very carefully."

He and his colleagues acknowledge that the study depends on self-reports and demonstrates only associations, not cause and effect. Moreover, the researchers had no data on the type of e-cigarette device used, the flavors added or the size of the nicotine dose.

Q&A: The ABCs of E-Cigarettes

BY JAN HOFFMAN | NOV. 15, 2018

As vaping grows more popular, especially among teens, here are answers to some basic questions about its health effects.

THE TERM "electronic cigarette" refers to a battery-powered device that heats a tank or cartridge of liquid usually containing nicotine, flavorings and other chemicals, but not the cancer-causing tar found in tobacco cigarettes. Users inhale and exhale the vapor. The devices come in numerous shapes, including ones that look like pens, flash drives and hookahs. Many consumers are confused about the health implications of e-cigarettes. This is a primer about what research so far shows about these devices.

ARE THEY SAFER THAN TRADITIONAL CIGARETTES?

Yes. But that does not mean they are safe.

E-cigarettes contain far fewer dangerous chemicals than those released in burning tobacco. Tobacco cigarettes typically contain 7,000 chemicals, including nearly 70 known to be carcinogenic. E-cigarettes also don't release tar, the tobacco residue that damages lungs but also contributes to the flavor of tobacco products. In the United States, cigarettes are associated with 480,000 deaths a year from coronary heart disease, stroke and numerous cancers, among other illnesses.

The research on e-cigarettes is young because the products have only been around for a little over a decade. Exacerbated by the voltage of a given device, certain e-cigarette flavors can irritate the airways, researchers say: benzaldehyde (added to cherry flavored liquids), cinnamaldehyde (gives cinnamon flavor), and diacetyl (a buttery flavor that can cause lung tissue damage called "popcorn lung.") Some flavors become irritants when added to vaping liquids. The process of turning liquid chemicals into vapor releases harmful particulates deep into the lungs and atmosphere, including heavy metals.

CAN THEY REALLY HELP SMOKERS QUIT?

It's unclear. The Food and Drug Administration has not yet approved the marketing of e-cigarettes as smoking cessation aids. Observational studies of their effectiveness reveal mixed results. Some show that a majority of adult users are former smokers, suggesting the devices are useful in helping them quit. Others reveal that many e-cigarette users also smoke conventional cigarettes. Still others say that a large percentage of e-cigarette users, particularly teenagers, never smoked traditional cigarettes. A 2018 study concluded that e-cigarettes did not help smokers quit at rates faster than smokers who did not use them. But this summer, a British Parliament committee resoundingly endorsed them, even going so far as to suggest that e-cigarettes be made available by prescription through the National Health Service.

DOES NICOTINE HAVE RISKS?

Nicotine is not known to cause cancer. It is a stimulant and a sedative, helping to release dopamine in the brain's pleasure centers. Some research suggests it can improve memory and concentration — although long-term smoking has been associated with cognitive decline. Inhaled nicotine can increase heart rate and blood pressure. The major cause for alarm is that nicotine is highly addictive. It is the chemical in tobacco and e-cigarettes that binds the user.

The nicotine in smoking cessation aids like gum, patches and lozenges is absorbed more slowly than in cigarettes.

"In tobacco smoke, the nicotine is delivered to the lungs, which have a large surface area," said Maciej Goniewicz, a pharmacologist and toxicologist at the Roswell Park Comprehensive Cancer Center in Buffalo, N.Y. "In one or two puffs, the smoker feels the nicotine go right to the brain." The e-cigarette brand Juul in particular "seems to closely match tobacco cigarettes in terms of the speed and amount of nicotine delivery," said Dr. Goniewicz, who studies the absorption of such chemicals.

WHAT ARE THE CONCERNS ABOUT TEENAGERS AND E-CIGARETTES?

The human brain develops into the mid-20s. Researchers worry that adolescents who vape will be most affected by nicotine addiction, which they can develop with less exposure than adults require.

Though studies have not conclusively shown that e-cigarettes can be relied upon to help adult smokers quit, there is substantial evidence that teenagers who use them have a higher risk of smoking cigarettes.

Teens are also using vapes to inhale marijuana. "It seems that kids who use e-cigarettes are more likely to use marijuana in general — smoked or vaped. Is there a gateway effect? We're just getting data now. But it's concerning," said Dr. Rachel Boykan, an associate professor at Stony Brook medical school who researches adolescence and tobacco control.

CAN PARENTS TELL IF THEIR TEENAGERS ARE VAPING?

"E-cig use can be very challenging to detect because they are discreet devices that don't emit much odor," said Dr. Sharon Levy, director of the adolescent substance use and addiction program at Boston Children's Hospital.

Parents can look online for photos of devices and pods. If you find those items in your child's room, pockets or backpack, "you should assume that your child is using it," Dr. Levy said, "not 'just holding it for a friend.'"

If children say they have only tried e-cigarettes a few times, Dr. Levy said, ask them to stop. Then tell them you will check their room and backpack. "And then do it. Kids who have used only sporadically should be able to stop without much intervention."

HOW CAN YOU TREAT TEEN NICOTINE DEPENDENCE?

There aren't widely accepted protocols for teenagers. Dr. Levy urges families to consult a medical professional. Limited interventions with nicotine replacement therapies like patches, gum or medications may be effective in older teens, she said. But "this should be done in conjunction with a good evaluation, since mental health disorders like depression and anxiety and use of other substances are common in kids with nicotine use disorder," she cautioned.

On Dec. 5, the Food and Drug Administration is holding a public hearing to discuss possible nicotine withdrawal therapies specifically for teenagers which, if restrictions on flavored e-cigarette brands proceed, could be an imminent challenge.

JAN HOFFMAN is a health behaviors reporter for Science, covering law, opioids, doctor-patient communication and other topics. She previously wrote about young adolescence and family dynamics for Style and was the legal affairs correspondent for Metro.

CHAPTER 2

Safe to Vape?

The promise that e-cigarettes delivered was that they were safer than cigarettes and that they could help free addicted smokers from the tyranny of tobacco. Without tar and many of the carcinogenic ingredients that go into cigarettes, vaping was marketed as a method to consume nicotine safely. However, this claim was made before the effects of vaping could be carefully studied. As vaping has exploded in popularity, scientists and researchers have rushed to evaluate the safety of e-cigarettes.

A Hot Debate Over E-Cigarettes as a Path to Tobacco, or From It

BY SABRINA TAVERNISE | FEB. 22, 2014

DR. MICHAEL SIEGEL, a hard-charging public health researcher at Boston University, argues that e-cigarettes could be the beginning of the end of smoking in America. He sees them as a disruptive innovation that could make cigarettes obsolete, like the computer did to the typewriter.

But his former teacher and mentor, Stanton A. Glantz, a professor of medicine at the University of California, San Francisco, is convinced that e-cigarettes may erase the hard-won progress achieved over the last half-century in reducing smoking. He predicts that the modern gadgetry will be a glittering gateway to the deadly, old-fashioned habit for children, and that adult smokers will stay hooked longer now that they can get a nicotine fix at their desks.

These experts represent the two camps now at war over the public health implications of e-cigarettes. The devices, intended to feed nicotine addiction without the toxic tar of conventional cigarettes, have divided a normally sedate public health community that had long been united in the fight against smoking and Big Tobacco.

The essence of their disagreement comes down to a simple question: Will e-cigarettes cause more or fewer people to smoke? The answer matters. Cigarette smoking is still the single largest cause of preventable death in the United States, killing about 480,000 people a year.

Dr. Siegel, whose graduate school manuscripts Dr. Glantz used to read, says e-cigarette pessimists are stuck on the idea that anything that looks like smoking is bad. "They are so blinded by this ideology that they are not able to see e-cigarettes objectively," he said. Dr. Glantz disagrees. "E-cigarettes seem like a good idea," he said, "but they aren't."

Science that might resolve questions about e-cigarettes is still developing, and many experts agree that the evidence so far is too skimpy to draw definitive conclusions about the long-term effects of the devices on the broader population.

"The popularity is outpacing the knowledge," said Dr. Michael B. Steinberg, associate professor of medicine at the Robert Wood Johnson Medical School at Rutgers University. "We'll have a better idea in another year or two of how safe these products are, but the question is, will the horse be out of the barn by then?"

This high-stakes debate over what e-cigarettes mean for the nation's 42 million smokers comes at a crucial moment. Soon, the Food and Drug Administration is expected to issue regulations that would give the agency control over the devices, which have had explosive growth virtually free of any federal oversight. (Some cities, like Boston and New York, and states, like New Jersey and Utah, have already weighed in, enacting bans in public places.)

The new federal rules will have broad implications for public health. If they are too tough, experts say, they risk snuffing out small e-cigarette companies in favor of Big Tobacco, which has recently entered the e-cigarette business. If they are too lax, sloppy manufacturing could lead to devices that do not work properly or even harm people.

And many scientists say e-cigarettes will be truly effective in reducing the death toll from smoking only with the right kind of federal regulation — for example, rules that make ordinary cigarettes more expensive than e-cigarettes, or that reduce the amount of nicotine in ordinary cigarettes so smokers turn to e-cigarettes for their nicotine.

"E-cigarettes are not a miracle cure," said David B. Abrams, executive director of the Schroeder National Institute for Tobacco Research and Policy Studies at the Legacy Foundation, an antismoking research group. "They need a little help to eclipse cigarettes, which are still the most satisfying and deadly product ever made."

Smoking is already undergoing a rapid evolution. Nicotine, the powerful stimulant that makes traditional cigarettes addictive, is the crucial ingredient in e-cigarettes, whose current incarnation was developed by a Chinese pharmacist whose father died of lung cancer. With e-cigarettes, nicotine is inhaled through a liquid that is heated into vapor. New research suggests that e-cigarettes deliver nicotine faster than gum or lozenges, two therapies that have never quite taken off.

Sales of e-cigarettes more than doubled last year from 2012, to $1.7 billion, according to Bonnie Herzog, an analyst at Wells Fargo Securities. Ms. Herzog said that in the next decade, consumption of e-cigarettes could outstrip that of conventional cigarettes. The number of stores that sell them has quadrupled in just the last year, according to the Smoke Free Alternatives Trade Association, an e-cigarette industry trade group.

"E-cigarette users sure seem to be speaking with their pocketbooks," said Mitchell Zeller, director of the F.D.A.'s Center for Tobacco Products.

Public health experts like to say that people smoke for the nicotine but die from the tar. And the reason e-cigarettes have caused such a stir is that they take the deadly tar out of the equation while offering the nicotine fix and the sensation of smoking. For all that is unknown about the new devices — they have been on the American market for only seven years — most researchers agree that puffing on one is far less harmful than smoking a traditional cigarette.

But then their views diverge.

Pessimists like Dr. Glantz say that while e-cigarettes might be good in theory, they are bad in practice. The vast majority of people who smoke them now also smoke conventional cigarettes, he said, and there is little evidence that much switching is happening. E-cigarettes may even prolong the habit, he said, by offering a dose of nicotine at times when getting one from a traditional cigarette is inconvenient or illegal.

What is more, critics say, they make smoking look alluring again, with images on billboards and television ads for the first time in decades. Dr. Glantz says that only about half the people alive today have ever seen a broadcast ad for cigarettes. "I feel like I've gotten into a time machine and gone back to the 1980s," he said.

Researchers also worry that e-cigarettes could be a gateway to traditional cigarettes for young people. The devices are sold on the Internet. The liquids that make their vapor come in flavors like mango and watermelon. Celebrities smoke them: Julia Louis-Dreyfus and Leonardo DiCaprio puffed on them at the Golden Globe Awards.

A survey from the Centers for Disease Control and Prevention found that in 2012, about 10 percent of high school students said they had tried an e-cigarette, up from 5 percent in 2011. But 7 percent of those who had tried e-cigarettes said they had never smoked a traditional cigarette, prompting concern that e-cigarettes were, in fact, becoming a gateway.

"I think the precautionary principle — better safe than sorry — rules here," said Dr. Thomas Frieden, director of the C.D.C.

E-cigarette skeptics have also raised concerns about nicotine addiction. But many researchers say that the nicotine by itself is not a serious health hazard. Nicotine-replacement therapies like lozenges and patches have been used for years. Some even argue that nicotine is a lot like caffeine: an addictive substance that stimulates the mind.

"Nicotine may have some adverse health effects, but they are relatively minor," said Dr. Neal L. Benowitz, a professor of medicine at the University of California, San Francisco, who has spent his career studying the pharmacology of nicotine.

Another ingredient, propylene glycol, the vapor that e-cigarettes emit — whose main alternative use is as fake smoke on concert and theater stages — is a lung irritant, and the effects of inhaling it over time are a concern, Dr. Benowitz said.

But Dr. Siegel and others contend that some public health experts, after a single-minded battle against smoking that has run for decades, are too inflexible about e-cigarettes. The strategy should be to reduce harm from conventional cigarettes, and e-cigarettes offer a way to do that, he said, much in the way that giving clean needles to intravenous drug users reduces their odds of getting infected with the virus that causes AIDS.

Solid evidence about e-cigarettes is limited. A clinical trial in New Zealand, which many researchers regard as the most reliable study to date, found that after six months about 7 percent of people given e-cigarettes had quit smoking, a slightly better rate than those with patches.

"The findings were intriguing but nothing to write home about yet," said Thomas J. Glynn, a researcher at the American Cancer Society.

In Britain, where the regulatory process is more developed than in the United States, researchers say that smoking trends are heading in the right direction.

"Motivation to quit is up, success of quit attempts are up, and prevalence is coming down faster than it has for the last six or seven years," said Robert West, director of tobacco studies at University College London. It is impossible to know whether e-cigarettes drove the changes, he said, but "we can certainly say they are not undermining quitting."

The scientific uncertainties have intensified the public health fight, with each side seizing on scraps of new data to bolster its position.

One recent study in Germany on secondhand vapor from e-cigarettes prompted Dr. Glantz to write on his blog, "More evidence that e-cigs cause substantial air pollution." Dr. Siegel highlighted the same study, concluding that it showed "no evidence of a significant public health hazard."

That Big Tobacco is now selling e-cigarettes has contributed to skepticism among experts and advocates.

Cigarettes went into broad use in the 1920s — and by the 1940s, lung cancer rates had exploded. More Americans have died from smoking than in all the wars the United States has fought. Smoking rates have declined sharply since the 1960s, when about half of all men and a third of women smoked. But progress has slowed, with a smoking rate now of around 18 percent.

"Part of the furniture for us is that the tobacco industry is evil and everything they do has to be opposed," said John Britton, a professor of epidemiology at the University of Nottingham in England, and the director for the U.K. Center for Tobacco and Alcohol Studies. "But one doesn't want that to get in the way of public health."

Carefully devised federal regulations might channel the marketing might of major tobacco companies into e-cigarettes, cannibalizing sales of traditional cigarettes, Dr. Abrams of the Schroeder Institute said. "We need a jujitsu move to take their own weight and use it against them," he said.

Dr. Benowitz said he could see a situation under which the F.D.A. would gradually reduce the nicotine levels allowable in traditional cigarettes, pushing smokers to e-cigarettes.

"If we make it too hard for this experiment to continue, we've wasted an opportunity that could eventually save millions of lives," Dr. Siegel said.

Dr. Glantz disagreed.

"I frankly think the fault line will be gone in another year," he said. "The evidence will show their true colors."

Race to Deliver Nicotine's Punch, With Less Risk

BY BARRY MEIER | DEC. 24, 2014

NEUCHATEL, SWITZERLAND — Deep inside a modernist research center on the edge of a mountain lake here, automated smoking machines sample the future of nicotine.

Scientists at Philip Morris International are experimenting with ways to deliver nicotine — Big Tobacco's addictive lifeblood — that are less hazardous than cigarettes but still pack the drug's punch and smoking's other pleasures. The smoking carousels, stuffed with burning cigarettes or glowing electronic devices, are among dozens of high-tech instruments being used.

The rush by Philip Morris and other tobacco companies to develop new ways of selling nicotine is occurring as more consumers are trying e-cigarettes, devices that heat a nicotine-containing fluid to create a vapor that users inhale. While only a small percentage of smokers have switched to the devices — experts say early e-cigarettes did not deliver enough nicotine to satisfy a smoker's cravings — major tobacco companies are deploying their financial resources and knowledge in a bid to dominate a potentially huge market for cigarette alternatives.

In recent months, several tobacco companies have ramped up nicotine levels in their e-cigarette brands, while others, like Philip Morris International, are starting to introduce slender, tubelike devices that will give users as much nicotine as the real thing by heating, not burning, tobacco. A few months ago, another cigarette maker, British American Tobacco, won approval from British drug regulators to market an inhalable nicotine spray.

"Our efforts are guided by two objectives," said Dr. Patrick Picavet, the director of clinical assessment for Philip Morris International. "To develop a range of products that can be scientifically substantiated to

NIELS ACKERMANN FOR THE NEW YORK TIMES

Scientists at the Philip Morris International research center in Neuchatel, Switzerland, are developing alternatives to cigarettes.

reduce risks and that are acceptable substitutes for smokers who can't or aren't willing to quit."

The entry of Big Tobacco into the e-cigarette business has set off alarm bells. Public health advocates, pointing to the industry's documented history of deception about the risks of smoking, question whether cigarette makers want to develop devices to help smokers quit or find new ways to sell nicotine to young people who have never smoked.

"Developing products that satisfy a smoker's addiction will increase the risk that they will be highly addictive to nonsmokers," said Matthew L. Myers, the president of the Campaign for Tobacco-Free Kids, an advocacy group in Washington, D.C.

These are not Big Tobacco's first efforts at mitigating tobacco's considerable health risks. Beginning in 1980s, Philip Morris and R.J. Reynolds Tobacco made stabs at introducing "safer" cigarettes designed to produce fewer carcinogens. But those products never caught on, and the tobacco industry was seemingly caught flat-footed when upstart companies started selling e-cigarettes, mostly made in China.

The new e-cigarette industry is still tiny, with global sales this year of $5 billion compared with more than $800 billion for tobacco products, according to estimates by Wells Fargo Securities. Still, cigarette companies have hedged their bets by acquiring e-cigarette makers or stepping up their own research efforts.

Along with replicating important sensory aspects of smoking, like taste, the biggest hurdle for the new devices, experts say, is delivering nicotine with the efficiency of a cigarette. Within seconds of taking a drag, a smoker feels the nicotine's soothing effects because compounds that are produced when tobacco burns are perfectly sized to carry nicotine deep into the lungs allowing the drug to quickly reach the brain. Those same compounds, which are collectively known as tars, also cause cancer and other diseases.

By comparison, the type of vapor generated by e-cigarettes, experts say, is a less efficient carrier of nicotine than smoke. "There is more deposition in the mouth" with vapor, said Jeffrey S. Gentry, the chief scientific officer of R.J. Reynolds, a division of Reynolds American.

A study published last year showed that one e-cigarette brand, Njoy, produced levels of nicotine in a user's blood significantly lower than the amount produced by a cigarette like a Marlboro. As a result, e-cigarette users have frequently turned to larger devices known as vape pens that have bigger batteries that can produce more heat. But more heat to increase nicotine levels may also result in higher levels of toxins and carcinogens, experts say.

Tobacco companies have rushed to increase nicotine levels in their vapor devices.

About a year after Altria, which sells Marlboro, introduced the MarkTen e-cigarette brand, it increased the concentration of nicotine by about 65 percent. Blu eCigs, which is owned by Lorillard, has raised the nicotine output of its latest device by 50 percent through a variety of changes such as increasing its nicotine concentration and incorporating a larger battery to produce higher heat. Njoy, which only makes e-cigarettes, is using a pharmaceutical ingredient in a new version of its device that is supposed to increase vapor absorption in the lung and elevate nicotine delivery to about 70 percent of a cigarette, according to company data.

At Philip Morris International's research center here, where about 300 scientists work, the nicotine chase is headed in several directions. The company says it has spent about $2 billion since 2008 researching cigarette alternatives with much of that effort focused on devices that use tobacco, but heat it, rather than burn it. Though the "safer" cigarettes that Philip Morris and R.J. Reynolds introduced decades ago were also heat-not-burn devices — and flopped with smokers — the new products, Philip Morris officials say, are more technologically advanced.

Last month, Philip Morris International began test marketing the first of these new devices, called iQOS, in Japan. The device has three components; a pocket-size charger, a heating element and a short stick containing tobacco and other ingredients. The tobacco sticks are heated to a point below combustion, producing an aerosol-like vapor that has about same amount of nicotine as a cigarette. The company plans to introduce another heat-not-burn device in 2016; the heating element of that device can be lit with a match, like a cigarette, but the tobacco stick does not burn.

Some public health researchers are critical of heat-not-burn products, saying that even heating tobacco produces carcinogens. Philip Morris International officials, like Dr. Picavet, counter that the safest nicotine delivery system has little value unless smokers want to use it. Heat-not-burn products, they argue, give consumers what they want with what appear to be lower health risks.

Company scientists are trying to quantify those risks through experiments that use a traditional cigarette as the toxic yardstick. The smoking machines in a laboratory here are used to draw on cigarettes and heat-not-burn devices and then send the resulting smoke or vapor through a series of tubes to a machine in an adjoining room. Cells resembling those found in the human lung are grown in the machine. After the smoke or vapor hits the cells, they are cultured and taken to other laboratories in the building where researchers examine them for biological or genetic changes.

Company officials report that the test results show far less cell damage with heat-not-burn-devices than with cigarette smoke — though they emphasize that laboratory tests do not translate into less disease in humans. To try to get at that risk, Philip Morris is also running clinical studies to measure the level of toxic compounds in the blood and urine of people who use the new devices.

The first study, conducted in 2013 in Poland, showed that levels of some of the most toxic contaminants in tobacco smoke were substantially lower in users of the iQOS heat-not-burn device than in smokers, though they were somewhat higher than in those who abstained. That study, however, lasted only five days. Scientists have not yet published results from a second study, which involved 160 people and lasted three months, company officials said. A third study, which is expected to last six to 12 months, has yet to begin, they said.

Assuming positive results from the human studies, Philip Morris International says it expects to eventually apply to the Food and Drug Administration for agency support for a claim that iQOS poses a "modified risk" to smokers when compared with a cigarette. If the device is approved, Altria will market it in the United States. (Philip Morris International was once part of Altria and the companies have an agreement that allows them to sell each other's products.)

R.J. Reynolds is poised to release Revo, a rebranded version of its heat-not-burn device originally called Eclipse and first marketed in 1996. Last year, a Vermont state judge ordered the cigarette maker to pay $8.3 million in fines after a finding that the company had misleadingly claimed in marketing that the device could lower a smoker's risk of contracting cancer, emphysema and other diseases. Those claims were made before the F.D.A. gained regulatory oversight of tobacco-related health claims. A spokesman for R.J. Reynolds, David Howard, said it plans to initially claim only that Revo "offers less cigarette smoke smell and no ashes" when compared with a cigarette. He declined to say whether the company plans to eventually seek a modified health risk claim with the F.D.A. for Revo.

Despite the proliferation of cigarette alternatives, industry critics fear that Big Tobacco, given its mastery of nicotine, will manipulate drug levels in new devices so that smokers end up using them, not as quitting aids, but as a way to get nicotine where smoking is prohibited. Public health experts also fear the devices will create a new generation of nicotine addicts.

Cigarette makers dismiss such suggestions. But the newest nicotine delivery devices hitting the market suggest the shape of things to come. Several years ago, Philip Morris International bought the rights to a novel form of inhalable nicotine. The idea was developed by outside researchers including Dr. Jed Rose of Duke University, a co-inventor of the nicotine skin patch.

In the past, smoking replacement products like gums and patches have generally failed because they released nicotine too slowly or in amounts too low to satisfy smokers. And on one point, both cigarette industry executives and their critics appear to agree. If the newest alternative products are to succeed from both a financial and a public health standpoint, they will have to deliver nicotine at levels comparable to a cigarette.

Is Vaping Worse Than Smoking?

OPINION | BY JOE NOCERA | JAN. 27, 2015

SO I SUPPOSE you heard about the latest e-cigarette study, the one that said that the vapors e-cigarette users inhale contain multiple forms of formaldehyde. It was much in the news last week, after its authors, five scientists from Portland State University, published a peer-reviewed letter outlining their findings in the prestigious New England Journal of Medicine.

"Before You Vape: High Levels of Formaldehyde Hidden in E-Cigs," said the headline at NBC.com. "Can You Guess What Cancer-Causing Agent Researchers Just Found in Electronic Cigarettes?" asked The Motley Fool. "E-Cigarettes Not Safer Than Ordinary Cigarettes," claimed the online publication Tech Times. The New England Journal of Medicine chimed in with a tweet of its own: "Chemical analysis of e-cigs' vapor show high levels of formaldehyde," it read. "Authors project higher cancer risk than smoking."

The study focused on a device known as a premium vaporizer that heats a flavored liquid containing nicotine. The heat causes the liquid to turn into vapor, which the user inhales. Most of these devices also allow the user to control the voltage. These devices have become increasingly popular as a way to ingest nicotine without smoking.

In the study, the Portland State scientists ran the device at both a low voltage and a high voltage. At the low voltage, they did not detect formaldehyde. But at the high voltage, they found some. Formaldehyde is, indeed, a known carcinogen, which also exists, among hundreds of other toxic chemicals and dozens of cancer-causing agents, in combustible cigarettes. The authors concluded that someone who was a heavy user of a vaporizer at the high voltage was five to 15 times more likely to get cancer than a longtime smoker. Or so they seemed to say.

There is not much doubt that studies like this have an impact on the public perception of e-cigarettes. Even though cigarettes result in 480,000 American deaths each year — and even though it is the tobacco, not the nicotine, that kills them — many in the public health community treat e-cigarettes as every bit as evil. Every dollop of news suggesting that vaping is bad for your health, much of which has been overblown, is irrationally embraced by anti-tobacco activists. One result is that, whereas 84 percent of current smokers thought e-cigarettes were safer than ordinary cigarettes in 2010, that number had dropped to 65 percent by 2013.

Worse, close to a third of the people who had abandoned e-cigarettes and returned to smoking did so because they were worried about the health effects of vaping, according to a study published last year in the journal Nicotine & Tobacco Research.

The Portland State study fits right into this dynamic. It is, on the one hand, factually true that vaping at an extremely high voltage will cause formaldehyde-releasing agents to develop.

But this conclusion is highly misleading. People don't vape at a high voltage because it causes a horrible taste — "a burning taste that occurs from overheating the liquid," wrote Konstantinos Farsalinos, a Greek scientist and vaping expert, in an email to me. Farsalinos has done human studies of vaping and discovered that above a certain voltage — lower than the high voltage test on the Portland State study — people simply couldn't inhale; the taste was unbearable.

Indeed, the study actually conveys good news. When used at normal voltage, vaping does not produce formaldehyde! "Rather than scaring people about the dangers of vaping and alarming them to the 'fact' that vaping raises their cancer risk above that of smoking, we should instead be regulating the voltage and temperature conditions of electronic cigarettes so that the problem of formaldehyde contamination is completely avoided," wrote Michael Siegel, a professor of public health at Boston University, on his blog. But given the way the Portland State authors characterized their research, it's no surprise that headline writers took away a different message.

When I spoke to David Peyton, one of the study's authors, he insisted that the study had been mischaracterized. All it was meant to do, he said, was compare the levels of formaldehyde in e-cigarettes versus cigarettes. "It is exceedingly frustrating to me that we are being associated with saying that e-cigarettes are more dangerous than cigarettes," he added. "That is a fact not in evidence." Well, maybe.

When I read him the tweet from the New England Journal of Medicine — "Authors project higher cancer risk than smoking" — he sounded horrified. "I didn't see the tweet," he said. "I regret that. That is not my opinion."

"There is a lot we don't yet know about e-cigarettes," said Peyton toward the end of our conversation. He is right about that; e-cigarettes are still so new that they need to be studied carefully. And he and his co-authors are planning further studies. Perhaps the next time, they will produce something that doesn't serve mainly as a scare tactic to keep smokers away from e-cigarettes.

JOE NOCERA is an Op-Ed columnist for The New York Times.

Smoking, Vaping and Nicotine

OPINION | BY JOE NOCERA | MAY 26, 2015

"WE NEED A national debate on nicotine," said Mitch Zeller.

Zeller is the director of the Center for Tobacco Products, a division of the Food and Drug Administration created in 2009 when Congress passed legislation giving the F.D.A. regulatory authority — at long last! — over cigarettes. In addition, the center will soon have regulatory authority over other tobacco products, including electronic cigarettes, which have become enormously controversial even as they have gained in use. Through something called a "deeming rule," the center is in the process of asserting that oversight over e-cigarettes.

Opponents of electronic cigarettes, which include many public health officials, hope that the center will treat these new devices like it treats cigarettes: taking steps to discourage teenagers from "vaping," for instance, and placing strict limits on the industry's ability to market its products.

Proponents, meanwhile, hope that the center will view e-cigarettes as a "reduced harm" product that can save lives by offering a nicotine fix without the carcinogens that are ingested through a lit cigarette. In this scenario, e-cigarette manufacturers would be able to make health claims, and adult smokers might even be encouraged to switch from smoking to vaping as part of a reduced harm strategy.

When I requested an interview with Zeller, I didn't expect him to tip his hat on which direction he wanted the center to go, and he didn't. Indeed, one of the points he made was that the F.D.A. was conducting a great deal of scientific research — more than 50 studies in all, he said — aimed at generating the evidence needed to better understand where to place e-cigarettes along what he calls "the continuum of risk."

Zeller is a veteran of the "tobacco wars" of the 1990s, working alongside then-F.D.A. Commissioner David Kessler, who had audaciously labeled cigarettes a "drug-delivery device" (the drug being nicotine) and had claimed regulatory authority. Zeller left the F.D.A. in 2000, after the Supreme Court ruled against Kessler's interpretation, and joined the American Legacy Foundation, where he helped create its hard-hitting, anti-tobacco "Truth campaign." After a stint with a consulting firm, Pinney Associates, he returned to the F.D.A. in early 2013 to lead the effort to finally regulate the tobacco industry.

"I am fond of quoting Michael Russell," Zeller said, referring to an important South African tobacco scientist who died in 2009. In the early 1970s, Russell was among the first to recognize that nicotine was the reason people got addicted to cigarettes. "He used to say, 'People smoke for the nicotine but die from the tar,'" Zeller recalled.

This is also why Zeller found e-cigarettes so "interesting," as he put it, when they first came on the market. A cigarette gets nicotine to the brain in seven seconds, he said. Nicotine gum or patches can take up to 60 minutes or longer, which is far too slow for smokers who need a nicotine fix. But e-cigarettes can replicate the speed of cigarettes in delivering nicotine to the brain, thus creating real potential for them to become a serious smoking cessation device.

But there are still many questions about both their safety and their efficacy. For instance, are smokers using e-cigarettes to quit cigarettes, or they using them to get a nicotine hit at times when they can't smoke cigarettes? And beyond that there are important questions about nicotine itself, and how it should be dealt with.

"When nicotine is attached to smoke particles, it will kill," said Zeller. "But if you take that same drug and put it in a patch, it is such a safe medicine that it doesn't even require a doctor's prescription." That paradox helps explain why he believes "there needs to be a rethink within society on nicotine."

Within the F.D.A., Zeller has initiated discussions with "the other side of the house" — the part of the agency that regulates drugs — to come up with a comprehensive, agency-wide policy on nicotine. But the public health community — and the rest of us — needs to have a debate as well.

"One of the impediments to this debate," Zeller said, is that the e-cigarette opponents are focused on all the flavors available in e-cigarettes — many of which would seem aimed directly at teenagers — as well as their marketing, which is often a throwback to the bad-old days of Big Tobacco. "The debate has become about these issues and has just hardened both sides," Zeller told me.

It's not that Zeller believes nicotine is perfectly safe (he doesn't) or that we should shrug our shoulders if teenagers take up vaping. He believes strongly that kids should be discouraged from using e-cigarettes.

Rather, he thinks there should be a recognition that different ways of delivering nicotine also come with different risks. To acknowledge that, and to grapple with its implications, would be a step forward.

"This issue isn't e-cigarettes," said Mitch Zeller. "It's nicotine."

JOE NOCERA is an Op-Ed columnist for The New York Times.

Can E-Cigarettes Save Lives?

OPINION | BY JOE NOCERA | OCT. 16, 2015

TWO WEEKS AGO, I received an email from NJOY, a company that sells electronic cigarettes. Its purpose was to introduce the Daily, a new product that NJOY described as "a superior e-cigarette scientifically developed to deliver quick-and-strong nicotine satisfaction at levels close to an actual cigarette."

One reason many adult smokers haven't switched to e-cigarettes is that most e-cigarettes don't provide the same nicotine kick as a real cigarette. With some 42 million American adults still smoking, and 480,000 of them dying each year as a result, this is tragic. Though nicotine is addictive, it is the tobacco that kills.

An e-cigarette that could truly replicate the experience of smoking would dramatically reduce — not eliminate, but reduce — the dangers of smoking. NJOY claims that the Daily comes closer to that experience than anything on the market. When I spoke to Paul Sturman, NJOY's chief executive, he emphasized not only the nicotine aspect, but also the Daily's "feel," and "the intensity of the hit to the back of the throat." Sturman added that the company's target market is adult smokers who have tried, but rejected, e-cigarettes. He thinks it's a huge market.

As Sturman was describing the Daily, I thought to myself, "The tobacco-control community is going to hate this thing." Most anti-tobacco advocates view replicating the feel and satisfaction of a cigarette as an effort to "renormalize smoking." And though some believe that smokers should be encouraged to move to e-cigarettes, most refuse even to acknowledge the health benefits of "vaping" over smoking.

Indeed, thanks to this vociferous opposition, an increasing number of Americans view vaping as no safer than smoking, which is absurd. And e-cigarette manufacturers like NJOY can't set them straight: The law giving the Food and Drug Administration regulatory authority over tobacco products, which passed in 2009, prohibits e-cigarette companies from making reduced-harm claims unless they jump through some near-impossible hoops. Thus, NJOY has no way to convey to adult smokers the critical message that e-cigarettes could save their lives.

The undisputed leader of the tobacco-control community is Matt Myers, who helped found and is the president of the Campaign for Tobacco-Free Kids. Unlike many of his anti-tobacco peers, Myers is on the record as saying that if "responsibly marketed and properly regulated, e-cigarettes could benefit the public health." But, like many others, he also fears that e-cigarettes may hook a new generation of children on nicotine, and could lead them to start smoking. And in truth, those fears get far more prominence in the Campaign for Tobacco-Free Kids' various statements about e-cigarettes than its cautious support for them under the right circumstances.

One thing that particularly bothers Myers about e-cigarette companies is their advertising, which he believes employs the same tactics Big Tobacco once used to hook youths on cigarettes. But when I noted that NJOY can't market the Daily as a reduced-risk product, thanks to the 2009 law — and thus had to find less straightforward ways to induce smokers to try the product — Myers told me that I should blame the F.D.A., which, six years in, has yet to impose a single regulation on e-cigarettes. "I think the F.D.A. deserves to be pilloried," he said.

He may be right about that. On the other hand, it's hardly news that government agencies take forever to get things done — and meanwhile, nearly half a million smokers continue to die each year. It seems to me that if the tobacco-control community wants to start saving lives by employing the reduced-harm strategy that e-cigarettes offer, it needs to forget about the F.D.A. and take matters into its own hands.

That means engaging with companies like NJOY that profess to be trying to do the right thing. Instead of demonizing them, the tobacco control community needs to find common ground, and come up with a set of standards — for marketing, manufacturing, and keeping e-cigarettes away from kids — that both sides can agree to. If such a deal were put in place, perhaps with state attorneys general to oversee it, anti-tobacco advocates could talk about the reduced harm potential of e-cigarettes with a clear conscience, without the involvement of the federal government. They then could describe the benefits of e-cigarettes for smokers that the companies themselves can't.

It's happened before. Two decades ago, seeing a once-in-a-lifetime opportunity to impose real restrictions on Big Tobacco, Myers engaged in negotiations that included the states' attorneys general — and Steve Parrish, then a Philip Morris executive. It was an act of tremendous courage — Myers was pilloried when his involvement was revealed — but without his willingness to look the enemy straight in the eye, Big Tobacco would never have been brought to heel.

I believe the time has come for Myers to screw up his courage again. It could be the beginning of the end for one of the greatest scourges on earth.

JOE NOCERA is an Op-Ed columnist for The New York Times.

Smokers Urged to Switch to E-Cigarettes by British Medical Group

BY SABRINA TAVERNISE | APRIL 27, 2016

TAKING A STANCE sharply at odds with most American public health officials, a major British medical organization urged smokers to switch to electronic cigarettes, saying they are the best hope in generations for people addicted to tobacco cigarettes to quit.

The recommendation, laid out in a report published Thursday by the Royal College of Physicians, summarizes the growing body of science on e-cigarettes and finds that their benefits far outweigh the potential harms. It concludes resoundingly that, at least so far, the devices are helping people more than harming them, and that the worries about them — including that using them will lead young people to eventually start smoking traditional cigarettes — have not come to pass.

"This is the first genuinely new way of helping people stop smoking that has come along in decades," said John Britton, director of the U.K. Center for Tobacco and Alcohol Studies at the University of Nottingham, who led the committee that produced the report. E-cigarettes, he said, "have the potential to help half or more of all smokers get off cigarettes. That's a huge health benefit, bigger than just about any medical intervention."

That conclusion is likely to be controversial in the United States, where arguments about e-cigarettes have jolted the traditionally low-key public health community.

E-cigarettes deliver nicotine without the harmful tar and chemicals that cause cancer. Some public health experts see e-cigarettes as the first real chance in years for 40 million addicted Americans to quit. But others, including the federal Centers for Disease Control and Prevention, have focused on the potential dangers of e-cigarettes, for example that they could extend smoking habits, that they could be a gateway to traditional cigarettes for children, or that their vapor could turn out to have long-term health effects.

"These guys, in my view, are going off a cliff," said Stanton A. Glantz, a professor of medicine at the University of California who has been outspoken in his criticism of e-cigarettes. "They are taking England into a series of policies that five years from now they all will really regret. They are turning England into this giant experiment on behalf of the tobacco industry."

But some American public health experts applauded the report, saying the emphasis on policies that reduce harm, such as recommending that smokers try e-cigarettes or giving clean needles to drug users, would probably save more lives.

"This is two countries taking pretty much diametrically opposed positions," said Kenneth E. Warner, a professor of public health at the University of Michigan School of Public Health. "One is focused exclusively on the hypothetical risks, none of which have been established. The other is focusing on potential benefits."

He added, "The British are saying, 'Let's see how we can help the main smokers today, who by the way are largely poor and less educated, and let's not focus so much on kids, who may or may not be sickened by this 40 years down the line.' "

Smoking is still the largest cause of preventable death in the United States, with more than 480,000 people a year dying of smoking-related illnesses. In past decades, smoking was spread throughout society, but today in Britain and the United States, smokers tend to be poor, less educated, or mentally ill.

E-cigarettes, now a multibillion-dollar market, have gained popularity faster than the federal government has managed to regulate them. The Food and Drug Administration has not yet published final rules that would subject them to federal oversight.

A spokesman for the C.D.C. said the agency would not comment on any report other than its own. He reiterated the C.D.C. position on e-cigarettes: "There is currently no conclusive scientific evidence supporting the use of e-cigarettes as a safe and effective cessation tool at the population level. The science thus far indicates most e-cigarette users continue to smoke conventional cigarettes."

But the report cites evidence from Britain that e-cigarettes have helped with quitting. Robert West, director of Tobacco Studies at University College London, analyzed monthly household survey data going back to 2009 in England, and concluded that use of an e-cigarette during an attempt to quit was associated with a 50 percent increase in the chances of success, compared with using no aid or using a product such as nicotine patches without any professional counseling. He estimated that around 20,000 smokers in England quit smoking in 2014 because of e-cigarettes.

Professor Glantz cited his recent analysis as evidence that e-cigarettes in fact reduce the chances someone will quit smoking.

The Royal College of Physicians is a respected doctors' group that helps set medical standards in Britain. It issued a groundbreaking report on the dangers of smoking in 1962 that was seen as the precursor of the American surgeon general's report of 1964 that linked smoking with cancer. The organization's last major report on reducing harm from tobacco use came out in 2007, before e-cigarettes became mainstream, and its authors said the new one was an attempt to evaluate their benefits and harms.

The report walks through a decade of science, listing studies that find in favor of e-cigarettes as well as studies that do not. It asserts that e-cigarettes are only 5 percent as harmful as traditional cigarettes, a conclusion that some American experts say has been lost in the United States in the rush to condemn e-cigarettes. It states bluntly that long-term effects of nicotine are likely to be minimal.

"The emergence of e-cigarettes has generated a massive opportunity for a consumer as well as a health care-led revolution in the way that nicotine is used in society," the report said. As the technology of e-cigarettes improves, "so the vision of a society that is free from tobacco smoking, and the harm that smoking causes, becomes more realistic."

E-Cigarettes Are Safer, but Not Exactly Safe

BY AARON E. CARROLL | MAY 10, 2016

PEOPLE GET HOOKED on cigarettes, and enjoy them for that matter, because of the nicotine buzz. The nicotine doesn't give them cancer and lung disease, though. It's the tar and other chemicals that do the real harm.

A robust debate is going on among public health officials over whether electronic cigarettes, or e-cigarettes, can alleviate the harms of smoking tobacco, or whether they should be treated as negatively as conventional cigarettes. In other countries, such as Britain, officials are more in favor of e-cigarettes, encouraging smokers to switch from conventional to electronic.

Last week, the Food and Drug Administration issued new rules on e-cigarettes, banning their sale to anyone under 18 and requiring that adults under the age of 26 show a photo identification to buy them.

Electronic cigarettes carry the promise of delivering the nicotine without the dangerous additives. The use of e-cigarettes by youth has increased sharply in recent years. In 2011, about 1.5 percent of high school students reported using them in the last month. In 2014, more than 12 percent of students did. That means that nearly 2.5 million American middle and high school students used them in the past month.

The problem is that nicotine is generally considered less safe for children and adolescents than for adults. Poisoning is possible. It's thought that nicotine may interfere with brain development. Most worrisome, it's believed that becoming addicted to nicotine in any form makes smoking more likely later in life.

E-cigarettes are perceived to be less harmful than conventional cigarettes, and they are thought to be useful aids to quitting. These perceptions, however, are not always fully grounded in evidence.

There's enough research about e-cigarettes to have warranted a number of systematic reviews and meta-analyses. A 2014 study in the journal Circulation analyzed the data from a number of angles. For instance, researchers found that the aerosol from e-cigarettes was significantly lower in toxins than from conventional cigarettes, although toxins could be detected. Those exposed secondhand were also at much lower risk from e-cigarettes than from traditional ones, though some risk might still exist.

In other words, we shouldn't believe that e-cigarettes result in the inhalation of "harmless water vapor," but we can accept that they are most likely much safer than conventional cigarettes.

Another review published later that year came to somewhat similar conclusions, and noted that at least a third of the scientific articles on the topic had authors with conflicts of interest. It also reported that studies found worrisome compounds in the aerosol, especially in the flavorings and propylene glycol, which is often added as a humidifying agent. The authors concluded that e-cigarettes can't be deemed safe, though they are less harmful than conventional cigarettes. I conducted my own mini-review a couple of years ago and came to the same conclusion.

But public health officials believe that conventional cigarettes are one of the most significant public health threats, and electronic cigarettes don't appear to be in the same league.

Many of them have argued that e-cigarettes can help people to quit smoking cigarettes, much as nicotine patches or gum do. A 2015 study in PLoS One reviewed the evidence. Among 1,242 smokers of e-cigarettes, 18 percent reported quitting conventional cigarettes for at least six months, which was significantly better than those using placebos without nicotine in them. E-cigarette use was also associated with a reduction in the number of cigarettes smoked per day. Only two studies were randomized controlled trials, however, and they were of mixed quality.

Most important, these studies could not compare the usefulness of e-cigarettes for quitting against other measures, like medications or nicotine replacement therapy. It's possible that those are more powerful.

But others argue that e-cigarettes may be a gateway to conventional cigarette use. A meta-analysis from early this year examined how people use both types of cigarettes. It found that current smokers were significantly more likely to use e-cigarettes and conventional cigarettes together. This was even truer in adolescents, where the "use of e-cigarettes does not discourage, and may encourage, conventional cigarette use."

I admit to being conflicted here. Of course, I'd rather no adolescents use either conventional or e-cigarettes. But I am somewhat swayed by the argument of e-cigarettes for harm reduction.

Years ago, pediatricians used to urge parents to quit smoking because of the health risk for their children. Then, enterprising researchers showed that if smoking parents would just agree to smoke several yards away from their infant, it could reduce hospitalization of infants in their first 18 months of life significantly. Now pediatricians still exhort parents to quit, but they also talk about smoking outside, away from babies. We don't want to make the perfect the enemy of the good.

And, of course, most pediatricians would encourage adolescents to use condoms if they have sex rather than preach abstinence-only. We recognize gray areas when it comes to discussing harm reduction.

One question that few want to consider, however, is whether we'd rather young people smoke conventional cigarettes or e-cigarettes. Neither would be preferable. But a recent study in The Journal of Health Economics forces us to think about this dilemma.

Cigarette sales to minors have been dropping throughout the country for more than a decade. But in the states that introduced bans on sales of e-cigarettes to minors, the decrease in conventional cigarette use slowed significantly. In other words, more children still smoke conventional cigarettes in states that banned e-cigarettes than would be expected by looking at states without bans. The study author argues that banning e-cigarette sales to minors might increase teen smoking over all.

The overall goal should be to get children and adolescents to quit all types of smoking. Banning sales of e-cigarettes to minors may help achieve that goal, but it's also possible it may backfire.

Safer to Puff, E-Cigarettes Can't Shake Their Reputation as a Menace

BY SABRINA TAVERNISE | NOV. 1, 2016

WASHINGTON — A decade after electronic cigarettes were introduced in the United States, use has flattened, sales have slowed and, this fall, NJoy, once one of the country's biggest e-cigarette manufacturers, filed for bankruptcy.

It is quite a reversal for an invention once billed as the biggest chance to end smoking as we know it and take aim at the country's largest cause of preventable death. Use of the devices is slumping because they are not as good as cigarettes at giving a hit of nicotine. Dealing another strike against them, the country's top public health authorities have sent an unwavering message: Vaping is dangerous.

The warning is meant to stop people who have never smoked — particularly children — from starting to vape. But a growing number of scientists and policy makers say the relentless portrayal of e-cigarettes as a public health menace, however well intentioned, is a profound disservice to the 40 million American smokers who could benefit from the devices. Smoking kills more than 480,000 Americans a year.

"We may well have missed, or are missing, the greatest opportunity in a century," said David B. Abrams, senior scientist at the Truth Initiative, an antismoking group. "The unintended consequence is more lives are going to be lost."

American public health experts, led by the Centers for Disease Control and Prevention, have long been suspicious of e-cigarettes. The possible risks of vaping are vast, officials warn, including the potential to open a dangerous new door to addiction for youth. Scientists will not know the full effect for years, so for now, they caution, be wary.

But mounting evidence suggests vaping is far less dangerous than smoking, a fact that is rarely pointed out to the American public. Britain, a country with about the same share of smokers, has come to the opposite conclusion from the United States. This year, a prestigious doctors' organization told the public that e-cigarettes were 95 percent less harmful than cigarettes. British health officials are encouraging smokers to switch.

The American approach "is the same as asking, 'What are the relative risks of jumping out a fourth story window versus taking the stairs?' " said David Sweanor, a lawyer with the Center for Health Law, Policy and Ethics at the University of Ottawa. "These guys are saying: 'Look, these stairs, people could slip, they could get mugged. We just don't know yet.' "

E-cigarettes are much less harmful because they do not have the deadly tar found in regular cigarettes. They instead provide the nicotine fix smokers crave through a liquid that is heated into vapor and inhaled. There is no long-term data yet, but evidence does not show the vapor to be particularly harmful in the short term.

That e-cigarettes are less harmful is a message American smokers rarely hear, partly because American regulation prevents it. Companies are banned from making such claims unless they go through a long process to prove it, and so far, no e-cigarette maker has done so. More states are also passing laws that lump e-cigarettes in with traditional cigarettes, levying taxes on them and banning their use as part of local smoke-free rules.

"When they are regulated just like tobacco, people draw the conclusion that they are just as dangerous," said Daniel I. Wikler, an ethicist at the Harvard School of Public Health. "You didn't say it, but you didn't have to. People make that assumption and you don't try to disabuse them of it."

Last week, Georgia State University published a report finding that the percentage of Americans who thought e-cigarettes were as bad as cigarettes or worse than them had tripled, to 40 percent in 2015 from 13 percent in 2012.

If smokers have tried everything else, and use an e-cigarette to quit completely, "that's a good thing," said Dr. Thomas R. Frieden, the

MARK MAKELA FOR THE NEW YORK TIMES

Jesse McPherson, left, and Ryan Hopkins at Sababa Vapes, a store in Philadelphia. Mounting evidence suggests vaping is far less dangerous than smoking.

director of the C.D.C. He has heard anecdotes about that happening, he added.

"But the plural of anecdote is not data," he said. "And counterbalancing that good trend, there are at least three negative things that might be happening," like people who have never smoked using them, children picking them up as a path to smoking, or smokers using them to perpetuate their habit.

But smoking has been declining. The 2015 adult smoking rate dropped by more than 10 percent from the previous year, the biggest decline since the government began tracking the measure in 1965, said Kenneth E. Warner, a professor of public health at the University of Michigan, citing the government's National Health Interview Survey. Past dips have always been linked to some event, he said, like a tax. But there was no single event to explain this one, and some suspect e-cigarettes may have played a role.

Terry F. Pechacek, a professor of public health at Georgia State University, estimated that in 2015, more than four million Americans reported that e-cigarettes had helped them quit smoking over the past five years, up from about 2.4 million in 2014.

Youth cigarette smoking has gone down, too — by about half since 2007, around the time e-cigarettes started to be sold in the United States. In fact, youth smoking had its biggest-ever drop in 2015, Professor Warner said, citing Monitoring the Future, a federally funded survey. The rate is now 7 percent, a historical low. (Dr. Frieden noted that hookah use had been rising, as had the share of young people using e-cigarettes.)

Science is filling in the blanks, said Dr. Thomas Glynn, a consulting professor at Stanford University and the former director of cancer science and trends at the American Cancer Society. "We've been wringing our hands for years, saying we don't have enough research, but we're getting to the point where we can't say that anymore," he said.

British policy makers say that they were also skeptical of the devices at first, but that they have become more convinced of their benefit as data has accumulated. Rates of successful quitting are up. The smoking rate is down. Surveys by Action on Smoking and Health, a British antismoking group, have found that half of Britain's 2.8 million e-cigarette users no longer smoke real cigarettes. Among people who are trying to quit smoking, e-cigarette users are 60 percent more likely to succeed than those who use over-the-counter nicotine therapies like gum and patches, a British study found.

Americans tend to value abstinence above all else, an all-or-nothing approach that British advocates see as rooted in the United States' Puritan culture, said Deborah Arnott, the chief executive of Action on Smoking and Health.

"It's a bit fundamentalist in the U.S.," Ms. Arnott said, adding that the intense focus on children missed the potential utility of e-cigarettes for current smokers, often some of the poorest and least educated

A vape and a safety notice at Sababa Vapes in Philadelphia. The United States' top public health authorities have often discouraged vaping.

members of society. "What about the smokers? What about the people who are dying now as a result of this habit?"

Dr. Glynn said the American approach was well meaning, and had in the past achieved spectacular success. But it comes with a deep suspicion of the tobacco industry that goes back decades, he added.

"We know there's a big, bad tobacco industry, and that's the enemy," he said. "But e-cigarettes do not fit that narrative. We are fighting a 2016 insurgency with nuclear weapons from the 1980s."

Some researchers think they cannot speak openly, and in many organizations, "advocacy is leading the charge, as opposed to science," Dr. Glynn said. "Public health is suffering as a result."

Professor Wikler said, "You want to be married to the science, but in this case, I think there's been a kind of unmooring, and that's a somewhat dangerous game."

Some Older Smokers Turn to Vaping. That May Not Be a Bad Idea.

BY PAULA SPAN | DEC. 8, 2017

JEANNIE COX currently enjoys a flavor called Coffee & Cream when she vapes. She's also fond of White Lotus, which tastes "kind of fruity."

She buys those nicotine-containing liquids, along with her other e-cigarette supplies, at Mountain Oak Vapors in Chattanooga, Tenn., where she lives. A retired secretary in her 70s, she's often the oldest customer in the shop.

Not that she cares. What matters is that after ignoring decades of doctors' warnings and smoking two packs a day, she hasn't lit up a conventional cigarette in four years and four months.

"Not one cigarette," she said. "Vaping took its place."

Like Ms. Cox, some smokers have been able to stop smoking by switching to e-cigarettes, and many are trying. A recent study by the Centers for Disease Control and Prevention found that more smokers now attempt to quit by using e-cigarettes as a partial or total substitute for cigarettes than by using nicotine gum or lozenges, prescription medications or several other more established methods.

Her success is what researchers disdainfully call "anecdotal evidence," however. There's "no conclusive evidence" that e-cigarettes help people stop smoking long-term, said Brian King, deputy director of the C.D.C.'s Office of Smoking and Health.

At the moment, therefore, neither the C.D.C., the Food and Drug Administration nor the United States Preventive Services Task Force has approved or recommended e-cigarettes for smoking cessation. In fact, the rise of e-cigarettes has generated contentious debate among public health officials and advocates.

But while the proportion of Americans who smoke continues to decrease — down to 15.1 percent in 2015 — the decline has stalled among older adults.

People over age 65 have always been less likely to smoke than adults in general, in part because premature death means fewer smokers survive to older ages. In 1965, when the C.D.C. started tracking smoking rates, 18.3 percent of older adults were smokers. It took 20-plus years for the proportion to fall below 15 percent.

But over the last six years, that percentage has plateaued, bouncing between 8 percent and 9 percent. That still leaves millions of older smokers who probably know they should quit, and may want to, but haven't.

Might switching to vaping improve their health, even if they never become completely nicotine-free?

"Vaping is clearly less harmful than regular cigarettes," said Dr. Steven Schroeder, who directs the Smoking Cessation Leadership Center at the University of California, San Francisco, and is a co-author of a recent JAMA article reviewing tobacco control developments.

Some studies have estimated that e-cigarettes confer at least a two-thirds reduction in health risks, compared with smoking.

Nicotine, Dr. Schroeder pointed out, isn't the primary culprit in the long list of smoking-related diseases. It's the addictive ingredient that keeps smokers lighting up, but the thousands of other chemicals in combustible cigarettes, among them 70 known carcinogens, do most of the damage.

"If you could get nicotine in a safer form, like an F.D.A.-approved medication, even for the rest of your life, you'd be in far better shape," said David Abrams, a clinical psychologist at New York University who researches nicotine and smoking.

This argument, known as harm reduction, recognizes that the best course for older smokers is to quit both cigarettes and e-cigarettes — especially since questions remain about the latter's safety, for users and for those inhaling secondhand vapor.

But harm reduction proponents like Dr. Abrams maintain that given the difficulty of quitting altogether, vaping could provide a reasonable alternative. "Any smoker, especially an older smoker, who isn't thinking about switching is doing himself a major disservice," he said.

Ms. Cox wasn't actually thinking about switching. She had loved smoking ever since she was a teenager sneaking Marlboros, and although she had developed a nighttime cough, she wasn't trying to quit.

But she'd planned a fall visit to her nonsmoking children in Alaska in 2013, and standing outside their home to smoke sounded unappealingly chilly. Ms. Cox did some online research, tried several flavors at Mountain Oak and bought a starter kit.

"I'm not quitting smoking, I'm just trying this newfangled thing," she told herself. "Three days later, I realized I hadn't smoked a cigarette in three days. I thought, 'This is working out kind of nice. Quitting is not supposed to be this easy.' "

Usually, it's not. Although older smokers don't seem to have a harder time than others, stopping cigarettes cold-turkey only rarely works.

Would-be quitters can greatly increase their odds of success by using F.D.A.-approved nicotine replacement products, or a prescription drug like Chantix, and by seeking support from smoking cessation counselors or telephone quit lines like 1-800-NOBUTTS.

"We know what works," said Dr. King of the C.D.C. "We have 50 years of science showing what works." Still, smokers make an average 15 attempts before they become ex-smokers.

The fear that they'll stop trying to go nicotine-free, and vape instead, is one reason the C.D.C. and most public health groups don't embrace e-cigarettes.

In fact, the C.D.C. reports that most smokers don't entirely switch; they become "dual users" who continue to smoke while vaping. Because even a few conventional cigarettes daily increase the risks of mortality and cardiovascular disease, "you'll still get an adverse health effect," Dr. King said.

Further, the C.D.C. takes a broad view of what improves public health, and it worries about growing e-cigarette use by adolescents (though conventional smoking has declined in that age group), even if the products might help others stop.

Longtime suspicion of Big Tobacco plays a role in the e-cigarette controversy, too, as the industry muscles into a field now populated by hundreds of small vapor companies.

The F.D.A. had planned to begin regulating e-cigarettes next August, prompting an outcry that small manufacturers unable to afford the hefty costs of applying for approval would simply shut down, leaving the field to the likes of Philip Morris.

The agency has since pushed e-cigarette regulation back to 2022. "A delay of execution," said Gregory Conley of the American Vaping Association. For now, the industry can't advertise vaping products as safer than cigarettes or even as smoke-free.

The industry has not particularly targeted older smokers, Mr. Conley said, possibly seeing them as set in their purchasing habits, and unwilling to spend time in vape shops experimenting with vaporizers and liquids to find a satisfying substitute for cigarettes (and a cheaper one, after the initial equipment purchase).

But older smokers also have a greater need to give up cigarettes. Not only can quitting extend their lives, but it can ward off many of the debilitating effects of heart disease, diabetes and other chronic disorders. Nonsmokers respond better to surgery and chemotherapy, Dr. Schroeder noted, and older adults often face one or both.

Ms. Cox wasn't feeling ill, apart from that cough, when she switched to a vaporizer and unintentionally stopped smoking. But she felt better afterward.

"I could breathe easier," she said. "I was no longer coughing. I could sleep longer. I got happier."

She Couldn't Quit Smoking. Then She Tried Juul.

BY JAN HOFFMAN | NOV. 16, 2018

Millions embrace e-cigarettes as smoking cessation aids. Will restricting the devices for teenagers put former adult smokers who vape at risk to start again?

TRY AS SHE MIGHT, Brittany Kligman couldn't free herself of a pack-a-day cigarette habit, eight years in duration. And she ached to.

She was mortified the time that a taxi driver sniffed as she entered his cab and remarked, "You're a smoker, huh?" (And she had just showered!) She was getting more sinus infections. Because her chest felt uncomfortably tight when she exercised, she stopped high intensity interval training. Then SoulCycle classes. Finally, she quit working out.

Then Ms. Kligman, 33, tried Juul, the sleek vaping device she credits for her liberation. Since last January, it's been hello nicotine salts, goodbye tar. Juul gave her everything she enjoyed about cigarettes — the nicotine jolt as well as something ritualized to do with her hands — but without the stink, the stigma and the carcinogens.

"The last cigarette I smoked was on July 5 when I ran out of pods," Ms. Kligman said, referring to cartridges of mango-flavored liquid, as she took discreet hits while chatting at a downtown Manhattan cafe. "I couldn't finish it — it made me sick. And I thought, 'How did I used to do this?'"

But this week, under pressure to keep its products away from teenagers, Juul announced it was suspending sales of many of its flavors (including Ms. Kligman's beloved mango) at retail stores. The next day, the Food and Drug Administration issued new requirements that stores can only sell flavored e-cigarettes from closed-off spaces that are inaccessible to minors, a stipulation that could force many outlets to stop carrying the products. The new restrictions make smokers-turned-vapers like Ms. Kligman uneasy.

JOSHUA BRIGHT FOR THE NEW YORK TIMES

Brittany Kligman vapes in her apartment in New York on Oct. 25, 2018.

"If you're going to sell an adult product, you have to be prepared to secure it," she said. "But it also seems like they're making a lot of steps and loops for people like me. They're taking away a flavor I used for smoking cessation. "

She not only intends to stock up on mango at her corner smoke shop, but is working up a Plan B: "I'll switch to Juul's tobacco flavor. I can get around this. Just like the kids will — they can always find a way."

Nicotine, the chemical in tobacco cigarettes that creates the addictive stranglehold that is so difficult to break, is most likely a signature reason that Juul and other e-cigarettes help former smokers like Ms. Kligman quit. In making the switch, smokers can satisfy their nicotine hunger without inhaling the dozens of cancer-causing carcinogens released by a burning cigarette.

Juul in particular may work better than nicotine patches and gum not only because of the amount of nicotine in a Juul pod, but because an e-cigarette's means of delivery — into the lungs and brain — is more immediate than through skin or saliva. Although studies of e-cigarettes are increasing, they, like the devices themselves, are still in the early stages. The first e-cigarettes arrived in the United States around 2006, but most versions now on the market are far more recent.

And while these products were conceived as smoking alternatives, the Food and Drug Administration has not yet formally approved them as smoking cessation aids, and research is mixed about their effectiveness.

The Centers for Disease Control and Prevention suggest that they can be effective in helping smokers quit "if used as a complete substitute for all cigarettes and other smoked tobacco products." Like Ms. Kligman, about 30 percent of adult users do exactly that, but nearly 60 percent use both, the C.D.C. said.

According to a national health survey released earlier this month by the C.D.C., the number of adult cigarette smokers in the United States dropped to about 34 million last year, while the number of adult e-cigarette users rose to about seven million. But the report didn't find sufficient evidence to link the two.

Though e-cigarettes are supposedly safer in most respects than combustible cigarettes, they are not benign. Nicotine is not known to cause cancer. It can induce feelings of pleasure and alleviate stress. But in addition to its powerful addictive properties — researchers suggest that the average smoker tries to quit 15 times over a lifetime, with many as much as 30 — nicotine can irritate bronchial pathways and raise heart rates.

According to a 2018 comprehensive evaluation of e-cigarettes by the National Academies of Sciences, Engineering and Medicine, the products are particularly challenging to study because mechanisms and content vary widely. The report said that in addition to nicotine, the long-term effects of the products' metals, chemicals in the aerosol and flavorings could be problematic.

Now regulators are struggling with how to address competing concerns — weighing the benefits of e-cigarettes for tobacco smokers against the risks for cigarette-naive adolescents, whose developing brains are especially vulnerable to nicotine. The overwhelming majority of smokers start as teenagers, but Ms. Kligman began smoking at 25, when she was a graduate student in biomedical science. Still, the moment of induction seemed purely adolescent: She and her sister wanted an escape during a soporific visit to their grandparents.

"It's cool," Ms. Kligman's sister assured her. "And it'll make you skinnier."

After smoking one cigarette, Ms. Kligman felt sweaty and nauseous. So she tried a second.

She began smoking every chance she got. It swiftly became a soothing oral fixation. When she felt nervous at parties or bars, cigarettes gave her an excuse to step outside. Moving to New York from Atlanta, she found that the people she was befriending were smokers. Defiantly, they stood in solidarity when nonsmokers made withering remarks.

Of course she was well aware of the health risks. She's a medical researcher. Doctors have been in her family for generations. One boyfriend announced that she couldn't smoke around him. "It caused me stress," Ms. Kligman recalled, "because I craved the nicotine when I was with him and I couldn't get it."

She tried so many ways to quit: Rationing cigarettes. Cold turkey. Nicotine gum. A boyfriend even bought her an unwieldy, old-school vape. It leaked and didn't fit in her purse — a nonstarter. Then, a prescription for a smoking cessation medicine.

But she never had a strategy — chewing straws? doing pushups? — to substitute when the urge to smoke came on. Each time she abstained, the irritability overwhelmed her.

"When it's bad, you're supposed to hang in there for 20 minutes," Ms. Kligman said. "But I'd say, 'I'm so done with this feeling. I'll have just one cigarette. Or two.'"

She told herself: "At least it's nicotine and not heroin."

Last January, at a dinner party, she asked a good friend to join her outside for a smoke after the meal. Four people at the table said, "We don't smoke anymore. We Juul."

JOSHUA BRIGHT FOR THE NEW YORK TIMES

Ms. Kligman said she couldn't finish the last cigarette she tried, in July. "It made me sick," she said. "And I thought, 'How did I used to do this?'"

Embarrassed that she was still smoking, she tried a hit of someone's Juul. She was underwhelmed, but allowed that it sort of worked. The next day she bought one. She used it for four days, then put it in a drawer and went back to cigarettes.

A month later, for a weekend visit to her friend Amy's cottage upstate, she packed the Juul. It was seriously cold outside. When she needed a cigarette break, another guest, a runner, intervened, saying, "Just Juul inside!"

She spent that weekend indoors, juuling nonstop to get a constant "nic fix." "I began to think, 'This is working. It's really working!" And it was so easy.

Back at home, she tried a cigarette. Gross.

So she continued to vape. For weeks she coughed up murk and muck that had attached to her airways. And then … it stopped.

Now her eyes are clear. Teeth gleam. Skin looks rejuvenated. And the money! The cigarette brand she smoked daily was about $17 a pack; a package of four cartridges could run about $17. Making the switch put back about $85 a week in her pocket. With the savings, she recently bought a celebratory pair of running shoes.

She now vapes about the same amount that she had smoked — a cartridge a day, roughly the nicotine equivalent to a pack. Soon she plans to try Juul's new lower-nicotine cartridges, hoping someday to be completely weaned. The device has overtaken her life much as cigarettes had. "I'm a hard-core Juuler," she said.

Almost all her friends vape now. Sunday mornings at Amy's cottage — six friends sitting around with mimosas, fresh-baked cinnamon rolls and Juuls. They have group texting chats, sending around Juul memes and news, sharing pictures of the latest accessories, like the casing wraps and charging stations. They shrug off health concerns that are being raised about e-cigarettes.

"After 18 years of smoking cigarettes," Amy said, "I'm not exactly worried about nicotine addiction."

Only one friend has quit vaping. He was going through three pods a day and landed in the hospital with a rapid heartbeat. Doctors said the cause was excessive nicotine.

"His husband smashed the Juul with a hammer and told him never to vape again," Ms. Kligman said.

"So he went back to smoking cigarettes."

JAN HOFFMAN is a health behaviors reporter for Science, covering law, opioids, doctor-patient communication and other topics. She previously wrote about young adolescence and family dynamics for Style and was the legal affairs correspondent for Metro.

CHAPTER 3

The Risks of Vaping

Even as e-cigarettes have grown in popularity and developed the reputation as safer alternatives to cigarettes, public health professionals have been divided on the risks posed by vaping. While vaping does appear to reduce the likelihood of certain lung cancers, e-cigarettes also contain a host of toxic ingredients that pose a threat to consumers in addition to higher concentrations of nicotine. The articles in this section address the various risks posed by e-cigarettes and vaping, and the challenges health professionals face in identifying exactly what those risks are.

Selling a Poison by the Barrel: Liquid Nicotine for E-Cigarettes

BY MATT RICHTEL | MARCH 23, 2014

A DANGEROUS NEW FORM of a powerful stimulant is hitting markets nationwide, for sale by the vial, the gallon and even the barrel.

The drug is nicotine, in its potent, liquid form — extracted from tobacco and tinctured with a cocktail of flavorings, colorings and assorted chemicals to feed the fast-growing electronic cigarette industry.

These "e-liquids," the key ingredients in e-cigarettes, are powerful neurotoxins. Tiny amounts, whether ingested or absorbed through the skin, can cause vomiting and seizures and even be lethal. A teaspoon of even highly diluted e-liquid can kill a small child.

But, like e-cigarettes, e-liquids are not regulated by federal authorities. They are mixed on factory floors and in the back rooms of shops, and sold legally in stores and online in small bottles that are kept casually around the house for regular refilling of e-cigarettes.

Evidence of the potential dangers is already emerging. Toxicologists warn that e-liquids pose a significant risk to public health, particularly to children, who may be drawn to their bright colors and fragrant flavorings like cherry, chocolate and bubble gum.

"It's not a matter of if a child will be seriously poisoned or killed," said Lee Cantrell, director of the San Diego division of the California Poison Control System and a professor of pharmacy at the University of California, San Francisco. "It's a matter of when."

Reports of accidental poisonings, notably among children, are soaring. Since 2011, there appears to have been one death in the United States, a suicide by an adult who injected nicotine. But less serious cases have led to a surge in calls to poison control centers. Nationwide, the number of cases linked to e-liquids jumped to 1,351 in 2013, a 300 percent increase from 2012, and the number is on pace to double this year, according to information from the National Poison Data System. Of the cases in 2013, 365 were referred to hospitals, triple the previous year's number.

Examples come from across the country. Last month, a 2-year-old girl in Oklahoma City drank a small bottle of a parent's nicotine liquid, started vomiting and was rushed to an emergency room.

That case and age group is considered typical. Of the 74 e-cigarette and nicotine poisoning cases called into Minnesota poison control in 2013, 29 involved children age 2 and under. In Oklahoma, all but two of the 25 cases in the first two months of this year involved children age 4 and under.

In terms of the immediate poison risk, e-liquids are far more dangerous than tobacco, because the liquid is absorbed more quickly, even in diluted concentrations.

"This is one of the most potent naturally occurring toxins we have," Mr. Cantrell said of nicotine. But e-liquids are now available almost everywhere. "It is sold all over the place. It is ubiquitous in society."

The surge in poisonings reflects not only the growth of e-cigarettes but also a shift in technology. Initially, many e-cigarettes were disposable devices that looked like conventional cigarettes. Increasingly, however, they are larger, reusable gadgets that can be refilled with liquid, generally a combination of nicotine, flavorings and solvents. In Kentucky, where about 40 percent of cases involved adults, one woman was admitted to the hospital with cardiac problems after her e-cigarette broke in her bed, spilling the e-liquid, which was then absorbed through her skin.

The problems with adults, like those with children, owe to carelessness and lack of understanding of the risks. In the cases of exposure in children, "a lot of parents didn't realize it was toxic until the kid started vomiting," said Ashley Webb, director of the Kentucky Regional Poison Control Center at Kosair Children's Hospital.

The increased use of liquid nicotine has, in effect, created a new kind of recreational drug category, and a controversial one. For advocates of e-cigarettes, liquid nicotine represents the fuel of a technology that might prompt people to quit smoking, and there is anecdotal evidence that is happening. But there are no long-term studies about whether e-cigarettes will be better than nicotine gum or patches at helping people quit. Nor are there studies about the long-term effects of inhaling vaporized nicotine.

 Unlike nicotine gums and patches, e-cigarettes and their ingredients are not regulated. The Food and Drug Administration has said it plans to regulate e-cigarettes but has not disclosed how it will approach the issue. Many e-cigarette companies hope there will be limited regulation.

"It's the wild, wild West right now," said Chip Paul, chief executive officer of Palm Beach Vapors, a company based in Tulsa, Okla., that operates 13 e-cigarette franchises nationwide and plans to open 50 more this year. "Everybody fears F.D.A. regulation, but honestly, we kind of welcome some kind of rules and regulations around this liquid."

Mr. Paul estimated that this year in the United States there will be sales of one million to two million liters of liquid used to refill e-cigarettes, and it is widely available on the Internet. Liquid Nicotine Wholesalers, based in Peoria, Ariz., charges $110 for a liter with 10 percent nicotine concentration. The company says on its website that it also offers a 55 gallon size. Vaporworld.biz sells a gallon at 10 percent concentrations for $195.

Mr. Paul said he was worried that some manufacturers outside the United States — China is a major center of e-cigarette production — were not always delivering the concentrations and purity of nicotine they promise. Some retailers, Mr. Paul said, "are selling liquid and they don't have a clue what is in it."

Cynthia Cabrera, executive director of Smoke Free Alternatives Trade Association, said she would also favor regulations, including those that would include childproof bottles and warning labels, and also manufacturing standards. But she said many companies already were doing that voluntarily, and that parents also needed to take some responsibility.

"You wouldn't leave a bottle of Ajax out," she said. Advocates of e-cigarettes sometimes draw comparisons between nicotine and caffeine, characterizing both as recreational stimulants that carry few risks. But that argument is not established by science, and many health advocates take issue with the comparison.

"There's no risk to a barista no matter how much caffeine they spill on themselves," said Dr. Neal L. Benowitz, a professor at the University of California, San Francisco, who specializes in nicotine research. "Nicotine is different."

Without proper precautions, like wearing gloves while mixing e-liquids, these products "represents a serious workplace hazard," he said.

The nicotine levels in e-liquids varies. Most range between 1.8 percent and 2.4 percent, concentrations that can cause sickness, but rarely death, in children. But higher concentrations, like 10 percent or even 7.2 percent, are widely available on the Internet. A lethal dose at such levels would take "less than a tablespoon," according to Dr. Cantrell, from the poison control system in California. "Not just a kid. One tablespoon could kill an adult," he said.

Some E-Cigarettes Deliver a Puff of Carcinogens

BY MATT RICHTEL | MAY 3, 2014

ELECTRONIC CIGARETTES appear to be safer than ordinary cigarettes for one simple — and simply obvious — reason: people don't light up and smoke them.

With the e-cigarettes, there is no burning tobacco to produce myriad new chemicals, including some 60 carcinogens.

But new research suggests that, even without a match, some popular e-cigarettes get so hot that they, too, can produce a handful of the carcinogens found in cigarettes and at similar levels.

A study to be published this month in the journal Nicotine and Tobacco Research found that the high-power e-cigarettes known as tank systems produce formaldehyde, a known carcinogen, along with the nicotine-laced vapor that their users inhale. The toxin is formed when liquid nicotine and other e-cigarette ingredients are subjected to high temperatures, according to the study. A second study that is being prepared for submission to the same journal points to similar findings.

The long-term effects of inhaling nicotine vapor are unclear, but there is no evidence to date that it causes cancer or heart disease as cigarette smoking does. Indeed, many researchers agree that e-cigarettes will turn out to be much safer than conventional cigarettes, an idea that e-cigarette companies have made much of in their advertising.

The website for Janty, a company that manufactures popular tank systems, says the benefits of e-cigarettes include having "no toxins associated with tobacco smoking."

Nonetheless, the new research suggests how potential health risks are emerging as the multibillion-dollar e-cigarette business rapidly evolves, and how regulators are already struggling to keep pace. While the Food and Drug Administration last month proposed sweeping new rules that for the first time would extend its authority to e-cigarettes, the F.D.A. has focused largely on what goes into these products — currently, an unregulated brew of chemicals and flavorings — rather than on what comes out of them, as wispy plumes of flavored vapor.

The proposed rules give the F.D.A. the power to regulate ingredients, not emissions, although the agency said it could consider such regulations in the future. Even so, some experts contend that the current approach is akin to examining the health risks associated with tobacco leaves rather than with cigarette smoke.

"Looking at ingredients is one thing, and very important," said Maciej L. Goniewicz, who led the first study, which is scheduled to be published on May 15. "But to have a comprehensive picture, you have to look at the vapor."

Both studies focused on tank systems, fast-growing members of the e-cigarette family. Unlike disposable e-cigarettes, which tend to mimic the look and feel of conventional smokes, tank systems tend to be larger devices heated with batteries that can vary in voltage, often resembling fountain pens or small flashlights. Users fill them with liquid nicotine, or e-liquid, and the devices are powerful enough to vaporize that fluid quickly, producing thick plumes and a big nicotine kick.

Dr. Goniewicz, an assistant professor of oncology at the Roswell Park Cancer Institute in Buffalo, said people using the systems "want more nicotine, but the problem is they're also getting more toxicants."

Complicating the issue is that the tank systems are made by a variety of manufacturers, many overseas, and then sometimes tinkered with and modified by retail shops or users. Still, e-cigarette makers should be measuring emissions, said Josh Rabinowitz, chief scientist at NJoy, a maker of more traditional e-cigarettes, not tank systems.

"We don't just evaluate the purity of what goes in, but also the purity of the emitted vapor because that's what the user is exposed to," said Dr. Rabinowitz. He said NJoy had significantly lower levels of formaldehyde than regular cigarettes.

Like Dr. Goniewicz's study, which has been subjected to peer review, the second study also centered on the impact of increased heat generated by the systems. In that study, the focus was on how people use the devices to create more — and more potent — vapor. Rather than fill their tank systems with e-liquid, experienced users often trickle drops of the fluid directly onto the device's heating element, a practice known as "dripping."

But with dripping, the e-liquid heats with such intensity that formaldehyde and related toxins "approach the concentration in cigarettes," said Dr. Alan Shihadeh, a project director at the Virginia Commonwealth University's Center for the Study of Tobacco Products and an associate professor of mechanical engineering at American University in Beirut, who led the research.

Both studies point to the same phenomenon: Intense heat can change the composition of e-liquids, creating new chemicals. Importantly, the researchers said, the chemical reactions apply not only to the liquid nicotine, but also to two other crucial ingredients in most e-liquids: vegetable glycerin and propylene glycol.

Precisely what level of heat causes the reaction is difficult to pinpoint. The Roswell research found, generally, that when battery voltage increased to 4.8 volts from 3.2 volts, toxin levels increased markedly.

"This finding suggests that in certain conditions, E.C.s might expose their users to the same or even higher levels of carcinogenic formaldehyde as tobacco smoke," the Roswell study says.

Both studies examined only a handful of carcinogens. Traditional cigarettes, by contrast, create thousands of chemicals and dozens of carcinogens, according to Prue Talbot, professor of cell biology at the University of California, Riverside. E-cigarettes do not tend to generate enough heat to create combustion, which is a big reason that many

SANDY HUFFAKER FOR THE NEW YORK TIMES

A study suggests that e-cigarette vapor can contain toxins.

public health officials and researchers predict they will prove less harmful than cigarettes.

"If I was in a torture chamber and you said I had to puff on something, I'd choose an e-cigarette over a regular cigarette," Dr. Shihadeh said. "But if you said I could choose an e-cigarette or clean air, I'd definitely choose clean air."

He added: "And I definitely wouldn't drip."

Whatever the health effects of the new systems, they are exploding in popularity and reshaping the market, according to a report issued in March by Bonnie Herzog, a tobacco-industry analyst for Wells Fargo Securities. In 2013, Ms. Herzog projected domestic sales of e-cigarettes at $1.7 billion a year but, based on surveys with makers and marketers of e-cigarettes, she now expects "in excess of $2 billion."

Demand for tank systems, Ms. Herzog wrote, is "accelerating" and "undeniably a key growth driver." She estimated that the new systems now represent 35 percent of the market, but they are growing twice as fast as the previous models.

Experts say tank systems appeal to young people who like products that can be customized with flavors and power, and are comfortable with fast-changing technology.

At Sky City Vapor in San Diego, the owner, Chris Hayek, said consumers clearly are gravitating toward the more powerful systems and away from the "ciga-likes."

"The ones shaped like a cigarette, that style doesn't do it for them," Mr. Hayek said. "It's not harsh, it doesn't produce as much vapor." He said that only about 5 percent of his customers are regular "drippers" but that the trend in the industry is toward tank systems that produce large amounts of strong vapor.

Some health data seems promising for e-cigarette users, such as a previous study led by the researchers at Roswell Park Cancer Institute. That research, published in 2012 in the journal Tobacco Control, found that the level of some toxic substances in 12 e-cigarette brands was significantly lower than in cigarette smoke. However, Dr. Goniewicz said that the technology is moving so quickly that many of the products tested are outdated — and some are no longer even on the market.

"Technology is way ahead of the science," Dr. Shihadeh concurred. "We're creating this stuff, and we don't understand the implications."

Dire Warnings by Big Tobacco on E-Smoking

BY MATT RICHTEL | SEPT. 28, 2014

TOBACCO COMPANIES, long considered public health enemy No. 1, have suddenly positioned themselves as protectors of consumer well-being in the digital age.

They are putting out among the strongest health warnings in the fledgling e-cigarette industry, going further even than the familiar ones on actual cigarettes, a leading cause of death. It has left the industry's critics scratching their heads and deeply skeptical.

One warning, from Altria, maker of Marlboros, reads in part: "Nicotine is addictive and habit forming, and is very toxic by inhalation, in contact with the skin, or if swallowed."

Another, from Reynolds American, maker of Camels, says the product is not intended for persons "who have an unstable heart condition, high blood pressure, or diabetes; or persons who are at risk for heart disease or are taking medicine for depression or asthma."

They appear on the packaging for the companies' e-cigarettes, which are part of a fast-growing industry that the tobacco companies are maneuvering to dominate.

The warnings, which are entirely voluntary and are seen by some as attempts to reduce legal liability or burnish corporate reputations, generally exceed what amounts to modest cautions, silence or even positive health claims from smaller e-cigarette makers.

One on a pack of nicotine cartridges for MarkTen e-cigarettes, for instance, the brand Altria is introducing nationwide, runs more than 100 words. People with heart disease, high blood pressure and diabetes should not use the product, the label says. Neither should children. It goes on to say that nicotine can cause dizziness, nausea and stomach pains, and may worsen asthma.

"When I saw it, I nearly fell off my chair," said Dr. Robert K. Jackler, a professor at the Stanford School of Medicine where he leads research into cigarette and e-cigarette advertising. MarkTen also warns that e-cigarettes are not a smoking cessation product, a warning that also appears on Vuse from Reynolds.

"Is this part of a noble effort for the betterment of public health, or a cynical business strategy? I suspect the latter," Dr. Jackler said.

Experts with years studying tobacco company behavior say they strongly suspect several motives, but, chiefly, that the e-cigarette warnings are a very low-risk way for the companies to insulate themselves from future lawsuits and, even more broadly, to appear responsible, open and frank. By doing so, the experts said, big tobacco curries favor with consumers and regulators, earning a kind of legitimacy that they crave and have sought for decades. Plus, they get to appear more responsible than the smaller e-cigarette companies that seek to unseat them.

The reason the strategy is low risk, experts said, is that many people don't read the warnings anyway.

But the companies say their reasoning is straightforward. William Phelps, a spokesman for Altria, said the warnings on MarkTen, made by the subsidiary NuMark, reflect "a goal to openly and honestly communicate about health effects" and that the warnings are based on "scientific research" and "previously developed warnings" on nicotine products. As part of a new national rollout, the MarkTen is in 60,000 stores in the western half of the United States and will be nationwide by year's end, the company said.

The R. J. Reynolds Vapor Company, which makes Vuse, had less to say about the origin of its e-cigarette warnings, which note, among other things, that nicotine is addictive and the product should not be used by people with heart conditions or high blood pressure. A company spokesman said the warning reflected the fact that Vuse did not contain tobacco leaf and did not undergo "combustion," like tobacco in cigarettes.

In a previous interview with The New York Times, the president of R. J. Reynolds Vapor Company, Stephanie Cordisco, said that her e-cigarette division aimed to make a break with the negative reputation of the cigarette industry. "We're here to make sure we can put this industry on the right side of history," she said in the interview. Reynolds is one of the companies that has sued, successfully, to stop more graphic warnings on cigarette packages.

The fact these companies are voluntarily warning about e-cigarettes is "totally Orwellian," said Robert N. Proctor, a Stanford history professor who studies the tobacco industry. He added, "They do everything for legal reasons, otherwise they'd stop making the world's deadliest consumer products," he said of tobacco companies.

When it comes to e-cigarettes, public health experts and regulators are struggling with deep contradictions and questions, the most fundamental of which is whether e-cigarettes will lure thousands of cigarette smokers away from a deadly habit or actually lead to a new generation of nicotine addicts.

In a report issued last month, the World Health Organization urged stronger restrictions on e-cigarettes, including indoor smoking bans, and also expressed "grave concern" at the growing role of tobacco companies in the industry.

Smaller e-cigarette companies are skeptical too. "To the uninitiated, it looks like they are responsible corporate citizens," said Cynthia Cabrera, executive director of the Smoke-Free Alternatives Trade Association, an e-cigarette industry group. She considers the warnings "disingenuous," particularly the MarkTen claim that nicotine is "very toxic" when inhaled, swallowed or brought into contact with the skin. That is not true of the doses in e-cigarettes, she said.

Ms. Cabrera said she believed that the big tobacco companies had an ulterior motive, perhaps to appear to regulators and lawmakers as more credible than the small e-cigarette companies. She speculated that big tobacco companies would then be able to lobby for rules and laws that would favor them. She said some lobbyists were telling legislators that prepackaged, uniform e-cigarettes had lesser health risks than the ones sold, sometimes in made-to-order fashion, in independent vapor shops. In terms of warnings, Ms. Cabrera's group has called for childproof packaging on e-liquids, which are used to fill e-cigarettes, and they favor warnings calling nicotine addictive and listing other ingredients.

For now, there are hundreds of smaller e-cigarette companies, many selling online, and their claims and warnings run the gamut. Some make health claims that Dr. Jackler said were wild and unsubstantiated, claiming to be sex stimulants, beneficial for insomniacs or even a way to promote weight loss. Dr. Jackler speculated that one motivation for Big Tobacco could be discouraging smokers from using a competing product.

Mr. Phelps, from Altria, dismissed that idea. "We want that category to be successful, and NuMark has taken a number of steps to be a leader," he said.

The warnings on the MarkTen are far more elaborate than those on a pack of Marlboros, which note, for instance, that "smoking by pregnant women may result in fetal injury, premature birth and low birth weight." The warning does not include other risks, like the addictive nature of cigarettes, which are known to cause cancer and other deadly diseases. Mr. Phelps said that Altria was putting out cigarette warnings mandated by the government. The government mandate does not, however, preclude stronger warnings from appearing on Marlboros.

Dr. Jackler asked: "Why wouldn't you warn about 'very toxic' nicotine on your cigarettes when you do so on e-cigarettes?"

Whatever the warnings say, they are typically disregarded by consumers, according to Allan M. Brandt, professor of the history of medicine and science at Harvard University and an expert in the tobacco industry.

Big tobacco companies "know that even these types of very serious warnings have generally not put significant dents in their sales," he said. But, he said, the warnings do appear to be part of an age-old practice by the industry: creating scientific gray areas. That tactic, he said, lets them forestall decisive action by consumers and regulators, as it did with cigarettes. "It's an incredibly effective and duplicitous practice in inventing additional new uncertainties and, at the same time, appearing to be cooperative," Mr. Brandt said. "They've done this before," he added. "It buys them time. It bought them 40 years with traditional tobacco products."

Vaping Can Be Addictive and May Lure Teenagers to Smoking, Science Panel Concludes

BY SHEILA KAPLAN | JAN. 23, 2018

WASHINGTON — A national panel of public health experts concluded in a report released on Tuesday that vaping with e-cigarettes that contain nicotine can be addictive and that teenagers who use the devices may be at higher risk of smoking.

Whether teenage use of e-cigarettes leads to conventional smoking has been intensely debated in the United States and elsewhere. While the industry argues that vaping is not a steppingstone to conventional cigarettes or addiction, some antismoking advocates contend that young people become hooked on nicotine, and are enticed to use cancer-causing tobacco-based cigarettes over time.

The new report by the National Academies of Sciences, Engineering and Medicine is the most comprehensive analysis of existing research on e-cigarettes. The report also cited conclusive proof that the devices are safer than traditional smoking products and may help smokers quit, citing conclusive proof that switching can reduce smokers' exposure to deadly tar, dangerous chemicals and other carcinogens.

But it stopped short of declaring that e-cigarettes are safe, noting there are no long-term scientific studies of the devices' addictive potential or their effects on the heart, lungs or on reproduction.

The panel found evidence among studies it reviewed that vaping may prompt teenagers or young adults to try regular cigarettes, putting them at higher risk for addiction, but that any significant linkage between e-cigarettes and long-term smoking has not been established. It said it was unable to determine whether young people were just trying cigarettes or becoming habitual smokers.

"When it got down to answering the questions about what the impacts on health are, there is still a lot to be learned," said David Eaton, of the University of Washington, who led the committee that reviewed existing research and issued the report. "E-cigarettes cannot be simply categorized as either beneficial or harmful."

The report was commissioned in 2016, after the F.D.A. gained the authority to regulate tobacco products that had previously been outside its jurisdiction, such as e-cigarettes and cigars.

Mitch Zeller, head of the agency's tobacco division, said the committee was assigned to assess the existing science, and to point out gaps in research. The report will aid the agency in its review of applications for lower-risk tobacco products and the potential harm or benefits those pose to individuals and the public.

On Wednesday, an F.D.A. advisory panel will review an application from Philip Morris International for iQOS, an electronic device that, unlike e-cigarettes, contains tobacco in a stick that the company says heats it but does not burn it. It releases nicotine vapor, which the company says is less hazardous than smoke. If approved, Philip Morris would be the first company allowed by the government to claim its product is less harmful than cigarettes.

Also this week, on Friday, the agency's new nicotine steering committee will hold a public hearing on over-the-counter therapeutic products, among them gums, patches and lozenges, designed to help smokers quit.

Cessation was one area where the committee's report did give the booming e-cigarette industry some good news. It pointed out the benefits for smokers trying to quit. But people who continue to smoke cigarettes, alternating with e-cigarettes, do not gain the same health benefits, the committee said. That's especially important given that most adults who vape also still smoke or use other tobacco products. The report also said the evidence was limited on whether e-cigarettes were effective for quitting smoking.

While there is no evidence at this time that e-cigarettes or their components cause cancer, the committee recommended more long-term research. Some e-cigarettes contain chemicals and metals whose long-term effects — including on pregnancy — also need further study, the committee said.

Smoking rates among adults and teenagers have declined significantly over the last few decades. In 2015, the last year for which the Centers for Disease Control and Prevention has statistics, about 37 million Americans, 15 percent of adults aged 18 and older, smoked cigarettes. The number has declined from nearly 21 percent of every 100 adults in 2005; and 42 percent in 1965.

With that decline, the e-cigarette industry has emerged as a potential substitute and Big Tobacco has been among the device developers enjoying new profits from the tobacco alternatives. Bonnie Herzog, a Wells Fargo tobacco analyst, predicted the industry will grow about 15 percent to $5.1 billion in retail sales in the United States, in 2018.

The vaping industry, as well as traditional tobacco companies, are gearing up for a lengthy fight with the F.D.A. over the campaign by the agency's commissioner, Dr. Scott Gottlieb, to slash levels of nicotine in traditional cigarettes to nonaddictive or minimally addictive levels.

Dr. Gottlieb is expected to issue an initial proposal, calling for public comment on lower nicotine levels, in the near future.

The new report reflects the complexity of the issues surrounding e-cigarettes and the balancing act regulators face over the pros and cons of the alternatives to conventional cigarettes.

Adam Leventhal, a professor of preventive medicine at the University of Southern California, and an author of the report, said his group did an exhaustive literature search, reviewing all studies on youths and e-cigarette use from around the world. Of those, 10 studies were deemed strong enough to address the question. But they did not show that using e-cigarettes caused teens to move on to tobacco, only that the use of e-cigarettes was associated with later smoking of at least one traditional cigarette. The report noted that more than 11 percent of all high school students — nearly 1.7 million youths — reported using e-cigarettes within the past month.

"The evidence was substantial that this association was consistent across a number of research methodologies, age ranges, locations, and research groups in and outside the U.S.," Mr. Leventhal said.

This conclusion is at odds with the findings of the British Royal College of Physicians, which asserts that e-cigarettes are not a gateway to smoking.

"Concerns about e-cigarettes helping to recruit a new generation of tobacco smokers through a gateway effect are, at least to date, unfounded," the organization notes on its website.

More intriguing was the newest report's finding of moderate evidence that youths who use e-cigarettes before trying tobacco are more likely to become more frequent and intense smokers.

Critics have long contended that the flavored liquids for the devices are luring adolescents to the habit, at a time when nicotine is especially hazardous for their brain development. Three of the top-selling flavors at e-liquid.com, a large online retailer, include "Unicorn Milk" (strawberries and cream), "TNT" (strawberry, apple and peach) and "I Love Donuts" (blueberries and pastry).

The authors of the new report cite conclusive evidence that vaping can be addictive, and that exposure to nicotine from e-cigarettes is highly variable, depends on the characteristics of the device, as well as how it is used. They also cited conclusive proof that in addition to nicotine, most e-cigarettes contain and emit potentially toxic substances.

In terms of second-hand vapor, the committee said there was conclusive evidence that e-cigarette use increases airborne concentrations of particulate matter and nicotine indoors.

The report concluded that much of the current research on e-cigarettes is flawed, either in methodology or because of industry-financed bias. In addition, the levels of nicotine and other chemicals, including metals, vary in e-cigarettes from brand to brand.

"And for kids who initiate on e-cigarettes, there's a great chance of intensive use of cigarettes. As the regulator, we've got to factor all that in," Mr. Zeller said.

In July, the F.D.A. delayed the deadline at least four years for e-cigarette companies to apply for approval to keep their products on the market, largely by showing some public health benefit.

Several major tobacco companies that produce e-cigarettes declined to comment on the report. R.J. Reynolds Tobacco Company issued a statement saying it was encouraged by the report's findings, and highlighted the committee's point that e-cigarettes "are likely to be far less harmful than conventional cigarettes."

But public health advocates who objected to the July delay said this report gave them further concern.

"What the report demonstrates is that despite the popularity of e-cigarettes, little is known about their overall health effects, and there is wide variability from product to product," said Matthew L. Myers, president of Campaign for Tobacco-Free Kids. "That makes the case even stronger for F.D.A. regulation."

The vaping industry was cautiously optimistic about the report. Gregory Conley, president of the American Vaping Association, a non-profit that advocates for vapor products, said the findings were consistent with those reached by the Royal College of Physicians and other institutions in Britain that have issued reports indicating e-cigarettes are less dangerous than traditional smoking and help with cessation.

"In the wake of this report, it is more apparent than ever that true leadership is needed in public health to ensure that adult smokers have access to truthful information about the benefits of switching to smoke-free products," he said.

As for the F.D.A., Dr. Gottlieb said the report would play a critical role.

"We need to put novel products like e-cigarettes through an appropriate series of regulatory gates to fully evaluate their risks and maximize their potential benefits," he said.

This May Be a First: Exploding Vape Pen Kills a Florida Man

BY JACEY FORTIN | MAY 16, 2018

AN ELECTRONIC CIGARETTE exploded and killed a man in Florida this month, the authorities said, in what appears to be the first death attributed to vaping products in the United States.

The man, Tallmadge D'Elia, was at his home in St. Petersburg, Fla., on May 5 when the device, also known as a vape pen, exploded, according to William A. Pellan, the director of investigations at the medical examiner's office for Pinellas County.

He confirmed that the cause of the accidental death was a "projectile wound to the head," and that Mr. D'Elia, 35, had suffered burns on about 80 percent of his body. It appeared that the explosion had started a fire in the bedroom where he was found.

One of the pieces removed from his head featured the logo of Smok-E Mountain Mech Works, which is based in the Philippines.

The company's owner did not immediately respond to an email requesting comment on Wednesday, but a representative told ABC Action News that its devices do not explode, adding that the problem may have stemmed from the battery.

Smok-E Mountain makes a particular type of vape pen called a mechanical mod.

Compared with more common types of vape pens, mechanical mods typically give users more direct access to the battery and do not use inner circuitry to regulate the voltage.

"Today, the products are overwhelmingly used by hobbyists," Gregory Conley, the president of the American Vaping Association, said of mechanical mods. He added that the e-cigarettes used by most people who vape have more built-in safety features.

"Millions of adults use vapor products regularly and tragic events like this are rare," Mr. Conley added. "The vast majority of vaping devices on the market carry the same fire risk as other products that use lithium-ion batteries, such as cellphones and laptops."

A report from the United States Fire Administration last year reviewed 195 reports of e-cigarette-related fires and explosions from 2009 to 2016, none of which resulted in deaths. It pointed specifically to electronic cigarettes that use lithium-ion batteries as a "new and unique hazard" because those are more prone to explosion.

"No other consumer product places a battery with a known explosion hazard such as this in such close proximity to the human body," the report said. "It is this intimate contact between the body and the battery that is most responsible for the severity of the injuries that have been seen. While the failure rate of the lithium-ion batteries is very small, the consequences of a failure, as we have seen, can be severe and life-altering for the consumer."

Supporters of vaping say that e-cigarettes with nicotine can help people quit smoking. Others worry that vape pens have gained appeal among young people and might make them more likely to smoke conventional cigarettes later.

Research suggests that while electronic cigarettes can be addictive, e-cigarette users have far less exposure to potentially toxic substances than do conventional smokers.

Vaping Is Big Tobacco's Bait and Switch

OPINION | BY JENEEN INTERLANDI | MARCH 8, 2019

Cigarettes hooked generations of teenagers. Now e-cigarettes might do the same.

I WAS 15 when I started smoking, and so were most of my friends. We smoked to rebel against our parents but also to identify with them — of course they smoked, even as they told us not to. We smoked because it was feminine and sexy, and also masculine and tough. Because celebrities did it, and they looked cool. Because the prissy kids *didn't* do it, and we weren't them. Because cigarettes were both forbidden and easy to get: ten quarters in a cigarette vending machine, which you could still find in most pizza joints and doughnut shops in suburban New Jersey in the early 1990s.

All of that — the appeal, the access, the illicitness of cigarettes — was by design. By the time my friends and I were born, cigarette makers had stitched their products into the fabric of our culture so thoroughly that not even a century's worth of research tying those products to an array of slow, painful deaths was enough to deter many of us.

Tobacco companies made cigarettes a diet tool and a matter of high fashion. They made smoking a feminist act. They didn't just assure the public that it was safe to smoke; they used doctors to push their brands. And the more they came to understand their own product, the more they advertised cigarettes to the young. Most people who don't start smoking by the end of adolescence never will. The cigarette makers knew that. They used cartoon camels, pictures of Santa Claus and larger-than-life cowboys in their ads.

It helped that their key ingredient was highly addictive. It also helped that they were willing to lie. When concerns emerged about nicotine dependence, cancer and heart disease, they kept regulators at bay by playing up scientific uncertainty. Then they bought off scientists and disguised corporate propaganda as independent research. By the time their deceptions were exposed, a new generation of smokers — promising billions of dollars in industry revenue — was already hooked.

In the late 1990s, Big Tobacco was finally brought to account for its practices, and a string of public health policies were put in place that over the past three decades have all but eliminated the scourge of teen smoking. But many of us who became tobacco consumers at 13, 14, 15 remain so at 39, 40, 41. And in recent years, we have watched history repeat itself.

The tobacco industry is pushing a new kind of smoking device — the e-cig or vape pen — that it says is far healthier than traditional cigarettes: no tobacco, no tar, just nicotine and flavored vapor. These devices, the industry says, will finally help us adult smokers quit or curb our habit. But here's the rub: E-cigs have brought smoking back into vogue for teenagers. As a result, the cost of this new cure may be another generation exposed to the same addiction we are still fighting.

Tobacco remains the leading cause of preventable death in the United States. Smoking kills some 480,000 people a year — more than AIDS, car accidents, illegal drugs and suicide combined — and costs $170 billion in annual health care expenditures, according to the Centers for Disease Control and Prevention. E-cig makers say, and some health experts believe, that e-cigs could help lower these terrible numbers, because they contain far fewer toxins than traditional tobacco cigarettes. The thinking goes that if all current smokers switched to these devices, the burden of disease and death could be dramatically cut.

Few have been more captivated by this argument than Scott Gottlieb, the departing commissioner of the Food and Drug Administration, the federal agency responsible for regulating tobacco and nicotine products.

Since he assumed his role at the agency two years ago, Dr. Gottlieb has tried to strike a balance between encouraging adult smokers to switch to e-cigs and keeping the devices away from minors. Children and teenagers face disproportionate risk from smoking, in part because nicotine is known to harm the developing brain. In 2016, the F.D.A. prohibited the sale of e-cigs to minors, and issued a string of new regulatory requirements for vaping devices. Then, under Dr. Gottlieb's tenure, the agency extended the deadline for meeting those requirements by several years, while also announcing plans to curb the nicotine content of regular cigarettes.

That plan backfired last year, when teen vaping reached epidemic proportions. Dr. Gottlieb has since tried to put the industry in check by, among other things, forcing e-cig makers to devise plans for keeping their products away from kids and issuing thousands of warning letters to retailers caught selling nicotine products to minors.

E-cig makers have responded to that pressure with a bait-and-switch that would make their Big Tobacco predecessors proud.

Juul, the company most responsible for the surge in teen vaping, scrubbed its Facebook and Instagram accounts and agreed to dramatically restrict sales of its most youth-friendly flavors, like mango, crème and fruit. But the company also received a $12.8 billion minority investment in December from the tobacco giant Altria, a move that will allow Juul products to be displayed alongside regular cigarettes in the nation's brick and mortar retail outlets. For its part, Altria volunteered to withdraw all of its flavored-pod products from the market until the youth vaping epidemic was resolved. Dr. Gottlieb and others say the Juul combination with Altria severely undercuts that promise.

Dr. Gottlieb's boldest antismoking efforts, which include reducing nicotine levels and banning menthol flavors in traditional cigarettes, are still in the planning stages. It's unclear whether his successor will shepherd them into policy.

In the meantime, according to Reuters, a slew of Juul copycats are making their way into convenience stores in defiance of an F.D.A. rule banning the sale of new e-cig products after August 2016. Juul is promoting itself as a health-conscious company, even as it develops new, potentially more addictive vaping products. And Philip Morris International has created a nonprofit — the Foundation for a Smoke-Free World — through which it has tried to partner with the World Health Organization. The foundation's stated goal is to reduce the global health burden of cigarette use. But according to tobacco industry watchdogs, leaked P.M.I. documents suggest that its true aim is to promote the company's own vaping products.

None of this should come as a surprise. The tobacco industry was built around a product that is inherently dangerous and unhealthy. And it has a long history of duplicity.

There are still many unanswered efficacy and safety questions about e-cigs. It's unclear how well they work as a smoking cessation tool. And while they are almost certainly safer than regular cigarettes, they are not necessarily safe. Health officials know next to nothing about the flavorings or about other chemicals generated by the heating of e-liquids. They also don't know how many teenagers who start using e-cigs will move on to tobacco products.

In the absence of such information, some e-cig proponents have fallen back on a trope from the previous tobacco wars: Smoking should be a matter of personal choice and personal responsibility. That argument is not entirely wrong. Nicotine and tobacco are, after all, legal substances, and if e-cigs do prove safer than regular cigarettes, adult smokers should be encouraged to switch.

But the next F.D.A. commissioner would be wise to carry out the work that Dr. Gottlieb started — to keep all nicotine products from reaching underage users. I take full responsibility for choosing to smoke. But I wish that someone would have made it harder for 15-year-old me to do so. I hope the powers that be will do at least that much for the teenagers of today.

JENEEN INTERLANDI has been a member of the Times editorial board since 2018, and a contributor to The New York Times Magazine since 2006. She writes about health, science and education.

First Death in a Spate of Vaping Sicknesses Reported by Health Officials

BY MATT RICHTEL AND SHEILA KAPLAN | AUG. 23, 2019

A PATIENT IN ILLINOIS is the first to die of a mysterious lung illness linked to vaping, public health officials announced on Friday.

The death occurred as doctors and hospitals nationwide report an increasing number of vaping-related respiratory illnesses this summer: 193 cases have now been reported in 22 states, including 22 cases in Illinois, officials said.

They have been stumped in recent weeks by the cause. State investigators have not found a common link — other than vaping in general — among the patients turning up in emergency rooms.

Many patients, including some in Illinois, have acknowledged vaping of tetrahydrocannabinol, or (T.H.C.), the high-inducing chemical in marijuana, according to statements from federal and state health agencies.

But officials don't know whether the ailments have been caused by marijuana-type products, e-cigarettes, or some type of street concoction that was vaped, or whether a contaminant or defective device may have been involved.

The Illinois patient's death was disclosed during a news conference held by officials at the Centers for Disease Control and Prevention, the Food and Drug Administration and the state of Illinois.

They did not provide details about the patient's identity, saying only that the person was an adult who had vaped recently and then succumbed to a severe respiratory illness.

Health officials did not say what product the patient had used, whether an e-cigarette or other vaping device; nor did they specify what substance was vaped.

Amid the lack of information, investigators are scrambling to find shared links to the respiratory problems. Officials said earlier this week that many patients, most of whom were adolescents or young adults, had described difficulty breathing, chest pain, vomiting and fatigue.

The most seriously ill patients have had extensive lung damage that required treatment with oxygen and days on a ventilator. Some are expected to have permanent lung damage.

"More information is needed to know what is causing these illnesses," said Ileana Arias, an official with the C.D.C., said on Friday.

The Illinois patients have ranged in age from 17 to 38, according to the state health department.

State health departments are handling most investigations into the respiratory illnesses.

"We're at a relatively early stage of understanding," Mitchell Zeller, director for the Center for Tobacco Products at the F.D.A., said on Friday. The collective agencies were throwing "a lot of resources at this," he added, but part of the problem was that state investigations are not always complete, making it difficult to form a clear picture.

One theory, as of yet unproved, is that illnesses may result from substances that are thought or known to be toxic in vaping products, which use heat to vaporize nicotine and other inhalants.

Brian King, deputy director of research translation at the Office on Smoking and Health at the C.D.C., said that potential irritants include "ultrafine particulates, some heavy metals, such as lead," and, he said, there "are also concerns about some flavorings."

But, he added, "We haven't specifically linked any of those ingredients to specific cases."

Dr. Michael Lynch, medical director of the Pittsburgh Poison Center at the University of Pittsburgh Medical Center, said the lung injuries doctors there are seeing are consistent with chemical inhalation injuries.

Dr. John Holcomb, a pulmonologist in San Antonio, Tex., noted that the F.D.A. has no control over the ingredients used in vaping products.

"The problem is we don't know what's being inhaled through these devices, of which there are five or six hundred different kinds," he said. "We have to assume that some of them may be dangerous and some may not be dangerous."

Others suggested that individuals are emptying out commercial nicotine pods and filling them up with a combination of T.H.C. oil and other chemicals.

If the respiratory illnesses can be traced to T.H.C.-laced vapors, public health officials and doctors expressed concern that it may signal the emergence of a second front in the battle against youth vaping: the growing use of unregulated, bootleg or black market cannabis liquids.

"We believe that they are getting empty cartridges from somewhere and filling them with their own products," said Nancy Gerking, assistant director of public health in Kings County, Calif., which has had numerous cases. "We don't know what they are cutting it with or anything else."

Until recently, these cases have been off the radar of most doctors and public health officials, who were already struggling to stop youths from vaping standard e-cigarettes. But cannabis liquids and oils have become more widely available online and in many stores. And because the ingredients may not be disclosed at all, unsuspecting consumers may be exposed to a cocktail of hazardous chemicals.

The e-cigarette market has broadened to counterfeiters and a range of devices that can be packed with different substances, including marijuana, but also various flavors and concoctions that may be mixed inexpertly.

Public health officials, however, declined to say if they yet are seeing a pattern that would make clear whether the problematic products are made by mass-market companies or counterfeiters, or whether the inhalants involved are standard to many vaping products or made or mixed by consumers themselves.

The recent revelations could also further complicate the tarnished image of the growing e-cigarette market. For several years, the industry and top-selling companies, like Juul, have faced scrutiny because of the rising popularity of e-cigarettes among teenagers, which threatens to create a new generation of nicotine addicts who may become eventual cigarette smokers.

MITCH SMITH contributed reporting from Chicago.

CHAPTER 4

Teens Vaping

Of the various concerns posed by the rise of vaping, perhaps the most worrisome is its popularity with young people. As e-cigarettes have grown in popularity, schools, parents and public health officials have looked to federal regulation and educational programs to stem the spread of the devices among teenagers. And yet, vaping has only continued to rise among young people, developing its own cultural cache.

E-Cigarettes, by Other Names, Lure Young and Worry Experts

BY MATT RICHTEL | MARCH 4, 2014

SAN FRANCISCO — Olivia Zacks, 17, recently took a drag of peach-flavored vapor from a device that most people would call an e-cigarette.

But Ms. Zacks, a high school senior, does not call it that. In fact, she insists she has never even tried an e-cigarette. Like many teenagers, Ms. Zacks calls such products "hookah pens" or "e-hookahs" or "vape pipes."

These devices are part of a subgenre of the fast-growing e-cigarette market and are being shrewdly marketed to avoid the stigma associated with cigarettes of any kind. The products, which are exploding in popularity, come in a rainbow of colors and candy-sweet flavors but, beneath the surface, they are often virtually identical to e-cigarettes, right down to their addictive nicotine and unregulated swirl of other chemicals.

The emergence of e-hookahs and their ilk is frustrating public health officials who are already struggling to measure the spread of e-cigarettes, particularly among young people. The new products and new names have health authorities wondering if they are significantly underestimating use because they are asking the wrong questions when they survey people about e-cigarettes.

Marketers of e-hookahs and hookah pens say they are not trying to reach young people. But they do say that they want to reach an audience that wants no part of e-cigarettes and that their customers prefer the association with traditional hookahs, or water pipes.

"The technology and hardware is the same," said Adam Querbach, head of sales and marketing for Romman Inc. of Austin, Tex., which operates several websites that sell hookahs as well as e-cigarettes and e-hookahs. "A lot of the difference is branding."

Sales of e-hookahs have grown "exponentially" in the last 18 months, Mr. Querbach said.

Public health authorities worry that people are being drawn to products that intentionally avoid the term "e-cigarette." Of particular concern is use among teenagers, many of whom appear to view e-cigarettes and e-hookahs as entirely different products when, for all practical purposes, they are often indistinguishable.

Indeed, public health officials warn that they may be misjudging the use of such products — whatever they are called — partly because of semantics. A survey by the Centers for Disease Control and Prevention found that 10 percent of high school students nationwide said that they had tried e-cigarettes in 2012, double the year before. But the C.D.C. conceded it might have asked the wrong question: Many young people say they have not and will not use an e-cigarette but do say they have tried hookah pens, e-hookahs or vaping pens.

The C.D.C. is sending a tobacco-use survey to 20,000 students nationwide that asks about e-cigarette experimentation but does not identify the devices by other names. The state of California, through a nonprofit partner called WestEd, is asking virtually the same question of 400,000 students.

Brian King, senior adviser to the Office on Smoking and Health at the C.D.C., said the agency was aware of the language problem. "The use of hookah pens could lead us to underestimate overall use of nicotine-delivery devices," he said. A similar problem occurred when certain smokeless tobacco products were marketed as snus.

Other health officials are more blunt.

"Asking about e-cigarettes is a waste of time. Twelve months ago, that was the question to be asking," said Janine Saunders, head of tobacco use prevention education in Alameda County in Northern California.

In October, Ms. Saunders convened a student advisory board to discuss how to approach "e-cigs." "They said: 'What's an e-cig?' " Ms. Saunders recalled, and she showed what she meant. "They said: 'That's a vape pen.' "

Health officials worry that such views will lead to increased nicotine use and, possibly, prompt some people to graduate to cigarettes. The Food and Drug Administration is preparing to issue regulations that would give the agency control over e-cigarettes, which have grown explosively virtually free of any federal oversight. Sales of e-cigarettes more than doubled last year from 2012, to $1.7 billion, according to Wells Fargo Securities, and in the next decade, consumption of e-cigarettes could outstrip that of conventional cigarettes. The number of stores that sell them has quadrupled in just the last year, according to the Smoke Free Alternatives Trade Association, an e-cigarette industry trade group.

The emergence of hookah pens and other products and nicknames seems to suggest the market is growing well beyond smokers. Ms. Zacks was among more than 300 Bay Area high school students who attended a conference focused on health issues last month on the campus of the University of California, Berkeley. Many students talked about wide use of e-hookahs or vaping pens — saying as many as half

Cigarette

e-Cigarettes
Njoy Traditional Flavor

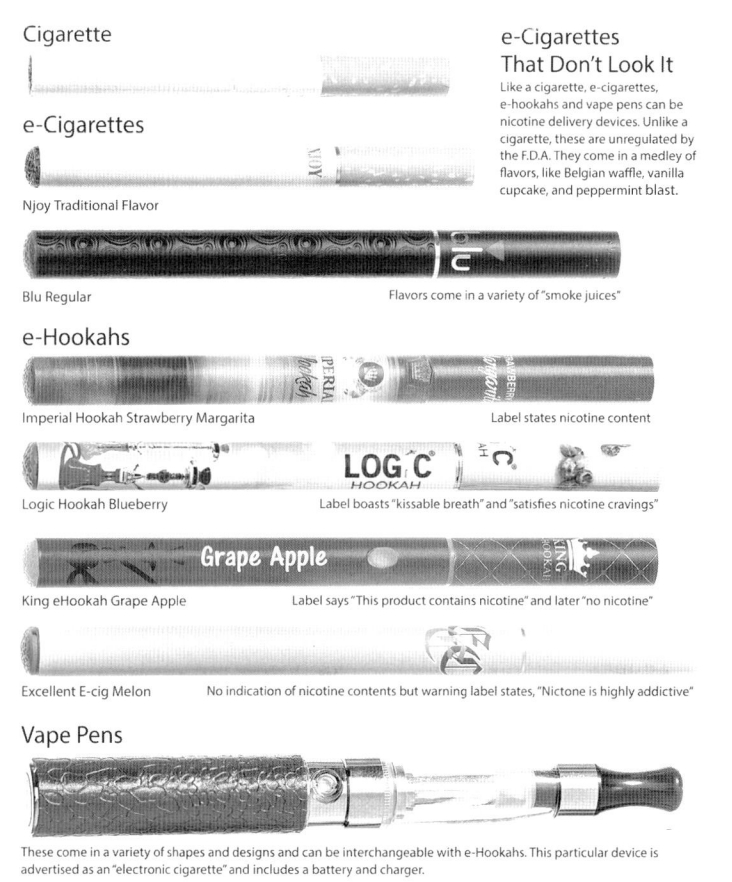

Blu Regular

e-Cigarettes That Don't Look It
Like a cigarette, e-cigarettes, e-hookahs and vape pens can be nicotine delivery devices. Unlike a cigarette, these are unregulated by the F.D.A. They come in a medley of flavors, like Belgian waffle, vanilla cupcake, and peppermint blast.

Flavors come in a variety of "smoke juices"

e-Hookahs
Imperial Hookah Strawberry Margarita — Label states nicotine content

Logic Hookah Blueberry — Label boasts "kissable breath" and "satisfies nicotine cravings"

King eHookah Grape Apple — Label says "This product contains nicotine" and later "no nicotine"

Excellent E-cig Melon — No indication of nicotine contents but warning label states, "Nictone is highly addictive"

Vape Pens
These come in a variety of shapes and designs and can be interchangeable with e-Hookahs. This particular device is advertised as an "electronic cigarette" and includes a battery and charger.

THE NEW YORK TIMES

of their classmates had tried one — but said that there was little use of e-cigarettes.

Ms. Zacks said the devices were popular at her high school here. "E-cigarettes are for people trying to quit smoking," she said, explaining her understanding of the distinction. "Hookah pens are for people doing tricks, like blowing smoke rings."

James Hennessey, a sophomore at Drake High School in San Anselmo, Calif., who has tried a hookah pen several times, said e-hookahs were less dangerous than e-cigarettes. He and several Drake students estimated that 60 percent of their classmates had tried the devices, that they could be purchased easily in local stores, and that they often were present at parties or when people were hanging out.

"E-cigarettes have nicotine and hookah pens just have water vapor and flavor," said Andrew Hamilton, a senior from Drake.

Actually, it is possible for e-cigarettes or e-hookah devices to vary in nicotine content, and even to have no nicotine. Mr. Querbach at Romman said that 75 percent of the demand initially was for liquids with no nicotine, but that makers of the liquids were expanding their nicotine offerings. Often, nicotine is precisely the point, along with flavor.

Take, for example, the offerings of a store in San Francisco called King Kush Clothing Plus, where high school students say they sometimes buy their electronic inhalers. On a counter near the back, where tobacco products are sold, are several racks of flavored liquids that can be used to refill e-cigarettes or hookah pens. The flavors include cinnamon apple, banana nut bread, vanilla cupcake, chocolate candy bar and coconut bomb. They range in nicotine concentration from zero to 24 milligrams — about as much as a pack of 20 ordinary cigarettes — but most of the products have some nicotine. To use the refills, it is necessary to buy a hookah pen, which vary widely in price — around $20 and upward.

It is also possible to buy disposable versions, whether e-cigarettes or hookah pens, that vary in nicotine content and flavor. At King Kush, the Atmos ice lemonade-flavored disposable electronic portable hookah promises 0.6 percent nicotine and 600 puffs before it expires.

Emily Anne McDonald, an anthropologist at the University of California, San Francisco who is studying e-cigarette use among young people, said the lack of public education about the breadth of nicotine-vapor products was creating a vacuum "so that young adults are getting information from marketing and from each other."

"We need to understand what people are calling these before we send out large surveys," Dr. McDonald said. Otherwise the responses do not reflect reality, "and then you're back to the beginning.

E-Cigarette Use by U.S. Teenagers Rose Last Year, Report Says

BY SABRINA TAVERNISE | APRIL 14, 2016

WASHINGTON — E-cigarette use continued to rise among young teenagers and preteens in the United States last year, according to new federal data, but cigarette smoking overall did not increase, suggesting that, at least so far, fears that the devices would hook a new generation on traditional cigarettes have not come to pass.

Experts said it was too soon to answer the essential question about e-cigarettes: Will they cause more or fewer people to smoke? But the broad trend in youth cigarette smoking has been down in recent years, and researchers have been taking note of that.

"We do not have any strong evidence that it is encouraging smoking among kids but neither do we have good evidence that it won't over time," said Kenneth E. Warner, a professor of public health at the University of Michigan.

About 5 percent of middle-school students reported using e-cigarettes in 2015, up from about 4 percent in 2014, according to data from the Centers for Disease Control and Prevention. That is a substantial increase from 2011, when less than 1 percent of middle schoolers used the devices.

Use for high-school students was also trending up, with 16 percent reporting using the devices in 2015, up from 13 percent in 2014. But the change was not statistically significant because of technical reasons having to do with the sizes and distributions of the samples. In 2011, the rate was just 1.5 percent for high schoolers.

Policy makers have worried that increased e-cigarette use could make it more likely young people would shift to traditional tobacco cigarettes, which are more toxic. But that does not seem to be happening yet. About 9 percent of high schoolers reported smoking cigarettes in 2015, unchanged from 2014, and down from 16 percent in 2011.

Among middle schoolers, about 2 percent reported smoking traditional cigarettes in 2015, statistically unchanged from 2014. In 2011, about 4 percent of middle schoolers smoked traditional cigarettes.

The popularity of electronic cigarettes has soared since they were introduced in the mid-2000s and the devices have swept through the market so quickly that they have outpaced the federal government's intention to regulate them. (Final rules from the Food and Drug Administration, which regulates tobacco products, have been expected for months.) Bonnie Herzog, an analyst with Wells Fargo, estimates the total vapor market, including e-cigarettes and other related products, such as liquids and personal vaporizers, totaled about $3.3 billion in the United States 2015.

E-cigarettes, designed to deliver nicotine without the toxic tar of conventional cigarettes, have prompted a split among public health experts with some saying the devices will hook new generations of smokers and undo hard-won progress on smoking rates and others saying they will help older, addicted smokers quit.

The answer is not yet clear, in part because there is not enough data on use to tell. But it is important: Cigarette smoking is still the single largest cause of preventable death in the United States, killing about 480,000 people a year. While smoking rates have dropped drastically since the 1960s, there are still more than 40 million Americans who smoke.

Professor Warner said what stood out was the fact that the rate of e-cigarette use had slowed from its earlier more rapid rise, a shift that he said was too early to interpret and that smoking of traditional cigarettes, after many years of declines, had not gone down.

"I'm disappointed, and a bit surprised, not to see another decline in cigarette smoking, even if small," he said. As for e-cigarettes, "If anything, use seems to be flattening out."

Young people are a particularly vulnerable bunch, and many public health experts agree that with so little known about the long-term effects of e-cigarettes, the fact that so many youths have started using them is worrying, even if they do not use them as a bridge to traditional cigarettes. Others argue that even nicotine can be harmful. In all, about three million middle and high school students used e-cigarettes in 2015, the data showed, up from 2.46 million in 2014.

"No form of youth tobacco use is safe," said Dr. Thomas R. Frieden, the director of the C.D.C. in a statement. "Nicotine is an addictive drug and use during adolescence may cause lasting harm to brain development."

The data, from the National Youth Tobacco Survey, which is a pencil-and-paper questionnaire administered to a large sample of middle- and high-school students across the country, had a bright spot: Hookah use declined for high school students, falling to about 7 percent from about 9 percent in 2014.

Plain Old Vaping Gives Way to 'Dripping' Among Teenagers, Study Says

BY JACEY FORTIN | FEB. 7, 2017

TEENAGERS HAVE FOUND a new way to worry their parents. Never mind plain old vaping — now, it's all about dripping.

The term refers to the practice of applying nicotine liquid directly to the heated coils of an e-cigarette or other vaporizer to produce thick clouds of nicotine vapor.

A new Yale University study of high school students in Connecticut, published in the journal Pediatrics, suggested that the approach was gaining favor among teenagers as a way to produce more flavorful clouds of vapor and "a stronger throat hit."

Of the teenagers who reported using e-cigarettes, about a fourth said they had hacked the devices to allow dripping.

The study defines e-cigarettes, which come in a variety of forms, as tools that "electrically heat and vaporize e-liquids to produce inhalable vapors." Those liquids typically contain nicotine and are available in different flavors.

In dripping, the liquid is manually applied to the e-cigarette's heated inner coil, rather than allowing it to flow there via an automatic wick system.

The study was based on anonymous surveys of 7,045 high school students in Connecticut. A full 1,874 said they had indulged in vaping with e-cigarettes at some point, though researchers counted only 1,080 after winnowing out some surveys with inconsistent answers. Of those, 282 said they had tried dripping.

Dr. Suchitra Krishnan-Sarin, a psychiatry professor at Yale and lead author of the study, wasn't surprised about the prevalence of vaping. "Teens are certainly drawn to both the novelty of the product and the availability of different flavors," she said.

A CBS News report and other summaries of the Yale findings may have been the first that many parents had heard of the practice. But Blake Brown, 32, who blogs extensively about vaping, said in a phone interview that dripping is nothing new.

"There's a side of vaping that's super simple, and that's what most of the public sees," he said. "There's also a different side to vaping where people like to tinker around with things, take things apart."

Manufacturers, he added, have already caught on to the dripping trend and created vaping devices that feature exposed coils, allowing users easier access to drip their liquid manually.

"You're getting more of a smooth draw and the flavor is enhanced greatly," he said. "Compared to the standard e-cigs you can get, it's like, you can go buy a Prius or you can go buy a Corvette."

Mr. Brown emphasized, however, that vaping is for adults — not teenagers.

The Yale study was not designed to investigate health risks, but Dr. Krishnan-Sarin pointed to recent research from the American University of Beirut suggesting that dripping — which can expose the nicotine liquid to higher temperatures than normal — may release higher levels of carcinogens.

She said more research is necessary to fully understand the long-term effects of vaping and e-cigarettes.

Lawmakers have scrambled to regulate vaping, which gained popularity only recently as an alternative to traditional methods of smoking and chewing tobacco. According to a history compiled by the Consumer Advocates for Smoke Free Alternatives Association, modern e-cigarettes did not make their way to the United States until 2006. (The organization also documents a smattering of prototype patents dating as far back as 1930.)

Differing state approaches led to a patchwork of regulations until last year, when federal law made it illegal to sell e-cigarettes to anyone under 18.

But as the Yale study makes clear, teenagers — in Connecticut, at least — are undeterred by the law.

"My message to parents always is: It's not a good idea for your kids to use these e-cigarettes until we know more about the safety and toxicity of these products," Dr. Krishnan-Sarin said.

Marijuana and Vaping Are More Popular Than Cigarettes Among Teenagers

BY JAN HOFFMAN | DEC. 14, 2017

CIGARETTE SMOKING HAS dropped so sharply among American teenagers that vaping and marijuana use are now more common, according to a national survey of adolescent drug use released Thursday.

The report, sponsored by the federal government's National Institute on Drug Abuse and administered by the University of Michigan, found that 22.9 percent of high school seniors said they had used marijuana within the previous 30 days and 16.6 percent had used a vaping device. Only 9.7 percent had smoked cigarettes.

The survey of 43,703 eighth-, 10th- and 12th-grade students in public and private schools nationwide raised concerns about the popularity of vaping devices, available in countless styles to appeal to different social groups. But it was otherwise optimistic. It found that teenagers' consumption of most substances — including alcohol, tobacco, prescription opioids and stimulants — has either fallen or held steady at last year's levels, the lowest rates in 20 years.

By contrast, rates of marijuana use have remained largely consistent, with occasional small shifts, in recent years. (Studies show, however, that marijuana rates have risen among young adults in the last decade.)

"We're impressed by the improvement in substance use by all teenagers," said Dr. Wilson Compton, deputy director of the institute.

Still, Dr. Compton continued, "we don't yet know about the health problems in vaping."

Vaping devices, which typically vaporize substances into an inhalant, are perceived by some experts as a healthier alternative to traditional cigarettes because they do not include carcinogens that come with burning tobacco. But Dr. Compton said, "The concern is that it may represent a new route for exposure to nicotine and marijuana."

The devices are typically sold with nicotine. But when 12th-graders were asked what they believed was in the mist they had vaped most recently, 51.8 percent said "just flavoring." When asked about use in the past month, one in 20 12th-graders said they had used marijuana in vaping devices and one in 10 said nicotine.

Cassie Poncelow, a school counselor at Poudre High School in Fort Collins, Colo., has noticed an upsurge in vaping across all social groups.

"We're seeing a ton of it," she said. The devices are readily accessible and easy to conceal, she added.

"Kids are taking hits on their vape pens in the hallways and nobody notices," Ms. Poncelow said, noting that some devices resemble flash drives, which students plug into laptops to recharge.

But educators and public health officials praised the drop in tobacco use. Dr. Compton noted that in 1996, 10.4 percent of eighth graders reported smoking cigarettes daily. By 2017, that figure fell to 0.6 percent. In 1997, daily smoking among 12th graders peaked at 24.6 percent. By 2017, only 4.2 percent smoked cigarettes daily.

Thomas J. Glynn, a former director of cancer science at the American Cancer Society and an adjunct lecturer at Stanford University School of Medicine, hailed the continuing tobacco decline as "an astounding accomplishment in public health."

"But," he added, "it doesn't mean we close the door and go home now."

While noting that the data on vaping devices as a gateway to cigarettes is inconclusive, he added, "I think we have to have alarms out."

Dr. Compton attributed the tobacco decline to many factors, including strong public health antismoking campaigns, higher cigarette prices and peer pressure not to smoke. Students in all grade levels reported that they viewed cigarettes and alcohol as distasteful and a serious health risk.

Similar explanations have been given for dropping rates of alcohol use, especially binge drinking. Students have become more self-conscious about the possibility of their drunken images being posted on social media, experts say, which can tarnish reputations and college eligibility.

But marijuana? Not so much.

In the report, only 14.1 percent of 12th graders said they saw a "great risk" from smoking marijuana occasionally. In 1991, 40.6 percent of seniors held that view. In 2017, nearly 24 percent of students in all three grades said they had used marijuana over the past year, a rate that has stayed relatively stable in recent years.

Allison Kilcoyne, who directs a health center at a high school in a Boston suburb, has seen firsthand the evidence of the survey's marijuana findings. Persuading students about marijuana's risk is tricky, said Ms. Kilcoyne, a family nurse practitioner, especially in a state that permits medical marijuana.

"They perceive there are no negative effects," Ms. Kilcoyne said. "I talk about the impact on their developing brain and the risk of learning to smoke marijuana as a coping mechanism. We have other interventions, I say. But the problem is that for them, it works. They're feeling immediate relief of whatever symptoms they have. They're medicating themselves."

Yet while marijuana use among high school seniors has not declined, it has also not increased in recent years. Given that fewer students hold marijuana in disregard, researchers are perplexed but relieved that use of marijuana has not kept pace with attitudes toward it.

"Drug use tends to go hand in hand with perceptions of risk and approval," said Ty S. Schepis, an associate professor of psychology at Texas State University who studies adolescent and young adult drug use.

But approving of marijuana may not necessarily translate in such a manner, he said. "I've had friends who like to go sky diving. I would never go sky diving. There are certain activities that we may quietly condone or tacitly approve, even though the majority still may not want to engage in it."

'I Can't Stop': Schools Struggle With Vaping Explosion

BY KATE ZERNIKE | APRIL 2, 2018

THE STUDENT HAD BEEN caught vaping in school three times before he sat in the vice principal's office at Cape Elizabeth High School in Maine this winter and shamefacedly admitted what by then was obvious.

"I can't stop," he told the vice principal, Nate Carpenter.

So Mr. Carpenter asked the school nurse about getting the teenager nicotine gum or a patch, to help him get through the school day without violating the rules prohibiting vaping.

E-cigarettes have been touted by their makers and some public health experts as devices to help adult smokers kick the habit. But school officials, struggling to control an explosion of vaping among high school and middle school students across the country, fear that the devices are creating a new generation of nicotine addicts.

In his four years at Cape Elizabeth, Mr. Carpenter says he can't recall seeing a single student smoke a cigarette. But vaping is suddenly everywhere.

"It's our demon," he said. "It's the one risky thing that you can do in your life — with little consequence, in their mind — to show that you're a little bit of a rebel."

Schools say the problem sneaked up on them last fall, when students arrived with a new generation of easily concealed devices that have a sleek high-tech design. The most popular, made by Juul, a San Francisco-based company that has received venture capital money, resemble a flash drive and have become so ubiquitous students have turned Juul into a verb.

Tasting like fruit or mint, these devices produce little telltale plume, making it possible for some students to vape even in class.

"They can pin them on to their shirt collar or bra strap and lean over and take a hit every now and then, and who's to know?" said Howard Colter, the interim superintendent in Cape Elizabeth.

E-cigarettes are widely considered safer than traditional cigarettes, but they are too new for researchers to understand the long-term health effects, making today's youth what public health experts call a "guinea pig generation."

School and health officials say several things are clear though: Nicotine is highly addictive, the pods in vaping devices have a higher concentration of nicotine than do individual cigarettes, and a growing body of research indicates that vaping is leading more adolescents to try cigarettes.

Ashley Gould, the chief administrative officer of Juul, said that the company's products are intended solely for adults who want to quit smoking.

"We do not want kids using our products," she said. "Our product is not only not for kids, it's not for non-nicotine users."

She said schools and the e-cigarette industry need to work together to understand why teenagers are vaping, and suggested that stress is a big reason. To that end, she said, Juul has offered schools a curriculum that includes mindfulness exercises for students to keep them away from the devices the company sells.

"We saw the same thing from Philip Morris with the We Card program, and the evaluation was that those things don't work," Jennifer Kovarik, who runs tobacco prevention programs for Boulder County, Colo., said of the company's efforts to keep their products away from teenagers. "If they didn't want youth to use it, it would be sold in 18-and-over-only establishments. It's available at Circle K's across the country."

E-cigarettes deliver nicotine through a liquid that is heated into vapor and inhaled, cutting out the cancer-causing tar of combustible cigarettes. But vaping liquids contain additives such as propylene glycol and glycerol that can form carcinogenic compounds when they are heated. Diacetyl, a chemical used to flavor some vape "juice," has been

NICK COTE FOR THE NEW YORK TIMES

Liz Blackwell, a school nurse in Boulder, Colo., showed a collection of vape pens that had been confiscated from students during a presentation at Nevin Platt Middle School in March.

linked to so-called popcorn lung, the scarring and obstruction of the lungs' smallest airways. A study published in the journal Pediatrics in March found substantially increased levels of five carcinogenic compounds in the urine of teenagers who vape.

"I'm afraid that we're going to be hooking a new generation of kids on nicotine, with potentially unknown risks," said Dr. Mark L. Rubinstein, the lead author of the study and a professor of pediatrics at the University of California, San Francisco. "With cigarettes, we've been studying them for many years, we have a pretty good idea of what the risks are. We just don't know what the risks of inhaling all these flavorings and dyes are, and what we do know is already pretty scary."

The industry points to a 2016 British study that says that vaping does not lead nonsmokers to become smokers. But the 2016 Monitoring the Future study, sponsored by the federal government's National Institute on Drug Abuse, followed students who in 12th grade had never smoked a cigarette and found that a year later, those who used e-cigarettes were about four times as likely to have smoked a cigarette. A study released in January by the National Academies of Sciences, Engineering and Medicine similarly concluded that vaping led students to smoke cigarettes, although it did not determine whether they became habitual smokers or just experimented.

Schools and local officials have stiffened penalties for students caught with vaping devices, suspending and even expelling them, and sent home letters pleading with parents to be on the lookout for a waft of fruit smell and, as one superintendent wrote, " 'pens' that aren't pens."

Several school districts in New Jersey have recently adopted policies requiring any student caught with an e-cigarette to be drug tested, because the devices can be used to smoke marijuana.

Oak Ridge High School in Placerville, Calif., shut down all but two bathrooms during classes in November and placed monitors at the doors during lunch to make sure not too many students are in the bathroom together. (Juul devices, for example, contain as much nicotine as a pack of cigarettes, so they are easy to share.) New Trier High School in Chicago's northern suburbs is considering installing vaping detectors in bathrooms.

With so many students caught multiple times, some schools have moved from punishment to intervention, requiring students caught vaping to receive counseling or substance abuse treatment.

"Despite all of the boundaries set by families and parents and the schools, and at risk of even expulsion, students are continuing to use," said Liz Blackwell, a school nurse in the Boulder Valley School District in Colorado. "They don't want to be kicked out of school, they don't want to suffer any punishment or discipline, and they don't want to have a bad relationship with their parents. They continue to use because it's an addiction."

As part of her treatment plan, one of Ms. Blackwell's students asked if she could stand at the back of the class and shake her foot when she started to feel the twitch to vape.

Two years ago, Boulder surveyed its students and found that 45 percent of high school students had used e-cigarettes, with 30 percent as current users. Officials say they expect the most recent survey, taken last year, to show about 45 percent of middle school students have used e-cigarettes.

The 2017 Monitoring the Future survey on adolescent drug use found that 11 percent of 12th graders, 8.5 percent of 10th graders and 3.5 percent of 8th graders had vaped nicotine in the previous 30 days. Of those high school seniors, 24 percent reported vaping daily, which the study defined as vaping on 20 or more occasions in the previous 30 days, said Richard A. Miech, a professor at the Institute for Social Research at the University of Michigan and a principal investigator of the study. Nineteen percent reported vaping on 40 or more occasions during that period.

Fifty-six percent reported vaping only on one to five occasions. Gregory Conley, the president of the American Vaping Association, which supports what he calls "fair and sensible" regulation of e-cigarettes, said that number indicated that most students who are vaping are not becoming addicted. "You can't use the definition of dependence and apply it to anyone using only one to five days in the prior month," he said.

Schools say that unlike adults, most students who vape are starting out as nonsmokers.

"I have the same conversation with every student we catch vaping," said Scott Carpenter, the dean for discipline at Cumberland High School in Rhode Island. "I say, 'If I handed you a cigarette would you smoke it?' And 100 percent of them look at you like you're absolutely crazy for even suggesting that they'd do that."

Federal law prohibits the sale of e-cigarettes to anyone under 18, and Juul and some other e-cigarette companies ask web purchasers to check a box saying that they are 21 or older. But the growing vaping industry has many items and campaigns that seem to appeal specifically to youth. There are vaping cloud contests, a line of hoodies and backpacks called VaprWear that make it easy to conceal the devices, and labels of vape "sauce" that resemble the designs of well-known candy wrappers like those of Jolly Ranchers and Blow Pops.

In Millburn, N.J., one of the school districts that now require any student caught with a vaping device to be drug tested, teenagers said Juuls began showing up at parties last year, and by fall were at school and football games. Now, students post videos of themselves doing vapor tricks on social media.

At a local deli where seniors go for lunch, a dozen students interviewed said it was easy to buy a Juul online or at a gas station or convenience store, and to buy refill pods in the hallway at school. None would publicly admit to owning a device, but all said they had tried vaping.

Ryan Wenslau, 18, said he thought vaping started for most students as an occasional diversion, "something to do." A stern talk from his baseball coach had convinced him not to use, he said. But for those students who continue, "I wouldn't necessarily call it an addiction," he said, "but it's habitual."

While there might be chemicals in vaping, they argued, there are more in cigarettes.

"Technically, it's better," said Fares Alhabboubi, 17.

Schools lament that teenagers equate safer with safe. But many say the unfamiliarity of e-cigarettes has made it hard to convince parents of the risks as well.

"If I had a pack of cigarettes in my room as a kid, that would have been discovered, here we're dealing with, first of all, what's a Juul?" said Michael McAlister, the principal at Northgate High School in Walnut Creek, Calif. The school has about 1,600 students, but parent education nights on the issue have turned out only about 70 people. Yet, out of 53 suspensions last year, 40 were for vaping devices.

"We're losing a battle and to me, it's predatory," Mr. McAlister said. "There's no way you're going to suspend your way out of this."

Did Juul Lure Teenagers and Get 'Customers for Life'?

BY MATT RICHTEL AND SHEILA KAPLAN | AUG. 27, 2018

SAN FRANCISCO — The leaders of a small start-up, PAX Labs, gathered at a board meeting in early 2015 to review the marketing strategy for its sleek new electronic cigarette, called Juul. They watched video clips of hip young people, posed flirtatiously holding Juuls. And they talked about the name of the gadget, meant to suggest an object of beauty and to catch on as a verb — as in "to Juul."

While the campaign wasn't targeted specifically at teenagers, a former senior manager said that he and others in the company were well aware it could appeal to them. After Juuls went on sale in June 2015, he said, the company quickly realized that teenagers were, in fact, using them because they posted images of themselves vaping Juuls on social media.

The former manager said the company was careful to make sure the models in its original campaign were at least 21, but it wasn't until late 2016 or January 2017 that the company said it decided the models in all Juul ads should be over age 35 — to be "better aligned" with a mission of focusing on adult smokers. Only in June of this year did the company again change its policy, this time to using only real people who had switched from cigarettes to Juul.

The company recently modified the names of its flavors — using creme instead of crème brûlée and cucumber instead of cool cucumber. Juul said it "heard the criticism" that teenagers might be attracted to the flavors and "responded by simplifying the names and losing the descriptors."

The sales campaigns for Juuls — now hugely popular with teenagers across the nation — are at the heart of a federal investigation into whether the company intentionally marketed its devices to youth. The attorney general of Massachusetts, also investigating the company,

JASON HENRY FOR THE NEW YORK TIMES

Juul's current advertising is more explicitly adult.

contends that Juul has been luring teenagers to try the product and has introduced many to nicotine. Her investigation will examine Juul's efforts to audit its own website and other online retailers that sell its products to see how effective they are at preventing minors from accessing Juul or Juul-compatible products. (Federal law prohibits sales of e-cigarettes to anyone under 18.)

"From our perspective, this is not about getting adults to stop smoking," the Massachusetts attorney general, Maura Healey, said in an interview. "This is about getting kids to start vaping, and make money and have them as customers for life."

And Cult Collective, the marketing company that created the 2015 campaign, "Vaporized," claims on its website that the work "created ridiculous enthusiasm" for the campaign hashtag, part of a larger advertising effort that included music event sponsorships and retail marketing. A spokesman for Cult Collective declined to comment.

The company, now called Juul Labs, denies that it ever sought to attract teenagers. James Monsees, one of the company's co-founders, said selling Juuls to youth was "antithetical to the company's mission."

The original sales campaign was aimed at persuading adult smokers in their 20s and 30s to try an alternative to cigarettes, but it "failed to gain traction on social media and failed to gain sales" and was abandoned after five months, in the fall of 2015, said a company spokesman, Matt David.

Mr. David said sales didn't take off until 2017, after Juul had improved its sales and distribution expertise, and, by then, had a more sober online marketing campaign.

The former Juul manager, who spoke to The New York Times on the condition that his name not be used, saying he worried about facing the ire of the company, said that within months of Juul's 2015 introduction, it became evident that teenagers were either buying Juuls online or finding others who made the purchases for them. Some people bought more Juul kits on the company's website than they could individually use — sometimes 10 or more devices.

"First, they just knew it was being bought for resale," said the former senior manager, who was briefed on the company's business strategy. "Then, when they saw the social media, in fall and winter of 2015, they suspected it was teens."

The Food and Drug Administration announced it was investigating Juul's marketing efforts in April. Juuls and other e-cigarettes are regulated by the F.D.A. as tobacco products because nicotine derives from tobacco leaves. E-cigarette users inhale far fewer toxins than do smokers of traditional cigarettes. The nicotine inhaled while vaping is less a concern for adults than these toxins, but it remains a serious health issue for teenagers, whose brains are still developing.

The Juul story highlights a central dilemma in public health. Cigarettes remain the leading cause of preventable death in the United States, killing more than 480,000 people a year. But will it be possible to get people who are addicted to cigarettes to switch to e-cigarettes, which are less harmful, without enticing a new generation or non-smokers to try them?

The F.D.A. commissioned research, published in January, that found "limited evidence" that e-cigarettes lead smokers to quit. And some evidence now suggests that young people who use e-cigarettes are more likely to try cigarettes.

Juul, in a letter responding to the F.D.A.'s demand for documents, said it had converted one million smokers to Juul, but the company data is drawn from self-reported surveys on its website and is unverifiable.

Dr. Scott Gottlieb, who heads the F.D.A., declined to comment on the agency's investigation of Juul. But he has long been hopeful that e-cigarettes or other similar devices, properly regulated, will prove a safer alternative to smoking and help people quit the deadly habit. Before becoming F.D.A. commissioner, he served on the board of directors of Kure, a retailer that sells e-cigarette products.

"Two-thirds of adult smokers have stated they want to quit," he said. "They know it's hard, and they've probably tried many times to quit. We must recognize the potential for innovation to lead to less harmful products."

But Eric Lindblom, a former F.D.A. tobacco official who heads the tobacco control program at Georgetown Law, said Juul's internal concerns about teenage use demonstrate they are in some ways "no different than the cigarette industry."

"They are going to maximize their sales and profits any way they can," he said. "They are going to do that within the law, but they are going to press the gray areas as much as they can."

JUULING BECOMES A VERB

Over the last three years, Juul has had a meteoric rise. It has become the dominant seller of e-cigarettes, now controlling a remarkable 72 percent of the market, according to Nielsen data. In July, the company completed a round of fund-raising for $1.2 billion, putting it in rarefied air. From a virtual standing-start in 2015, it is now valued by investors at $16 billion.

Across the country, Juuls have become so popular that "Juuling" has indeed become a verb, and officials from several state governments have sent alerts to schools warning them about the problem.

A survey of adolescent drug use last year found that 11 percent of 12th graders, 8.2 percent of 10th graders and 3.5 percent of eighth graders had vaped nicotine in the previous 30 days.

Juul's other co-founder, Adam Bowen, said that he was aware early on of the risks e-cigarettes posed to teenagers, and that the company had tried to make the gadgets "as adult-oriented as possible," purposely choosing not to use cartoon characters or candy names for its flavors.

The F.D.A. has ordered Juul to turn over the company's research and marketing documents, including focus group data and toxicology reports, to determine whether it intentionally courted the youth market.

The day after receiving the F.D.A. letter, Juul announced it would spend $30 million to combat underage vaping and recruited Tom Miller, the attorney general of Iowa, who helped lead the multistate 1998 master settlement with tobacco companies, to run an advisory board to counsel Juul on its efforts. Mr. Miller said recommendations might include more controls on social media marketing and better surveillance of retail outlets, but the ultimate decision on how to spend the money remains with Juul.

Mr. Miller says he sees huge potential in e-cigarettes. He believes Juul and other e-cigarette companies have already helped lower the adult smoking rate to 13.9 percent in 2017 from 16.8 percent in 2014. "The only plausible explanation is e-cigarettes," he said.

A report from Citigroup, citing Nielsen data, said that sales of traditional cigarettes dropped 6 percent in the first quarter of this year and "it's impossible to say what has caused the change for sure but the most obvious case is Juul."

Juul recently deleted months of social media posts, including ones with images of cool-looking young people vaping Juuls. This spring it made major changes to its website, which had prominently displayed a Juul surrounded by luscious-looking images of fruit and the words

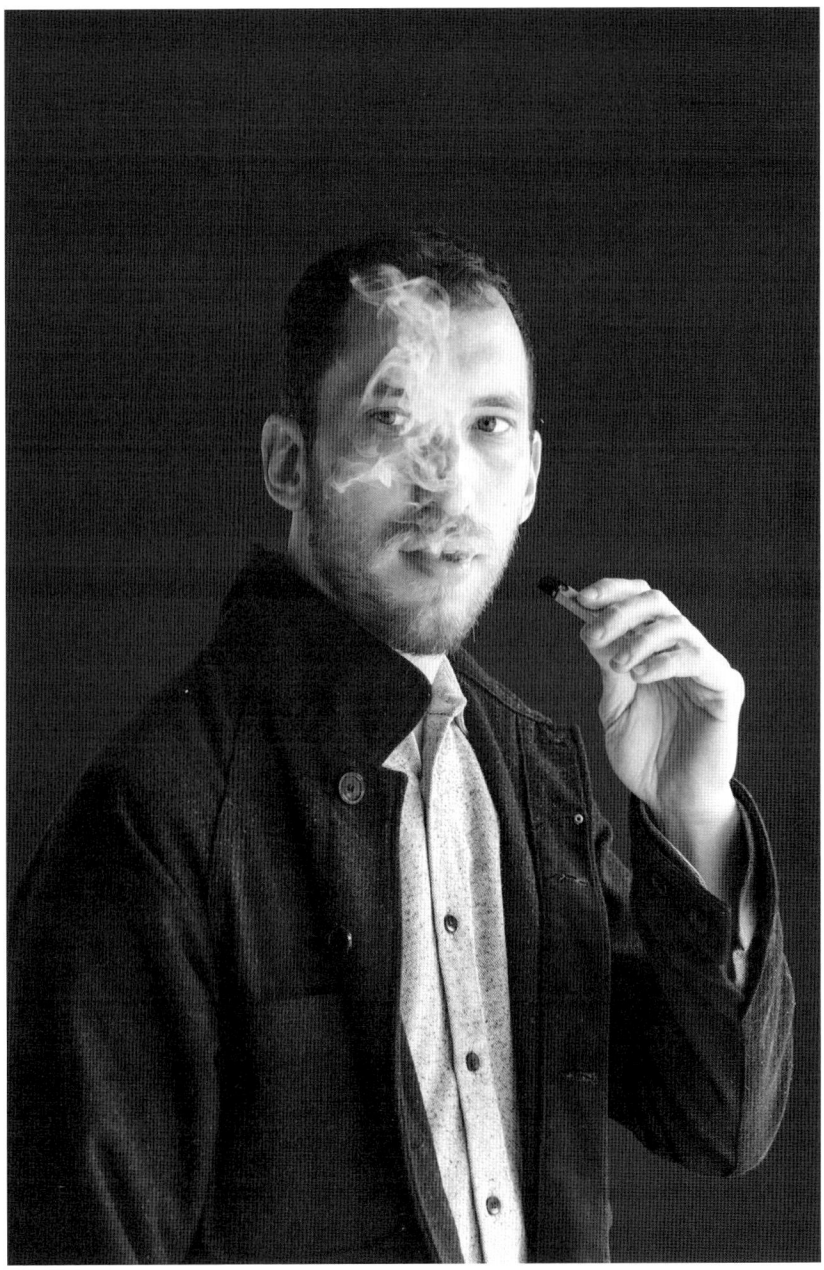

JASON HENRY FOR THE NEW YORK TIMES

James Monsees, one of Juul's co-founders, said selling Juul to youth was "antithetical to the company's mission."

"Mango, it's back." The site is now a more sober-looking affair, featuring video of adults vaping with a tagline "For smokers. By design." Across the top of the page, visitors are invited to "learn about our youth prevention efforts."

A NICOTINE FAD'S ORIGIN STORY

Mr. Bowen, 42, and Mr. Monsees, 38, the company's founders, met in 2003 in a graduate product-design program at Stanford University, bonding over brainstorming sessions and cigarettes. Both had been smokers since their teens, and both have since quit; Mr. Monsees regularly uses a Juul.

The culmination of the program was a masters thesis, and both had struggled to find a worthy subject. In 2004, about six months before the thesis was due, they got to talking about their smoking habits and, within days, were excitedly sending emails back and forth about developing an alternative to cigarettes.

Big tobacco companies were experimenting with e-cigarettes, but there was no real market for them until around 2010, when NJoy, an Arizona company, became the industry's first darling. By 2013, e-cigarettes were a $1.7-billion-a-year business, still only a small fraction of the $90 billion cigarette business.

But then NJoy gambled on an e-cigarette that looked virtually identical to a cigarette. It was a mistake, said Craig Weiss, the chief executive who pushed the so-called cigalike strategy and now consults for Juul. As NJoy's fortunes flagged, he said he realized that people didn't want a product that looked so much like a cigarette that it still left them with the stigma of being a smoker. NJoy filed for Chapter 11 bankruptcy in 2016, later re-emerging.

Juul initially developed a product in 2010 that looked like a fountain pen and distributed it in specialty vape shops. Its sales grew to a modest $30 million by 2015.

Then the company found its current design, a sleek stick that looks like a flash drive, and largely stumbled onto a new way of delivering nicotine: it mixes nicotine with a chemical called benzoic acid. The result is that when Juul users inhale, they get a very quick and powerful burst of nicotine. This gives smokers a more cigarette-like experience, but medical researchers say it also makes the product more addictive for youth.

The company launched its new product in June 2015, with starter kits costing $35, and packs of four nicotine refill cartridges selling for $16 — each roughly the equivalent of the cost of a pack of cigarettes. According to Nielsen, sales in the first month were roughly $1,500 and reached over $1 million that December. It began a steady climb, and then experienced explosive growth in the beginning of 2017, with sales rising 627 percent in the four weeks ending June 17, 2017, according to Nielsen and Wells Fargo Securities.

The company said that toward the end of 2016 and around the beginning of 2017, it changed its social marketing campaign and guidelines to require all models to be over the age of 35.

In the last two months, Juul has removed the flavor focus and now uses only "real people" who have used Juul to switch from smoking cigarettes, the company said.

Matt Myers, president of the Campaign for Tobacco-Free Kids, said that he was prepared to be a fan of a product like Juul if it is responsibly marketed and shown to help adults quit smoking. But he cited a Centers for Disease Control and Prevention report that in 2017 2.1 million high schoolers and middle schoolers used e-cigarettes — "and the reports about high school students using Juul are rampant," he said.

Mr. Myers observed that Juul "delivers nicotine so much better than any comparable product on the market," and so its popularity means that "both the hopes of the e-cig fans, and fears of those concerned about e-cigs and kids, rise exponentially."

A TOBACCO INDUSTRY TACTIC

On Jan. 23, The Boulder Daily Camera published a front-page story about the growing concerns of local educators in Colorado about student use of Juuls.

NICK COTE FOR THE NEW YORK TIMES

A presentation of various vape devices that were confiscated from students at a school in Boulder, Colo., in March. In January, the Colorado school system had received an offer from a former educator working with Juul to develop an anti-vaping curriculum.

Five days later, Carrie Yantzer, the principal at Nederland Middle-Senior High School, received an email that immediately struck her as suspicious. The writer introduced himself as Bruce Harter, a former educator working with Juul to develop an anti-vaping curriculum for schools.

"I read about the challenges you're having with Juul," Mr. Harter wrote. He offered a free, three-hour curriculum provided by Juul to discourage teens from using e-cigarettes by teaching them about their brains and giving them mindfulness exercises.

"What we've found from focus groups with teenage Juul users is that young people don't understand the dangers of nicotine addiction," the letter read. "They sometimes feel 'pushed' by friends to use e-cigarettes. We also found that they don't have operative ways to deal with stress and the emotional ups and downs of their lives right now."

Ms. Yantzer was angry. "It sounded preposterous," she said, and the company "deceptive."

She wasn't the only school administrator to get such a letter. The Boulder school district and, ultimately, the state of Colorado condemned the offer as a brand-building exercise that was tone-deaf at the very least.

"The way we see this is a fox guarding the henhouse," said Alison Reidmohr, tobacco communications specialist for the Colorado Department of Public Health. "A company that stands to profit from, and currently profit off, youth using a product can't be trusted to prevent use of this product."

Ashley Gould, Juul's chief administrative officer, said the company, because it has not built management around former tobacco-industry employees, was unaware the tactic had been used by cigarette companies. However, Juul's board of directors includes experienced investors, including Nicholas Pritzker, a billionaire whose family controlled one of the country's largest chewing tobacco companies, Conwood, which was acquired in 2006 by Reynolds American for $3.5 billion.

For its part, Juul said it was still deciding what to do with that school program. Ms. Gould said the company did not realize the curriculum would offend or that the idea harked to a tactic big tobacco companies used decades ago. "We didn't know," she said. "We should've known."

JUUL GOES TO WASHINGTON

Juul has a new innovation in the works, a Bluetooth-enabled version of its e-cigarette that it hopes could push more smokers to switch without risking youth uptake. Mr. Monsees called it a "smart" e-cigarette.

The Bluetooth-equipped Juul might provide a way for adult vapers to measure their nicotine use. It also might discourage teen use by disabling the device unless it's in the presence of its adult buyer, perhaps by linking it to the buyer's cellphone. The solution would still require effective controls on sales to minors at brick-and-mortar stores and online retail outlets.

Juul officials contend their ability to offer such innovations is hamstrung by regulatory policies. The company is building a high-powered operation in Washington to help it navigate such issues. It's run by Tevi Troy, a political strategist who worked with Dr. Gottlieb, the F.D.A. commissioner, at the Department of Health and Human Services under President George W. Bush and who wrote an opinion article with him for The Wall Street Journal.

The company has also hired Jim Esquea, who was an assistant secretary at the health department during the Obama administration, and Gerald Masoudi, a former F.D.A. chief counsel.

The company is also ratcheting up its lobbying efforts. It has reported spending $450,000 on lobbying so far in 2018 — substantially more than the $120,000 reported spent for all of 2017. It also recently started a political action committee, although no donations have yet been reported. In June, Kevin Burns, Juul's chief executive, gave $50,000 to the Republican congressional leadership fund.

The centerpiece of Dr. Gottlieb's tobacco control strategy is a plan that would potentially greatly benefit e-cigarette companies, including Juul. It would require tobacco companies to reduce nicotine levels in traditional cigarettes so much that they were no longer addictive. The proposal is still in the early discussion phase, with the tobacco industry strongly opposed. But it would potentially make Juul, a potent nicotine delivery device, far more appealing to smokers.

Mr. Monsees, a Juul co-founder, says he believes that e-cigarettes are a key to reducing smoking, and can be profitable without sales to teenagers.

"Yes, I want to make money," he said. "I'm on the board with a fiduciary duty that obligates me to make money."

But he added, "The best investor return in the long term comes from more adults turning away from combustible cigarettes."

ALEXANDRA YOON-HENDRICKS contributed reporting from Washington.

Addicted to Vaped Nicotine, Teenagers Have No Clear Path to Quitting

BY JAN HOFFMAN | DEC. 18, 2018

A HARVARD ADDICTION medicine specialist is getting calls from distraught parents around the country. A Stanford psychologist is getting calls from rattled school officials around the world. A federal agency has ordered a public hearing on the issue.

Alarmed by the addictive nature of nicotine in e-cigarettes and its impact on the developing brain, public health experts are struggling to address a surging new problem: how to help teenagers quit vaping.

Until now, the storm over e-cigarettes has largely focused on how to keep the products away from minors. But the pervasiveness of nicotine addiction among teenagers who already use the devices is now sinking in — and there is no clear science or treatment to help them stop.

"Nobody is quite sure what to do with those wanting to quit, as this is all so new," said Ira Sachnoff, president of Peer Resource Training and Consulting in San Francisco, which trains students to educate peers about smoking and vaping. "We are all searching for quit ideas and services for this new nicotine delivery method. It is desperately needed."

A harsh irony underlies the search for solutions: Devices that manufacturers designed to help adults quit smoking have become devices that teenagers who never smoked are themselves fighting to quit.

The Food and Drug Administration and the attorney general of Massachusetts are investigating Juul Labs, the maker of the most popular e-cigarettes, to determine whether it deliberately lured teenagers with its sleek packaging and flavors.

On Monday Monitoring the Future, an annual survey of American teenagers' drug use sponsored by the federal government's National Institute on Drug Abuse and conducted by the University of Michigan, reported that teen use of e-cigarettes soared in 2018.

ELIZABETH FRANTZ FOR THE NEW YORK TIMES

Dr. Susanne Tanski, a pediatrics professor at Dartmouth, holding pieces of a vape pen that can be worn on a lanyard.

The survey, which polls eighth, 10th and 12th graders across the country, found the rise in nicotine vaping was the largest spike for any substance recorded by the study in 44 years. About 21 percent of high school seniors had vaped within the previous 30 days, researchers found, compared to about 11 percent a year ago.

The survey also found that many students believe they are vaping "just flavoring." In fact, just about all brands include nicotine, and Juul has particularly high levels of it.

Over all, 3.6 million middle and high school students are now vaping regularly, according to a government study released last month.

The need for therapies dedicated to teenagers is pressing, said Marina Picciotto, a Yale neuroscientist who is president of the Society for Research on Nicotine and Tobacco. Adolescents are uniquely vulnerable to addiction.

ELIZABETH FRANTZ FOR THE NEW YORK TIMES

Dr. Tanski with an assortment of vaping products in her office at Dartmouth-Hitchcock Medical Center in Lebanon, N.H.

The brain's prefrontal cortex, which affects judgment and impulse, is still maturing. "When you flood it with nicotine, you are interrupting development," Dr. Picciotto said. Psychiatrists say that nicotine can exacerbate underlying mental health conditions; it can also lead to hyperactivity, depression and anxiety.

Pam Debono of Bloomfield Hills, Mich., is in the throes of helping her three children, ages 17 through 20, stop vaping for good.

"At first we thought, 'It's just a phase that takes wanting to quit, some self-discipline, and then it's done,' " Mrs. Debono said. Turning to standard carrot-stick methods, she and her husband began sanctions like grounding and then cutting off their children's allowances, so that the kids couldn't afford the flavored nicotine cartridges.

But the couple had to grimly acknowledge nicotine's physiological grip. "We sure wouldn't treat alcohol or prescription drug addictions that way," Mrs. Debono said.

They tried nicotine patches and gum, to no avail. They withstood howling windstorms of teenage irritability that come from common withdrawal symptoms: disrupted sleep, unbottled anxiety and ramped-up moodiness.

Even when the kids managed to stop, they would resume at moments of stress, using the vapes as a kind of self-soothing medication. Now Mrs. Debono resorts to home kits for random nicotine testing.

Unfortunately, methods for quitting cigarettes can't be grafted onto vapes. While cutting down on daily cigarettes can include simple math — cutting back, say, from the 20 cigarettes in a pack to 18 to 14 and so on — an analogous method doesn't readily apply to vaping.

That's because the amount of nicotine each person inhales and then absorbs through e-cigarettes is difficult to measure. A formula for reducing cigarettes doesn't readily translate to pods or cartridges.

Moreover, medications for breaking nicotine's hold over cigarette smokers, including nicotine patches and prescriptions, don't work for everyone and are mostly approved just for adults.

In short, establishing tapering protocols and cessation medications tailored to teenage vaping will require long-term studies, researchers say.

Absent formal guidance, pediatricians are stymied. "We are using our best judgment but we don't know exactly what to do. There's no sound science yet," said Dr. Susanne E. Tanski, who will represent the American Academy of Pediatrics at an F.D.A. hearing next year on vaping interventions.

Vicki, a mother in suburban Boston who requested that her last name be withheld to protect the family's privacy, asked her pediatrician for suggestions for her son, 17, who has long been trying to give up Juul. The doctor recommended several addiction centers.

"They were all for adults!" she said.

Jonathan Hirsch, a social studies teacher who oversees tobacco and vaping education at Redwood High School in Larkspur, Calif., where 36 percent of 11th graders say they vape, said that even students who want to quit struggle mightily to do so. They will purposely not take their Juuls to school, only to relent at lunchtime and rush home for a hit.

Mr. Hirsch said that although instilling a fear of disease can be a successful tool to prevent cigarette smoking, using fear to intercede with students already vaping does not work. Faced with losing their devices — their nicotine — they become furtive or lash out. One parent took away his son's vape, Mr. Hirsch said, and the boy got so worked up that he punched a tree and broke his hand.

Nor do habitual vapers stop because of the threat of consequences. "When I asked my students the other day if they know someone who routinely leaves the class to vape because they 'have to,' at least two-thirds raised their hands," Mr. Hirsch said.

The perception that everyone vapes points to the biggest obstacle in persuading teenagers to quit: the pugnacious, peer-glued nature of adolescence itself. It's stylish. Forbidden.

In addition, while making that first step in recovery — owning the addiction — is difficult for any addicted person, it's arguably harder for teenagers, who are loathe to admit dependence on anyone or anything.

"It's not often that you find a 16-year-old who says, 'Hey Mom and Dad, I'm addicted to vapes, can you take me to therapy?' " said Bonnie Halpern-Felsher, a Stanford professor and developmental psychologist who researches adolescent behavior around tobacco products. "Young people don't do that. And how many even know they're addicted?"

With little guidance, doctors are formulating individual approaches. Dr. Tanski, an associate pediatrics professor at Dartmouth's Geisel School of Medicine, begins her assessments indirectly. She'll ask, "Are your friends vaping?"

Language is essential, she said. If a doctor asks about "e-cigarettes," most teens will say no, because "cigarettes" are out of favor. To familiarize confounded parents with products, Dr. Tanski shows them an assortment of vapes that she's nicknamed "my petting zoo."

"So instead you say, 'Do you Juul? Vape? Use Lush? Phix?' "

Dr. Tanski's "petting zoo" of vaping products. It's important for parents to be familiar with the devices, she said.

When patients taunt, asking if she prefers that they smoke cigarettes, Dr. Tanski discusses the potential harm of the particles and chemicals in a vape's aerosol, which can harm the airways. "I'll say, 'We know a lot of bad stuff now about tobacco, but it took so long for those diseases to develop and for us to learn about them. I'm not willing to do this experiment on you.'"

Dr. Sharon Levy, an adolescent addiction expert at Boston Children's Hospital, will do "motivational interviewing" — educating teenagers so they will want to quit vaping for their own sake, not just to get parents off their backs. Cognitive behavioral strategies offer paths to redirect thoughts during cravings, she said. She also does mental health evaluations to determine whether the teen is vaping to ease underlying anxiety or depression.

Her practice admits up to 10 new patients weekly. "I'd say 75 percent have vapes as part of their story," she said.

The other day she was assessing a middle-schooler whose dependence was so severe that he had been skipping classes to vape in the bathroom.

"He's going to class now but sees himself as vulnerable, because he's worried he won't be able to resist the cravings," Dr. Levy said. "It's all he thinks about. It's like treating a patient who has stopped heroin but wants to inject himself with an empty needle."

She occasionally combines talk therapy with nicotine patches. Some doctors prescribe antidepressants to ease withdrawal. Dr. Levy also recommends deep breathing, yoga and exercise.

Typically, that initial intervention doesn't occur with a doctor. "Schools are usually the first to catch young people vaping and then try to figure out what to do," said Dr. Halpern-Felsher. She and her team developed a free online guide called the Tobacco Prevention Toolkit, which includes a major unit on vaping and Juuls. The program has reached 200,000 students.

One school told her that the kit's message about how manufacturers are manipulating teens inspired some indignant students to cut back.

Without a holy grail for vaping cessation, the toll on families is searing.

"I believe the companies who created these things should pay for treatment," Vicki, the suburban Boston mother, said through angry tears. "They targeted children. They said it was just about trying different flavors and having fun. Well, they're the devil to me."

CHAPTER 5

Trying to Quit

While e-cigarettes may pose fewer risks than traditional cigarettes, they remain highly addictive and habit-forming. As a result, there has been a surge of individuals who have found themselves addicted to vaping and eager to quit. The articles in this section detail the struggles of individuals seeking to overcome their increasing dependence on vaping and the political and industry reforms that aim to curb the spread of these products.

F.D.A. Imposes Rules for E-Cigarettes in a Landmark Move

BY SABRINA TAVERNISE | MAY 5, 2016

WASHINGTON — After years of debate about the health risks of electronic cigarettes, the federal government on Thursday made it final: They need to be regulated and kept out of the hands of children.

The Food and Drug Administration issued sweeping new rules that for the first time extend federal regulatory authority to e-cigarettes, banning their sale to anyone under 18 and requiring that adults under the age of 26 show a photo identification to buy them.

The long-awaited regulations, 499 pages of them, shifted the terms of the public debate over e-cigarettes, putting the federal government's heft behind a more restrictive approach to the devices. Many health experts fear that e-cigarettes will eventually hook a new generation on traditional cigarettes, while others worry that a tougher approach will make it harder for addicted smokers to get access to devices that may be their best hope of quitting.

"We've agreed for many years that nicotine does not belong in the hands of children," Sylvia Mathews Burwell, the secretary of the Department of Health and Human Services, said at a news conference on Thursday. "Progress has been made, but the context has changed so we need to act."

E-cigarettes were introduced about a decade ago as devices that deliver nicotine without the harmful tar and chemicals that cause cancer. They have since grown into a multibillion-dollar business, with nine million American adults using them, and while most health experts agree that they are less harmful than cigarettes, little is known about their long-term effects.

The rules, which take effect in 90 days, have broad implications for public health and the tobacco industry. They subject producers to federal regulation for the first time, requiring them to register with the F.D.A. and provide it with a detailed account of their products' ingredients and their manufacturing processes. Producers will also have to apply to the F.D.A. for permission to sell their products. That includes vape shops that mix their own e-cigarette liquid.

The move was applauded by public health experts who said the industry needed oversight and who had been waiting nearly seven years for the agency to provide it. But it infuriated many e-cigarette companies, which argued that the rules would crush smaller producers that could not afford the time and lawyers to complete an arduous federal applications process. That would have the effect of buoying big tobacco companies, some argued, many of which have gotten into the e-cigarette business.

"This is not regulation — it is prohibition," the American Vaping Association, a trade group for the industry, said in a statement. It said that submitting an application to get a product approved would take more than 1,700 hours and cost more than $1 million.

The growing use of e-cigarettes has sharply divided American public health experts. The central question is whether they help people stop smoking — or whether they are a gateway to traditional cigarettes, especially for younger people. Health experts in Britain have decided that they are effective in helping people quit, and have urged smokers there to switch to them. American experts have been more cautious, warning that e-cigarette use may eventually result in young people moving from vaping to traditional cigarettes.

But smoking rates for youth have declined since the devices were introduced in the mid-2000s, and some experts say that is proof enough that the fears — at least for now — have not come to pass.

"In terms of the health of the public, this action is a disaster," said Dr. Joel L. Nitzkin, senior fellow for tobacco policy at the R Street Institute, a conservative think tank in Washington. "This will move the debate into a new arena. I wouldn't be surprised if we started seeing lawsuits."

Smoking is the largest cause of preventable death, with more than 480,000 tobacco-related deaths each year in the United States. Forty million American adults smoke.

The regulations establish oversight of what has been a market free-for-all of products, including vials of liquid nicotine of varying quality and unknown provenance. Finalizing the rules has taken years. They stem from a major tobacco-control law Congress passed in 2009 and were first proposed in draft form in 2014.

"The process has started, and it has been incredibly difficult," said Matthew L. Myers, the president of the Campaign for Tobacco-Free Kids, a health advocacy group, who welcomed the rules.

Producers will be subject to F.D.A. inspections and will not be able to market their products as "light" or "mild" without agency approval. Companies will be prohibited from giving out free samples.

"There are retailers selling these products, but in the back room, they are also mixing," said Mitch Zeller, the director of the Center for Tobacco Products at the F.D.A. "That means under the law, they are manufacturers."

One of the central questions about the regulations was whether they would be so tough that it would be hard for smaller producers to remain on the market and thus bolster large tobacco companies, which have money and big legal departments to navigate the arduous federal application process.

Market analysts and industry groups seemed to be in broad agreement on Thursday that the regulations would have that effect. Some public health experts also expressed that concern.

"If the vape shops go out of business because they cannot afford to provide the information the F.D.A. needs, then the multinational tobacco companies will have less competition," said Gary A. Giovino, a professor of health behavior at the State University of New York at Buffalo.

But federal health officials countered that the industry would have ample time to respond to the rules. Companies with products on the market now, including vape shops that mix their own liquids, will have two years to submit an application to the F.D.A. for approval of a product. It can stay on the market for another year while the agency reviews the application.

Officials and public health experts said there was broad agreement — including in federal statute — that the industry needed to be regulated, not unlike the food industry, and that these rules were a thoughtful way to accomplish that. Mr. Zeller said that until now the industry had been the "wild, wild West."

"Today is a first step, a foundational step, to bring all these previously unregulated products into the world of being regulated," he said at the agency's briefing.

The rules also impose regulations on hookah and pipe tobacco, as well as all cigars, a tougher move than originally anticipated as the agency was pondering excluding so-called premium cigars.

The rules did not include specific bans on flavors in e-cigarettes, though health officials said they were working on new rules to extend the flavor ban for traditional cigarettes to cigars. Antismoking activists had been pressing the agency to prohibit flavors in all tobacco products, arguing that they appeal to young people, and the omission in the new regulations was a disappointment.

"The concern is for at least three years, flavored e-cigarette products will remain on the market no matter how many kids are using them," Mr. Myers said. He added that the F.D.A. left open the possibility of limiting the addition of flavors in the future, but that it would depend on how the agency interpreted the rules released Thursday.

New York State Bans Vaping Anywhere Cigarettes Are Prohibited

BY SARAH MASLIN NIR | OCT. 23, 2017

ELECTRONIC CIGARETTES, the popular vapor substitute to traditional tobacco cigarettes, will soon be banned from public indoor spaces in New York State — just like the real thing.

Gov. Andrew M. Cuomo on Monday signed a bill to ban vaping anywhere cigarettes are already prohibited, like workplaces, restaurants and bars. The ban goes into effect in 30 days.

E-cigs, as the products that vaporize a variety of oils into an inhalant are generally known, were added to the state's Clean Indoor Air Act this summer by the State Assembly, and the measure was approved by the Senate. The original act has been around since 2003, when smoking tobacco products in public indoor areas was first banned in the state, one of the country's first such measures.

New York has come down fiercely on e-cigs, even as their popularity grows: they now represent a $2.5-billion industry, according to the Centers for Disease Control and Prevention, which says that while the health consequences of the product are little understood, there are still reasons for concern, including nicotine addiction.

A 2016 study by the New York State Department of Health showed that 20 percent of children had tried the products, double from just two years prior. In July, the state banned e-cigs from all school grounds.

"These products are marketed as a healthier alternative to cigarettes, but the reality is they also carry long-term risks to the health of users and those around them," Mr. Cuomo said in a statement. "This measure closes another dangerous loophole in the law, creating a stronger, healthier New York for all."

In New York, around 70 percent of the state's municipalities already have bans in effect, according to the American Lung Association. New

York City's ban has been in place since 2013, when then-Mayor Michael R. Bloomberg included it in the city's Smoke Free Air Act.

But manufacturers have not gone quietly in the city. They have mounted several legal challenges, arguing that e-cigs do not qualify because technically they do not emit smoke. The most recent challenge to New York City's ban was rejected this year in the New York State Court of Appeals, which found that the inclusion of e-cigs in the law was valid.

Jeff Seyler, the executive vice president of the American Lung Association's Northeast region, said, "This new law not only protects public health by restricting the use of e-cigarettes and the public's exposure to smoke-cigarette emissions," but it also shields children, for whom the products are "just another tool reeling them into a dangerous and often lifetime of addiction to nicotine."

But proponents of devices like e-cigs and vaporizers — larger, cellphone-size gadgets — say they are a safer alternative to cigarettes and may help with smoking cessation. Studies so far have been limited and short term, and are not conclusive on either front.

At Long Island Vape, in Huntington Station, N.Y., the owner, Aman Singh, said the rules were unnecessary — the social mores that govern cigarette smokers already are in play when it comes to vapers, he said. "Our customers know that they can't be walking through a store vaping, or sitting at a bar vaping," he said. "They don't feel like doing it anyway because it's obnoxious."

Mr. Singh acknowledged that the product he sells may be a health risk, but he says it is a lesser evil; most customers use it as way to quit traditional cigarettes, he said.

"We're out here trying to help people," he said, adding he worries about the impact ever-tighter strictures on e-cigarettes would have on his customers. "I think people will start smoking cigarettes again."

Vaping Products That Look Like Juice Boxes and Candy Are Target of Crackdown

BY KATIE THOMAS | MAY 1, 2018

FEDERAL AUTHORITIES said on Tuesday they were issuing 13 warning letters to companies that sell vaping products like liquid nicotine in packaging that may appeal to children, including products that resemble juice boxes and candy.

The joint action by the Food and Drug Administration and the Federal Trade Commission is the latest step by the federal government to crack down on the vaping industry, particularly on devices that are popular with teenagers.

Last week, F.D.A. officials said they had started an undercover sting operation targeting retailers that sell the popular Juul products to minors and had asked the maker, Juul Labs, to turn over documents related to marketing practices and health research.

The action on Tuesday, against a group of manufacturers, distributors and retailers, focused on products that the agencies said were aimed at underage users or could be accidentally ingested by children. The products, sold through multiple online retailers, have names like One Mad Hit Juice Box, sold by NEwhere Inc., and Vape Heads Sour Smurf Sauce, sold by Lifted Liquids, which look like Warheads candy.

One product, the Twirly Pop, sold by Omnia E-Liquid, also came with a real lollipop, federal officials said.

Some of the companies also sold products to minors. Federal officials said even if the products were not sold to minors, a child could be mistakenly poisoned because the packaging so closely resembled food and candy.

"The images are alarming, and it's easy to see how a child could confuse these e-liquid products for something they believe they've consumed before," Dr. Scott Gottlieb, the F.D.A. commissioner, said in a telephone call with reporters on Tuesday.

Child poisonings from ingesting liquid nicotine have recently increased. Such poisonings can be deadly and can cause seizures, comas and respiratory arrest. There is no evidence the products under scrutiny this week caused any child deaths, officials said.

Nevertheless, "it takes a very small amount of these e-liquids, in some cases less than half a teaspoon, to be at the low end of what could be a fatal effect for a kid, and even less than that to make them very, very sick," said Mitch Zeller, the director of the F.D.A.'s Center for Tobacco Products.

Some of the products even smelled like the food they were imitating, said Maureen K. Ohlhausen, the acting chairwoman of the F.T.C. The apple juice product came in a cardboard box, with the corners sealed and folded over just like the shelf-stable boxes sold in supermarkets, according to the warning letter. It also smelled like apple juice, even without opening the package.

"These companies are marketing their e-liquids in a manner that makes the product particularly appealing to young children," she said.

Nick Warrender, the owner of Lifted Liquids, said he removed the Vape Heads product from his inventory and redesigned the packaging about six months ago to address officials' concerns over marketing such products. "It was something we already saw as a problem," he said.

He said that the products were never marketed to children, but were designed to appeal to adults' nostalgia. "Our goal is complete compliance with the F.D.A. and the F.T.C.," he said, but added that he also wanted to create products that will be attractive to consumers.

"Our goal is also to provide products that are going to give adult smokers the ability to get away from cigarettes and also something they are going to enjoy."

Mr. Warrender said his products are sold in childproof packaging and that any online sales go through a rigorous vetting system.

Jameson Rodgers, vice president of business development at NEwhere, Inc., said the company stopped manufacturing and shipping the apple juice product months ago, after deciding in early 2017 that it was "a way to be proactively responsible." Mr. Rodgers said that it was possible some retailers were continuing to sell remaining inventory of the product even though his company had stopped making or shipping it.

Other companies could not be reached immediately for comment. F.D.A. officials said all of the companies sent warning letters on Tuesday had recently sold the products.

Last summer, Dr. Gottlieb issued a reprieve to manufacturers of electronic cigarettes by delaying regulations that could have removed many of their products from the market, while at the same time announcing an initiative that will push tobacco cigarette makers to reduce the levels of nicotine in their products.

Dr. Gottlieb said the action on Tuesday, as well as the crackdown last week on the Juul products, were part of a longer-term campaign aimed at reducing the use of vaping products by minors.

While he said there is value in encouraging the development of alternatives that could lure smokers away from harmful cigarettes, public health officials needed to be vigilant about not addicting a new generation of young people to vaping products.

"These are just the initial steps in what is going to be a sustained campaign," Dr. Gottlieb said. "There are bad actors out there."

San Francisco Voters Uphold Ban on Flavored Vaping Products

BY JAN HOFFMAN | JUNE 6, 2018

The measure is considered the strictest in the nation. Voters backed it despite an expensive advertising campaign funded by a major tobacco company.

DESPITE A $12 MILLION AD blizzard by a giant tobacco company, voters in San Francisco resoundingly supported a new ban on the selling of flavored tobacco products, including vaping liquids packaged as candies and juice boxes, and menthol cigarettes.

The measure, known as Proposition E, is said to be the most restrictive in the country, and health groups predicted it could serve as a model for other communities.

The vote had been expected to be close, but the final tally was 68 percent to 32 percent in support of the ban. Those results reflected a big miscalculation by R. J. Reynolds Tobacco Company, which had saturated the city with multimedia ads in four languages, likening the ban to Prohibition and invoking a black market crime wave.

"They had a strategic chance there to show that they are actually walking the walk and talking the talk about moving smokers to non-smoker tobacco products," said Eric Lindblom, a Georgetown Law professor and former Food and Drug Administration tobacco official. "Instead they took this scorched earth approach, trying to eliminate the entire flavor ban. They failed and now other jurisdictions can say, 'Why should we compromise?'"

Although using electronic cigarettes, or vaping, is touted as a means of smoking cessation, parents, public health advocates and federal regulators have expressed deepening concern as some studies show that the products are gateways to smoking for teenagers. E-cigarettes give users a powerful hit of nicotine, but without the mix of toxins contained in traditional, combustible cigarettes.

Schools across the country have grown increasingly alarmed about the growing use of e-cigarettes among middle- and high school students, and some are taking harsh disciplinary measures, including suspensions, to curtail it.

Dr. Melissa Welch, a spokeswoman for the American Heart Association, one of several national organizations that fought to uphold the ban, said she hoped the San Francisco vote would be a first step toward ending "the sale of candy-flavored tobacco before nicotine addiction claims a new generation of young people."

Proponents of the ban pointed to some 7,000 products, including those with flavors said to be particularly alluring to young users like bubble gum, chicken and waffles, and unicorn milk.

San Francisco's Board of Supervisors unanimously approved the ban last year. It was to take effect in April. But R. J. Reynolds, which makes popular vaping products called Vuse, as well as Newport menthol cigarettes, propelled the campaign to block it by getting the initiative on Tuesday's ballot.

Jacob McConnico, a spokesman for R. J. Reynolds, called the vote "a setback for tobacco harm reduction efforts because it removes from the market many potentially reduced-risk alternatives."

Nevertheless, he added, the company would urge federal officials to draft regulations to restrict youths' access to the products while "preserving choice for adult smokers who are looking for alternatives to help them switch."

Juul Labs, maker of the top-selling vaping devices, which is based in San Francisco, did not have a prominent voice in the debate. The company did not respond to requests for comment.

A coalition of groups, including the American Cancer Society, the American Heart Association, the American Lung Association and Tobacco-Free Kids Action Fund, conducted a vigorous drive to uphold the ban. Their war chest was significantly smaller — $2.3 million, including a $1.8 million personal contribution from Michael R. Bloomberg, the former mayor of New York City.

In a statement, Mr. Bloomberg said the vote "shows that the tobacco industry, no matter how much money it spends on misleading ads, can be defeated. This vote should embolden other cities and states to act."

The United States has lagged behind other nations in regulating menthol cigarettes. The inclusion of menthol in the San Francisco ban was hailed by numerous groups, concerned about the booming sales of menthol cigarettes among minorities, who have seen disproportionately high mortality rates related to smoking.

"The ban on menthol cigarettes is a monumental step forward for health equity and social justice for communities of color," said Dr. Phil Gardiner, a co-chairman of the African-American Tobacco Control Leadership Council.

Canada banned the sale of menthol cigarettes last fall, and a similar measure for the European Union will take effect in 2020. In the United States, the F.D.A. banned cigarettes with flavors like chocolate, cinnamon and vanilla in 2009 and said it would look at menthol cigarettes. Though it has taken steps to regulate them as well, the agency has continued to allow them on the market.

A handful of other cities, including Chicago, New York and Providence, R.I., have some restrictions on flavored tobacco products, such as limiting their sale to adults-only stores.

Matthew Myers, president of the Campaign for Tobacco-Free Kids, said that some cities, including Duluth and St. Paul in Minnesota, have instituted more circumscribed bans than San Francisco's, but held off widening their reach when they saw the pushback from R. J. Reynolds.

"When Reynolds paid to put this on the ballot, other jurisdictions were cautious," he said. "The resounding vote in San Francisco is going to lead a lot of cities to take a closer look."

Such policies can be tough to manage, said Mark D. Meaney, a senior lawyer for the Public Health Law Center, which has helped draft tobacco restrictions. "But San Francisco certainly has the expertise and capacity to enforce them."

Oakland recently passed restrictions that will soon take effect, and outreach workers are contacting small retailers to educate them about the new ordinance. Just this week, the San Mateo County, Calif., Board of Supervisors unanimously approved a ban that very much resembles San Francisco's and one in small, rural Yolo County, Calif.

Although R. J. Reynolds led the attack on the ban, other groups joined in. Libertarians took up the protest, saying that the government was overreaching. Small business owners also fought back, saying that the ban would sharply reduce their profits.

"Anchor products allow us to stay competitive to big-box stores, and we will lose regular customers that keep our doors open," said Miriam Zouzounis, a board member of the Arab American Grocers Association, which represents over 400 businesses in San Francisco. She said the law would disproportionately affect Arab, Sikh and Asian store owners.

The ban is expected to take effect within days after the vote is officially certified.

SHEILA KAPLAN contributed reporting.

JAN HOFFMAN has been a Science reporter since 2013. Before that she wrote about young adolescence and family dynamics for Styles and was the legal affairs correspondent for Metro. She joined The Times in 1992.

Altria to Stop Selling Some E-Cigarette Brands That Appeal to Youths

BY SHEILA KAPLAN | OCT. 25, 2018

WASHINGTON — Under pressure to curb vaping among young people, the tobacco giant Altria announced on Thursday that it would discontinue most of its flavored e-cigarettes and stop selling some brands altogether.

The company also said, for the first time, that it would support federal legislation to raise the age to 21 for the purchase of any tobacco and vaping product.

The Food and Drug Administration launched a campaign earlier this year against the makers of e-cigarettes, including the blockbuster start-up Juul, as well as major tobacco companies, that were marketing their products in ways that appealed to teenagers. The agency issued warnings on Sept. 12 to several companies, giving them 60 days to prove they can keep their e-cigarette devices away from minors. It also warned 1,100 retailers to stop selling the devices to minors.

In addition, the agency conducted a surprise inspection of Juul's headquarters in San Francisco, seizing boxes of documents related to the company's marketing strategy.

In a letter to the F.D.A., Howard A. Willard III, chairman and chief executive of Altria Group, said he was alarmed at the epidemic levels of youth e-cigarette use, although he stopped short of saying that his company's products contributed to it.

"Although we do not believe we have a current issue with youth access to or use of our pod-based products, we do not want to risk contributing to the issue," Mr. Willard wrote.

He also said that e-cigarettes remain an important alternative for adults who want to stop smoking.

"The current situation with youth use of e-vapor products, left unchecked, has the potential to undermine that opportunity," Mr. Willard said.

KHUE BUI FOR THE NEW YORK TIMES

A MarkTen XL e-cigarette being recharged at Altria's research and technology center in Richmond, Va.

Altria's move could pressure other e-cigarette makers, including Juul, the dominant seller of the devices, to withdraw some products. Altria has a tiny slice of the market, while Juul, with its sleek device that looks like a flash drive, now controls more than 70 percent of the market, and is valued by investors at $16 billion, according to Nielsen data.

"I think Altria will be happy to try to look like the good guy and let Juul take the heat," said Desmond Jenson, a senior staff lawyer with the Public Health Law Center, based in Minnesota. "Juul selling well is actually to Altria's benefit.

"There's plenty of evidence that shows that e-cigarette use leads to combustible cigarette use among youth, and this year combustible use by high school students is up for the first time in 20 years," he added. "So if Juul is getting kids hooked and they end up switching to Marlboro, Altria wins."

Altria sells two types of vaping products through its Nu Mark subsidiary: the MarkTen and Green Smoke brand, which resemble traditional cigarettes, and the MarkTen Elite and Apex by MarkTen, which are larger and use an e-liquid pod inserted into a cartridge.

In its earnings call Tuesday, Altria said that 20 percent of its MarkTen and Green Smoke products feature flavors other than menthol, tobacco and mint. It plans to stop selling these flavors, which include Mardi Gras, Apple Cider and Strawberry Brulee. The company will continue to sell MarkTen and Green Smoke in menthol, tobacco and mint.

Altria has not given up completely on new flavors. In a note on the company's website, Mr. Willard said he believes that flavors do help adults switch from cigarettes to e-cigarettes, and that the company would introduce new ones with F.D.A. permission.

"We believe that pod-based products significantly contribute to the rise in youth use of e-vapor products," Mr. Willard conceded in his letter to the F.D.A.

The flavor-based pods are not a significant part of the company's e-cigarette portfolio at this point. The MarkTen Elite is sold in about 25,000 stores. The Apex is sold online in 10 states.

In a recent interview, the F.D.A. commissioner, Dr. Scott Gottlieb, said that while e-cigarettes may be a preferable alternative to combustible tobacco cigarettes, they are not risk free.

"Any time you inhale vape products, there is every reason to believe there are risks associated with it," he said.

Dr. Gottlieb also noted that he was revisiting the use of menthol in certain products, which has been of particular concern in African-American communities targeted by makers of menthol cigarettes like Newport and Kools in years past. "It was a mistake for the agency to back away on menthol," he said.

The F.D.A. is also moving on other fronts that threaten the tobacco industry. In response to a legal ruling, the agency said last month it would speed up release of new, graphic package warnings ordered years ago by Congress. It is also proposing to lower nicotine levels in cigarettes, rendering them nonaddictive.

Among Altria's other concerns is F.D.A. approval of IQOS, the penlike electronic device developed by Philip Morris International, which the company says heats tobacco sticks but does not burn them. Although Philip Morris has applied for approval, Altria would distribute the device in the United States.

A federal advisory committee in January recommended that the F.D.A. reject a bid to allow the product to be sold as safer than traditional cigarettes. The agency has not yet made a final decision on whether the product can be sold as a reduced harm product, or at all.

Altria has also recently stepped up its political donations. On Sept. 19, the tobacco company made its largest contribution of the year, $150,000 to the Congressional Leadership Fund, a so-called Super Pac aimed at electing Republicans to the House of Representatives, according to the Center for Responsive Politics, which tracks political spending. Last year, Altria gave the organization a total of $82,930.

F.D.A. spokesman Michael Felberbaum said that the agency appreciated any voluntary steps that companies were taking to address youth access and appeal of e-cigarettes, and would be taking additional action shortly.

Becky Wexler, a spokeswoman for the Campaign for Tobacco-Free Kids, was not impressed by the tobacco company's move.

"Altria's announcement makes them look good, but it will have little practical impact given their very small share of the pod e-cigarette market," Ms. Wexler said. "It is not a substitute for mandatory F.D.A. rules that apply to all e-cigarette manufacturers, including a ban on flavors that attract kids and enforcement of the requirement for F.D.A. review before new products go on the market."

Juul Suspends Selling Most E-Cigarette Flavors in Stores

BY SHEILA KAPLAN AND JAN HOFFMAN | NOV. 13, 2018

WASHINGTON — Facing mounting government pressure and a public backlash over an epidemic of teenage vaping, Juul Labs announced on Tuesday that it would suspend sales of most of its flavored e-cigarette pods in retail stores and would discontinue its social media promotions.

The decision by the San Francisco-based company, which has more than 70 percent of the e-cigarette market share in the United States, is the most significant sign of retrenchment by an industry that set out to offer devices to help smokers quit but now shoulders blame for a new public health problem: nicotine addiction among nonsmoking teens.

Juul's announcement effectively undercut the Food and Drug Administration's plan to unveil a series of measures aimed at curbing teenage vaping. The agency is expected later this week to announce a ban on sales of flavored e-cigarettes in convenience stores and gas stations and strengthen the requirements for age verification of online sales of e-cigarettes.

To prevent some users from reverting to menthol cigarettes, Juul said it would keep mint, tobacco and menthol flavors for its devices in retail stores.

In recent months, the F.D.A. has mounted an increasingly aggressive campaign against the major manufacturers of vaping products that appeal to young people, focusing particularly on Juul. The company's sleek device (nicknamed the iPhone of e-cigarettes) resembles a flash drive and comes with flavor pods like crème and mango, leading public health officials to criticize the company and others for appearing to market directly to teenagers, who are especially vulnerable to nicotine addiction.

JOSHUA BRIGHT FOR THE NEW YORK TIMES

More than three million middle and high school students reported using e-cigarettes in 2017, according to preliminary government data, with about one-third saying the flavors were a big factor in their choice.

E-cigarettes were originally developed to help smokers quit by giving them a way to satisfy their nicotine cravings without the tar and deadly carcinogens that come with burning tobacco.

"Our intent was never to have youth use Juul," said Kevin Burns, chief executive of Juul Labs in a statement emailed to reporters. "But intent is not enough. The numbers are what matter and the numbers tell us underage use of e-cigarettes is a problem."

But critics and public health advocates said the company had no choice, especially after the F.D.A. seized documents related to marketing strategies from the company's headquarters last month, and while some states were investigating whether its tactics were directly aimed at minors.

Caroline Renzulli, a spokeswoman for the Campaign for Tobacco-Free Kids, called Juul's announcement too little too late. "Juul's social media marketing fueled its popularity with kids," she said. "Now that it has captured 75 percent of the e-cigarette market, Juul no longer needs to do social media marketing because its young customers are doing it for them."

Maura Healey, the attorney general for Massachusetts, echoed that sentiment. "Unfortunately, much of the damage has already been done," she said. "Our investigation into Juul's practices, including if it was knowingly selling and marketing its products to young people, will continue."

In a tweet Tuesday afternoon, Dr. Scott Gottlieb, commissioner of the F.D.A. said: "Voluntary action is no substitute for regulatory steps #FDA will soon take. But we want to recognize actions by Juul today and urge all manufacturers to immediately implement steps to start reversing these trends."

The F.D.A. acknowledged earlier this year that it had been caught off-guard by the soaring popularity of vaping among minors, and also began targeting retail outlets that were selling them the products. In September, it gave Juul and manufacturers of a few other flavored e-cigarettes and vaping products 60 days to submit plans to prove they could keep them away from minors. That deadline passed this past weekend.

More than three million middle and high school students reported using e-cigarettes, according to preliminary, unpublished government data, with about one-third of them saying the flavors were a big factor in their choice.

Mr. Burns, the Juul executive, said that as of Tuesday, the company would stop accepting retail orders for mango, fruit, crème and cucumber Juul pods. Those account for about 45 percent of retail sales for the $16 billion company, according to some estimates.

Lower in the announcement, the company said it would renew sales of those products at retail outlets that invested in age-verification technology. A timetable for resuming those sales was not announced.

Juul also said it would improve its online age-verification system to ensure buyers are 21 or older. By the end of the year, Mr. Burns said,

Juul will add a real-time photo requirement to match a buyer's face against an uploaded government-issued ID. The company will also try to prevent bulk shipments to people who are distributing to minors, by restricting customers to two devices and 15 pod packages per month, and no more than 10 devices per year.

In addition, Juul said it would shut down its Facebook and Instagram accounts in the United States that promoted use of the flavored pods. According to its release, the company said it would ask the major social media companies, including Twitter and Snapchat, to help them "police" posts that promote the use of e-cigarettes or cigarettes by underage users.

Dr. Gottlieb said earlier that officials had met with several e-cigarette and tobacco companies to discuss ways to reduce youth vaping after threatening to take e-cigarettes off the market if the companies could not curb teenage sales.

Some companies have indicated they would heed the F.D.A.'s warnings. In October, Altria said it would discontinue most of its flavored e-cigarettes and stop selling some brands entirely. For the first time, the tobacco giant also said it would support a law raising the age to 21 for the purchase of all tobacco and vaping products, a proposal it had previously resisted.

R.J. Reynolds Tobacco Company, a subsidiary of British American Tobacco, also submitted plans to the F.D.A. on Friday that backed the higher age limit.

Michael Shannon, a spokesman for R.J. Reynolds, said it also agreed not to market products through social media influencers and would also require age-verification for access to the website where it sells the e-cigarette Vuse.

The tobacco company stopped short of promising to take Vuse, which comes in berry and other flavors, out of retail stores, but Mr. Shannon said the company would enforce contractual penalties for retailers that sell tobacco products to youths. In addition, it plans to start a mystery shopping program to check compliance.

On Tuesday, CNBC reported that Fontem Ventures, a unit of Imperial Tobacco Group, would raise the minimum age to buy pods on its website to 21. The company sells blu e-cigarettes, which come in various fruity flavors.

Since it came on the market in 2015, Juul has become all but irresistible to teenagers, who had been drilled since preschool days on the perils of cigarette smoking. The name itself sounded like a mash-up of "jewel" and "cool."

Unlike the clunky older vapes, the compact device could readily evade detection from parents and teachers. It not only looked like a flash drive, it could be recharged in a computer's USB port. The flavors were both alluring and sophisticated. And it offered a way for teenagers to rebel and appear hip, seemingly without causing cancer.

And so Juul became a fast, furious hit among high school and even middle school students. A comprehensive report on e-cigarettes in January by National Academies of Sciences, Engineering and Medicine noted that 11 percent of all high school students, or nearly 1.7 million, had vaped within the last month. Preliminary unpublished federal data estimates that number is now at least three million. By now, students have their own vocabulary built around Juul — "juuling" has become a verb.

Schools around the country were caught unaware. The aerosol mist from Juul is nearly odorless and dissipates within seconds. Students began juuling as teachers' backs were turned. They filled school bathrooms for juuling breaks. And for all that school officials knew, students were just diligently recharging flash drives on laptops.

Within 18 months of Juul's release, school officials began confiscating them and providing information sessions to parents. They had two paramount concerns: the increasing use of Juul and other vapes for marijuana and the amount of nicotine in Juul's pods. Nicotine, the naturally occurring chemical in tobacco, is the addictive element that binds smokers to cigarettes and vapers to Juul and other e-cigarettes.

Teenagers, whose brains are still developing, need less exposure to nicotine than adults in order to become addicted.

But perhaps most worrisome was a conclusion reached by the National Academies: that teenagers who use the devices may be at higher risk for cigarette smoking.

In its announcement on Tuesday, Juul emphasized its product's use among adults as an alternative to cigarette smoking and said it would continue to post testimonials on YouTube of adults who had switched to Juul from traditional cigarettes.

Later this week, the F.D.A. is expected to propose a ban on sales of flavored e-cigarettes, with a few exceptions; a pursuit of a ban on menthol cigarettes, which could take years to go into effect; and stricter controls of online sales to prohibit minors from accessing the products.

The Price of Cool: A Teenager, a Juul and Nicotine Addiction

BY JAN HOFFMAN | NOV. 16, 2018

E-cigarettes may help tobacco smokers quit. But the alluring devices can swiftly induce a nicotine habit in teenagers who never smoked. This is the tale of one person's struggle.

READING, MASS. — He was supposed to inhale on something that looked like a flash drive and threw off just a wisp of a cloud? What was the point?

A skeptical Matt Murphy saw his first Juul at a high school party in the summer of 2016, in a suburban basement crowded with kids shouting over hip-hop and swigging from Poland Spring water bottles filled with bottom-shelf vodka, followed by Diet Coke chasers.

Everyone knew better than to smoke cigarettes. But a few were amusing themselves by blowing voluptuous clouds with clunky vapes that had been around since middle school. This Juul looked puny in comparison. Just try it, his friend urged. It's awesome.

Matt, 17, drew a pleasing, minty moistness into his mouth. Then he held it, kicked it to the back of his throat and let it balloon his lungs. Blinking in astonishment at the euphoric power-punch of the nicotine, he felt it — what he would later refer to as "the head rush."

"It was love at first puff," said Matt, now 19.

The next day, he asked to hit his friend's Juul again. And the next and the next. He began seeking it out wherever he could, that irresistible feeling — three, sometimes four hits a day.

So began a toxic relationship with an e-cigarette that would, over the next two years, develop into a painful nicotine addiction that drained his savings, left him feeling winded when he played hockey and tennis, put him at snappish odds with friends who always wanted to mooch off his Juul and culminated in a shouting, tearful confrontation with his parents.

JOSHUA BRIGHT FOR THE NEW YORK TIMES

Matt Murphy outside his home in Reading, Mass.

He would come to hate himself for being dependent on the tiny device, which he nicknamed his "11th finger." Yet any thought of quitting made him crazy-anxious.

Experiences like Matt's have placed Juul at the epicenter of a national debate. On one side stand longtime adult smokers who celebrate the device as the aid that finally helped them quit smoking. On the other are teenagers who have never smoked a cigarette but who have swiftly become addicted to Juul's intense nicotine hits.

This week the Food and Drug Administration tried to walk a careful line between the two, announcing restrictions that only permit stores to sell most flavored e-cigarettes from closed-off areas that are inaccessible to customers under 18. But it stopped short of previous threats to ban stores from selling flavors altogether.

The agency has acknowledged that it was caught flat-footed by a tidal wave of teenage vaping. According to the 2018 National Youth Tobacco Survey, released this week, the number of middle and high school students who currently vape has soared to about 3.6 million. On Dec. 5, the F.D.A. will hold a public hearing about potential therapies to address teenage nicotine addiction.

The easily concealable Juul, which had barely come on the market when Matt tried it, has become wildly popular with teenagers and now accounts for more than 70 percent of the e-cigarette sales in the United States. The F.D.A. is investigating whether the company that makes it, Juul Labs, intentionally marketed its devices to youth. On Tuesday, under increasing pressure, Juul announced it would stop its social media promotions and suspend store sales of many of its flavors — except for tobacco, menthol and mint (Matt's favorite).

One pod, or cartridge, of Juul's flavored liquids contains an amount of nicotine roughly equivalent to a pack of cigarettes. That can be a benefit to smokers who get the nicotine fix they desperately seek without the carcinogenic smoke that comes from burning tar-laden tobacco. But the impact on teenagers, whose brains are still developing, is troubling.

"Nicotine may disrupt the formation of circuits in the brain that control attention and learning," said Dr. Rachel Boykan, a clinical associate professor of pediatrics at Stony Brook University School of Medicine and an executive member of the American Academy of Pediatrics' section on tobacco control. "And there is a higher risk of them subsequently becoming tobacco smokers."

The science about long-term effects of the other chemicals and small metals in the vaporized liquids is unsettled, not only because formulations vary widely and are often undisclosed, but because e-cigarettes have not been around long enough to study thoroughly.

Some research suggests disturbing risks. A joint project between Duke and Yale's Tobacco Center of Regulatory Science, published this fall in the journal Nicotine and Tobacco Research, found that when certain popular flavors are added to a common solvent in the vaping liquids, they produce chemicals that irritate airways and lungs. A 2016 study in the journal Chest said that smoking e-cigarettes had an effect

JOSHUA BRIGHT FOR THE NEW YORK TIMES

An advertisement for a Juul product, which accounts for more than 70 percent of e-cigarette sales.

on the heart and arteries which, while it was not as pronounced as that of combustible cigarettes, was still distinctive.

Perhaps what alarms public health experts most about e-cigarettes generally and Juul in particular is nicotine which, when vaporized, is absorbed by the body within seconds, much faster than when delivered by chewing gum or patches. Its potent addictive properties, doctors say, can be most pronounced in teenagers.

After a few weeks of bumming daily hits from friends (called "fiending"), Matt went on a family vacation out West. On his second day without a Juul, he found he wanted one desperately. On the third, he couldn't take it anymore.

He searched Juul's website to find a local store that sold it, and ordered an Uber to get there, mumbling a nonchalant excuse to relatives. Between the cost of the ride service plus the Juul "starter" kit, he spent $100 to sate his need.

Soon, he escalated to a daily pod, sometimes more. He was spending $40 a week, draining his Christmas and birthday money, and his paycheck from his part-time job at Chili's.

Matt doesn't come across as a cool alpha. He's an easy, approachable kid with a certain sweetness, voted "best personality" by his high school classmates. Focused on achieving academic and financial success, he stayed away from marijuana, alcohol and cigarettes. The Juul, he thought, was a harmless way to look like an edgy risk-taker.

It became stitched into his social identity, and bound him to his buddies, who would ride around town hitting their Juuls in one friend's 2002 Volvo. By the time he graduated from high school in 2017, four of his five closest friends were also daily Juulers.

He and other athletes noticed they would get out of breath more quickly. "We called it 'Juul lung,' " Matt said. "We knew it lowered our performance but we saw that as a sacrifice we were willing to make."

There is an art and artifice to being a teenage Juuler, Matt explained during numerous long conversations, including one over a recent lunch at a local pizza shop. You have to scope out which convenience stores will card you and which will look away, so long as you pay their inflated prices.

Near Matt's house in Reading, a middle-class Boston suburb, there are two convenience stores on West Street. The first won't sell you e-cigarettes unless you are 21. The second was just over the town line in neighboring Woburn, where the legal age until recently was 18. Turned away in Reading, Matt and his friends would simply saunter down the block, where they could pass scrutiny.

What he had initially derided as Juul's pitiful wisp of nearly odor-free vapor turned out to be a great advantage. Teachers were clueless. If his parents walked into his room five seconds after he exhaled, they wouldn't know. "The Juul was super, super sneaky and I loved it," he said.

But by the time he got to college, he began to admit to himself he had a problem. He was majoring in biochemistry at the University of

Vermont and feeling overwhelmed by the workload; the Juul was his only stress-escape. To limit his use, he kept it in his dorm room rather than carry it with him.

But soon, he realized: "All I wanted was to be in my room."

He had 40 minutes between classes: Ten minutes, bike to the dorm. Hit Juul, 20 minutes. Ten minutes, bike to next class. Repeat.

By now his vaping was about maintenance, keeping the craving irritability at bay. He knew things had gotten just ridiculous, but there was nothing to be done about it. He even fixed a Velcro strip on the dresser next to his dorm room bed and stuck the Juul on it, so that as soon as he opened his eyes in the morning he could just reach up for a hit: first, best, only head rush of the day.

One girl on his dorm hall sold Juul pods from stock she had bought from a guy who ordered armloads on the internet. Unlike back home in high school, college students vaped in public everywhere — in lecture halls, at hockey games, in the dorm common rooms.

"Matt was open about wishing he didn't do it," said Tucker Houston, his freshman roommate. "It was a constant battle for him. People would tell him that they'd want to buy a Juul and he'd be like, 'No! You don't want to, it's not cool, it's not fun.' He became known as the juuling anti-Juul advocate."

This past summer, Matt returned home to work construction for his father, a building contractor. In the full sway of his addiction, he stuck the empty pods in his backpack so they wouldn't be spotted in the household trash. He hid the Juul in his bedroom, doing without it on the job for up to six hours at a stretch.

That was rough.

"But I knew if my parents caught me, I couldn't do it again, and that represented a future of not doing it," Matt said. "I rationalized that it was better to do without it briefly, than forever."

Then he found that the delayed gratification from leaving it at home was fantastic. "If you wait an hour, it feels great. But if you wait five hours, it feels unbelievable."

At the end of the day, he would take a long, two-second draw, and keep it in his lungs, a practice called "zeroing," because his body absorbed all the vapor, exhaling none. He'd zero it four or five times, feel dizzy, blink about 10 times, and then be fine.

One day, Matt's mother walked into his room to collect his dirty laundry. There was his backpack, unzipped, open.

The confrontation with his parents was epic.

David Murphy, Matt's father, was startled by the extent of Matt's Juul concealment. He hadn't suspected something was amiss. Matt's behavior never seemed appreciably altered.

The vaping had to end, Mr. Murphy ordered. "I said, 'Nicotine is a lifelong burden. There's a big company with its hand in your pocket, distracting your thought process continuously. Juuling is a huge undocumented risk. Now, how do we come back together as a family and solve this problem?"

Two hours into the tearful conversation, Matt concluded: "I could not justify the addiction anymore. And I realized my parents were my allies. Because I wanted to stop and they wanted me to stop."

Because Juul is so new, there is no consensus protocol for how teenagers should withdraw. Matt devised a weaning regimen: every two hours, five short hits. Then longer breaks, fewer hits.

One June day he was riding shotgun in the Volvo with his old friends. As he was about to take a scheduled hit, he grew despairing and exasperated. He had tried quitting before but it had never worked; would he always be chained to this gadget? Impulsively, he tried to throw the Juul out the car window, but the window stuck. So he abruptly yanked back the sunroof and heaved it to the street.

One friend, sitting in the back, cheered and pumped his fist. But another scowled — he would happily have taken Matt's Juul.

"I felt strong for five minutes," Matt said. "And then I felt really weak. I only realized the magnitude of my addiction when I stopped."

Nicotine withdrawal, he said, was hell. He was overtaken with bouts of anxiety. Who was he without his 11th finger? He would get

JOSHUA BRIGHT FOR THE NEW YORK TIMES

Two gas stations on West Street, separated by a town line, where until recently one sold e-cigarettes to 18-year-olds, and another sold them to 21-year-olds.

the shakes, curl up in his bed, overcome with a sense of powerlessness.

"When Matt withdrew, he'd flip out a lot, especially when other people had it around him," said Jared Stack, a friend since elementary school. "They wouldn't stop doing it just because he had. They didn't care — because they were addicted too."

It was the whirring, the purring, the sound of their Juuls firing up, that would trigger Matt. Yet avoiding his friends was inconceivable.

After three weeks, the worst of it passed. Even still, Matt can tick off to the day how long it's been since he stopped on June 6: 163 days as of Friday.

He transferred to the University of Massachusetts in Lowell, majoring in business and living at home. Whenever he feels the Juul urge now, he tells himself, "I'd have to go through the whole horrible dark time that is being addicted and then quitting."

His eyes brightened as he gulped the last of his pizza, long limbs splayed everywhere. Instead, he said, he tries to help friends who want to quit. "They text me all the time when they're trying. They'll say, 'Did you experience this?'

"And I say, 'Yes,' because I want them to know I understand," he said. "And then I tell them, 'But it gets better.' Because it does."

JAN HOFFMAN is a health behaviors reporter for Science, covering law, opioids, doctor-patient communication and other topics. She previously wrote about young adolescence and family dynamics for Style and was the legal affairs correspondent for Metro.

How to Help Teenagers Quit Vaping

BY JAN HOFFMAN | DEC. 18, 2018

VAPING IS SURGING among American adolescents. According to one national survey, 3.6 million middle and high school students used e-cigarettes in 2018. Another found that the rise in vaping from 2017 to 2018 was the sharpest for any substance the researchers had investigated in the project's 44-year history.

While e-cigarettes swept onto the market about a decade ago on the perception that they were largely benign — useful tools, in fact, to help smokers quit tobacco — concerns are growing over the harm that might be caused by the particles and chemicals users inhale. But the chief worry is over the ingredient commonly found in vaping liquids: nicotine.

Nicotine is the addictive chemical that chains both cigarette smokers and vapers, compelling them to repeated use. Its grip is tough to break.

Teenagers, whose brains are still developing, are particularly susceptible. Parents and educators are discovering that, unfortunately, there are no established protocols to help teenagers quit vaping. But there are measures parents can take.

YOU JUST FOUND YOUR CHILD'S EMPTY VAPING PODS. NOW WHAT?

Don't panic. Also, don't go ballistic.

Before you confront, educate yourself.

WHAT ARE GOOD RESOURCES?

The Centers for Disease Control and Prevention has a useful website on what the federal government currently knows about vaping and e-cigarettes.

The Tobacco Prevention Toolkit, by researchers at Stanford, has a major unit on vaping and Juuls. It is not just for educators: Frequently updated, it has photos, charts and points of discussion that may help you engage your teenager.

NOW THAT I'VE GOT SOME FACTS, WHAT'S NEXT?

Try to see e-cigarettes from the perspective of teenagers. They know that on the scale of all things forbidden, lots of substances — prescription and street drugs, alcohol and cigarettes, to name a few — rank far higher than vapes. While adolescents are canny enough to hide their Juuls from you, they don't really believe that vaping is harmful.

So if you unleash an angry outburst, they will likely push back, thinking you are making a big deal over nothing.

Also realize that the defensiveness and fibbing you're hearing may not be just a child reacting to being caught — the sort of behavior that earns consequences and stern lectures. This is different.

Your teenager may be addicted to nicotine. If you take a draconian stance, you are essentially threatening to put an addicted person into abrupt withdrawal.

You need another approach.

HOW DO I REASON WITH A TEENAGE VAPER?

"The trick is not to try to scare them, because scare tactics don't work at this point," said Dr. Suchitra Krishnan-Sarin, a Yale professor of psychiatry who focuses on adolescent behaviors and tobacco products. "But explaining how these products are making them addicted is the way to go."

Involve them in a conversation. Try to get them to recognize the compulsive quality of their behavior. Show them what researchers know about nicotine addiction and the questions they are raising about the possible long-term harms of vaping.

The goal is to encourage them to want to quit for their own good, not just to give you lip service and continue behind your back.

ARE ALL TEENAGERS WHO TRY VAPING LIKELY TO BECOME ADDICTED?

Not necessarily. Some people can smoke one cigarette and have a glass of wine at a party — and that's it.

ELIZABETH FRANTZ FOR THE NEW YORK TIMES

Several brands of vaping devices. Parents should be able to recognize the different types of devices, experts say, and be on the lookout for them.

But nicotine addiction can happen swiftly and is extremely hard to extinguish. One factor is the amount of nicotine the user is exposed to. Some vaping devices, like Juul, provide high levels.

If there is a family history of addiction, or if other family members are using addictive substances like alcohol, tobacco or drugs at home, a teenager's vulnerability ratchets up.

Teenagers with anxiety or depression can also succumb more quickly. And, doctors note, withdrawing from nicotine can also set off anxiety and depression, at least temporarily.

WHAT'S THE BEST WAY TO QUIT?

Unfortunately, even the experts aren't sure.

"We as researchers are barely keeping up with the increased use and proliferation of these products," Dr. Krishnan-Sarin said. "We haven't started to scratch the surface."

Addiction medicine experts are beginning to suggest some approaches. Ask your pediatrician about them.

Cognitive behavioral therapy can help redirect thoughts when cravings hit. Talk therapy can address underlying anxiety or depression, which may be related to the reason the teen is vaping or have been triggered by quitting.

Other activities can calm an agitated mind in withdrawal, especially yoga, meditation and sports. A teenager can renew acquaintance with a passionate interest or hobby that might have fallen away.

Nicotine patches and prescription cessation medications might be worth exploring, though most are only approved for adults. Dr. Sharon Levy, an adolescent addiction medicine expert at Boston Children's Hospital, has begun prescribing nicotine replacement patches off-label for older teenagers who are motivated to quit.

Experts caution that there is no silver bullet. Instead, they suggest that you try a constellation of approaches.

You might also want to reach out to the school counselor: the struggle to quit could affect academic performance and classroom behavior.

Speaking of schools: Dr. Krishnan-Sarin also recommends that parents contact administrators not only to urge stricter policies toward vaping, but to insist that teachers and students receive vaping education.

THE BOTTOM LINE?

Many forces bore down to compel your child to vape, including social media, peer pressure and the easy accessibility of flavored products. It is really hard for any teenager to step away from those omnipresent enticements.

As your child struggles to break free, make sure they know you're not the enemy, but a steadfast ally.

JAN HOFFMAN is a health behaviors reporter for Science, covering law, opioids, doctor-patient communication and other topics. She previously wrote about young adolescence and family dynamics for Style and was the legal affairs correspondent for Metro.

F.D.A. Accuses Juul and Altria of Backing Off Plan to Stop Youth Vaping

BY SHEILA KAPLAN | JAN. 4, 2019

WASHINGTON — The Food and Drug Administration is accusing Juul and Altria of reneging on promises they made to the government to keep e-cigarettes away from minors.

Dr. Scott Gottlieb, the agency's commissioner, is drafting letters to both companies that will criticize them for publicly pledging to remove nicotine flavor pods from store shelves, while secretly negotiating a financial partnership that seems to do the opposite. He plans to summon top executives of the companies to F.D.A. headquarters to explain how they will stick to their agreements given their new arrangement.

Dr. Gottlieb was disconcerted by the commitments the companies made in the deal announced Dec. 19, under which Altria, the nation's largest maker of traditional cigarettes, agreed to purchase a 35 percent — $13 billion — stake in Juul, the rapidly growing e-cigarette start-up whose products have become hugely popular with teenagers. Public health officials, as well as teachers and parents, fear that e-cigarettes have created a new generation of nicotine addicts.

"Juul and Altria made very specific assertions in their letters and statements to the F.D.A. about the drivers of the youth epidemic," Dr. Gottlieb said in an interview. "Their recent actions and statements appear to be inconsistent with those commitments."

In October, after meeting with Dr. Gottlieb, Altria had agreed to stop selling pod-based e-cigarettes until it received F.D.A. permission or until the youth problem was otherwise addressed. In doing so, Howard A. Willard III, Altria's chief executive, sent the F.D.A. a letter agreeing that pod-based products significantly contribute to the rise in youth vaping.

But the new deal commits the tobacco giant to dramatically expanding the reach of precisely those types of products, by giving

SCOTT MCINTYRE FOR THE NEW YORK TIMES

Altria's deal to purchase 35 percent of Juul Labs gives the fast-growing e-cigarette start-up access to the tobacco giant's shelf space in 230,000 retailers.

Juul access to shelf space in 230,000 retail outlets where Marlboro cigarettes and other Altria tobacco products are sold. (Juul currently sells in 90,000 stores.)

It is a development that startled the F.D.A., which in September had threatened to pull e-cigarettes off the market if companies could not prove within 60 days that they could keep the products away from minors. Altria, Juul and three tobacco companies sent the detailed plans spelling out how they would comply with the agency's request. Now, those plans appear in jeopardy, Dr. Gottlieb said.

"I'm reaching out to both companies to ask them to come in and explain to me why they seem to be deviating from the representation that they already made to the agency about steps they are taking to restrict their products in a way that will decrease access to kids," Dr. Gottlieb said.

It is possible that the F.D.A. will pressure Altria to keep Juul flavor pods off its shelf space, but the tobacco company is not likely to consent.

David Sutton, an Altria spokesman, said the company is merely a minority investor in Juul, and does not control its business.

"We didn't buy Juul; we didn't merge with Juul," Mr. Sutton said. "They are an independent company. Our commitment to preventing youth from using any tobacco product including e-vapor is unchanged."

Chris Bostic, deputy director for policy at the Action on Smoking and Health, a nonprofit health advocacy group, was skeptical.

"This rings so many alarms," Mr. Bostic said. "It seems like this goes counter to what Altria promised. It's certainly not a different company when you are a major owner."

The requested meeting between Dr. Gottlieb and the companies is likely to take place as the agency releases guidelines for a tough new set of vaping industry restrictions that were first announced in November. Dr. Gottlieb has made ending the youth vaping epidemic the cornerstone of his term as commissioner. He also plans to ban menthol cigarettes and flavored cigars, and to reduce the amount of nicotine allowed in cigarettes to nonaddictive levels.

Victoria Davis, a spokeswoman for Juul, said the company is sticking to its plan to curb youth vaping.

"We are as committed as ever to preventing underage use of e-cigarettes, including Juul devices," Ms. Davis said. "We are moving full steam ahead on implementing our action plan to limit youth usage, and this is unchanged since we announced our plan in November. We will respond to the letter when we receive it, and look forward to a constructive dialogue with F.D.A."

The contretemps with the F.D.A. is only the latest headache in Washington for Juul, a company that has had much more success capturing market share in an emerging industry than in navigating the government scrutiny that comes with it.

Juul, based in San Francisco, has quickly captured more than 70 percent of the nation's e-cigarette business since its 2015 launch. But the company spent 2018 fending off federal regulators, lawmakers and parents who attacked Juul for the soaring rate of vaping and nicotine addiction among teenagers who have never smoked. According to the 2018 National Youth Tobacco Survey, released in November, the number of middle and high school students who vape has risen to about 3.6 million.

Juul also revamped its advertisements, and said it would suspend retail sales of teen-friendly flavors like mango, fruit and crème, restricting them to Juul's own site, which has an age verification system. Kevin Burns, the chief executive, said Juul would continue to sell only its mint, tobacco and menthol flavors in stores.

Although individual employees made political contributions earlier, the e-cigarette company first created a political action committee in 2018, and began making political contributions shortly thereafter. Preliminary data for last year shows that Juul and its employees donated about $200,500 to federal candidates and political parties, according to the Center for Responsive Politics, which tracks campaign spending. The company also spent nearly $900,000 in 2018 on lobbyists and advisers to reposition itself as a public health company eager to disrupt the tobacco business.

That's a fraction of what large tobacco companies spend. Altria spent more than $7 million on lobbying last year, and early reports for the 2017-18 campaign cycle, which have not all been filed, showed the company and its employees donated more than $2.8 million to federal candidates and political party committees, mostly Republican.

Juul had weak ties to the Trump administration and congressional Republicans and sought better connections.

Now, Juul will have access to Altria's deep lobbying pockets and more experienced government relations team, but such support cuts both ways.

"Altria should be very careful about using its significant investment to influence Juul policy," said Marc Scheineson, a partner at Alston & Bird, whose clients at the firm include small tobacco companies. "This development is likely to make F.D.A. even more skeptical," he said, of products like Juul and other alternative nicotine delivery systems that "are designed to wean smokers off combustible products and not create a new generation of dual-tobacco users."

Indeed, sources within the public health community fear that the inserts that Altria has agreed to include in Marlboro and other cigarette packs, advertising Juul, might encourage smokers to use both products, rather than quit.

After Altria purchased its stake in Juul, Precision Strategies, a public relations firm founded by former aides to President Barack Obama, ended its contract with the company.

KENNETH P. VOGEL contributed reporting.

Glossary

anecdotal Based on facts or observation rather than more rigorous modes of scientific study.

anomalous Inconsistent with what is normal or expected.

carcinogenic Possessing ingredients that contain the ability to cause cancer.

cessation The process of ending or quitting something.

detractor A person who criticizes or critiques someone or something.

e-cigarette A cigarette-shaped device containing liquid nicotine that is vaporized and inhaled, resembling the experience of smoking tobacco-based cigarettes.

enigmatic Difficult to understand or mysterious.

epidemiology The branch of medicine that deals with the study of the prevalence and patterns of health and disease conditions across a population.

formaldehyde A strong-smelling carcinogenic gas used primarily as a disinfectant and preservative. Found in tobacco cigarettes.

gateway An opening or means of access to a place or pattern. Used to denote a drug that may not be habit-forming in itself but has the potential to lead to the use of other addictive drugs.

opioids A class of highly addictive narcotic drugs that are intended to relieve pain.

palate A person's appreciation of taste and flavor.

particulate A very small bit of matter, such as dust or soot.

preposterous Contrary to reason or popular belief; utterly absurd or ridiculous.

regulation A rule or directive made by an authority intended to affect how something should be done.

stigma A mark of shame or disgrace associated with a particular behavior, quality, circumstance, or person.

stimulant A substance that raises the level of physiological or nervous energy in a person.

toxicants Toxic substances introduced into an environment.

ubiquitous Present or found everywhere.

vernacular The language or dialect spoken by ordinary people in a particular region or territory.

zeitgeist The defining mood or spirit of a particular era, shown by the ideas and beliefs of the time.

Media Literacy Terms

"Media literacy" refers to the ability to access, understand, critically assess and create media. The following terms are important components of media literacy, and they will help you critically engage with the articles in this title.

angle The aspect of a news story that a journalist focuses on and develops.

attribution The method by which a source is identified or by which facts and information are assigned to the person who provided them.

balance Principle of journalism that both perspectives of an argument should be presented in a fair way.

bias A disposition of prejudice in favor of a certain idea, person or perspective.

byline Name of the writer, usually placed between the headline and the story.

caption Identifying copy for a picture; also called a legend or cutline.

chronological order Method of writing a story presenting the details of the story in the order in which they occurred.

column A type of story that is a regular feature, often on a recurring topic, written by the same journalist, generally known as a columnist.

commentary A type of story that is an expression of opinion on recent events by a journalist generally known as a commentator.

credibility The quality of being trustworthy and believable, said of a journalistic source.

editorial Article of opinion or interpretation.

fake news A fictional or made-up story presented in the style of a legitimate news story, intended to deceive readers; also commonly used to criticize legitimate news that one dislikes because of its perspective or unfavorable coverage of a subject.

feature story Article designed to entertain as well as to inform.

impartiality Principle of journalism that a story should not reflect a journalist's bias and should contain balance.

intention The motive or reason behind something, such as the publication of a news story.

motive The reason behind something, such as the publication of a news story or a source's perspective on an issue.

news story An article or style of expository writing that reports news, generally in a straightforward fashion and without editorial comment.

op-ed An opinion piece that reflects a prominent individual's opinion on a topic of interest.

paraphrase The summary of an individual's words, with attribution, rather than a direct quotation of their exact words.

plagiarism An attempt to pass another person's work as one's own without attribution.

quotation The use of an individual's exact words indicated by the use of quotation marks and proper attribution.

reliability The quality of being dependable and accurate, said of a journalistic source.

source The origin of the information reported in journalism.

tone A manner of expression in writing or speech.

Media Literacy Questions

1. Identify the various sources cited in the article "A Hot Debate Over E-Cigarettes as a Path to Tobacco, or From It" (on page 61). How does Sabrina Tavernise attribute information to each of these sources in her article? How effective are Tavernise's attributions in helping the reader identify her sources?

2. In "Juul Suspends Selling Most E-Cigarette Flavors in Stores" (on page 188), Sheila Kaplan and Jan Hoffman directly quote Kevin Burns. What are the strengths of the use of a direct quote as opposed to a paraphrase? What are the weaknesses?

3. Compare the headlines of "E-Cigarettes, by Other Names, Lure Young and Worry Experts" (on page 132) and "Where Vapor Comes Sweeping Down the Plain" (on page 22). Which is a more compelling headline, and why? How could the less compelling headline be changed to better draw the reader's interest?

4. What type of story is "Is Vaping Worse Than Smoking?" (on page 73)? Can you identify another article in this collection that is the same type of story?

5. Does Kate Zernike demonstrate the journalistic principle of balance in her article " 'I Can't Stop': Schools Struggle With Vaping Explosion" (on page 146)? If so, how did she do so? If not, what could Zernike have included to make her article more balanced?

6. Does "The Price of Cool: A Teenager, a Juul and Nicotine Addiction" (on page 194) use multiple sources? What are the strengths of using multiple sources in a journalistic piece? What are the weaknesses of relying heavily on only one or a few sources?

7. "She Couldn't Quit Smoking. Then She Tried Juul." (on page 97) features photographs. What do these photographs add to the article?

8. What is the intention of the article "How to Help Teenagers Quit Vaping" (on page 203)? How effectively does it achieve its intended purpose?

9. Analyze the authors' reporting in "Did Juul Lure Teenagers and Get 'Customers for Life'?" (on page 152) and "Addicted to Vaped Nicotine, Teenagers Have No Clear Path to Quitting" (on page 163). Do you think the reporting is more impartial in one article than in the other? If so, why do you think so?

10. Often, as a news story develops, a journalist's attitude toward the subject may change. Compare "The E-Cigarette Industry, Waiting to Exhale" (on page 10) and "Dire Warnings by Big Tobacco on E-Smoking" (on page 112), both by Matt Richtel. Did new information discovered between the publication of these two articles change Richtel's perspective?

11. Identify each of the sources in "Did Juul Lure Teenagers and Get 'Customers for Life'?" (on page 152) as a primary source or a secondary source. Evaluate the reliability and credibility of each source. How does your evaluation of each source change your perspective on this article?

Citations

All citations in this list are formatted according to the Modern Language Association's (MLA) style guide.

BOOK CITATION

THE NEW YORK TIMES EDITORIAL STAFF. *Vaping: Big Business*. New York: New York Times Educational Publishing, 2020.

ONLINE ARTICLE CITATIONS

BAKALAR, NICHOLAS. "From 0 to 10 Million: Vaping Takes Off in the U.S." *The New York Times*, 31 Aug. 2018, https://www.nytimes.com/2018/08/31/health/vaping-cigarettes-nicotine.html.

BENNETT, JESSICA. " 'Vape' Joins Pot Lingo as Oxford's Word of the Year." *The New York Times*, 21 Nov. 2014, https://www.nytimes.com/2014/11/23/fashion/vape-joins-pot-lingo-as-oxfords-word-of-the-year.html.

CARROLL, AARON E. "E-Cigarettes Are Safer, but Not Exactly Safe." *The New York Times*, 10 May 2016, https://www.nytimes.com/2016/05/11/upshot/e-cigarettes-are-safer-but-not-exactly-safe.html.

FAUSSET, RICHARD. "Feeling Let Down and Left Behind, With Little Hope for Better." *The New York Times*, 25 May 2016, https://www.nytimes.com/2016/05/26/us/feeling-let-down-and-left-behind-with-little-hope-for-better.html.

FORTIN, JACEY. "Plain Old Vaping Gives Way to 'Dripping' Among Teenagers, Study Says." *The New York Times*, 7 Feb. 2017, https://www.nytimes.com/2017/02/07/health/ecigarettes-dripping-high-school-student.html.

FORTIN, JACEY. "This May Be a First: Exploding Vape Pen Kills a Florida Man." *The New York Times*, 16 May 2018, https://www.nytimes.com/2018/05/16/us/man-killed-vape-explosion.html.

HOFFMAN, JAN. "Addicted to Vaped Nicotine, Teenagers Have No Clear Path to Quitting." *The New York Times*, 18 Dec. 2018, https://www.nytimes.com/2018/12/18/health/vaping-nicotine-teenagers.html.

HOFFMAN, JAN. "How to Help Teenagers Quit Vaping." *The New York Times*, 18 Dec. 2018, https://www.nytimes.com/2018/12/18/health/vaping-teens-nicotine.html.

HOFFMAN, JAN. "Marijuana and Vaping Are More Popular Than Cigarettes Among Teenagers." *The New York Times*, 14 Dec. 2017, https://www.nytimes.com/2017/12/14/health/teen-drug-smoking.html.

HOFFMAN, JAN. "The Price of Cool: A Teenager, a Juul and Nicotine Addiction." *The New York Times*, 16 Nov. 2018, https://www.nytimes.com/2018/11/16/health/vaping-juul-teens-addiction-nicotine.html.

HOFFMAN, JAN. "Q&A: The ABCs of E-Cigarettes." *The New York Times*, 15 Nov. 2018, https://www.nytimes.com/2018/11/15/health/qna-ecigarettes-teenagers.html.

HOFFMAN, JAN. "San Francisco Voters Uphold Ban on Flavored Vaping Products." *The New York Times*, 6 June 2018, https://www.nytimes.com/2018/06/06/health/vaping-ban-san-francisco.html.

HOFFMAN, JAN. "She Couldn't Quit Smoking. Then She Tried Juul." *The New York Times*, 16 Nov. 2018, https://www.nytimes.com/2018/11/16/health/vaping-juul-nicotine-quit-smokers.html.

INTERLANDI, JENEEN. "Vaping Is Big Tobacco's Bait and Switch." *The New York Times*, 8 Mar. 2019, https://www.nytimes.com/2019/03/08/opinion/editorials/vaping-ecigarettes-nicotine-safe.html.

KAPLAN, SHEILA. "Altria to Stop Selling Some E-Cigarette Brands That Appeal to Youths." *The New York Times*, 25 Oct. 2018, https://www.nytimes.com/2018/10/25/health/altria-vaping-ecigarettes.html.

KAPLAN, SHEILA. "F.D.A. Accuses Juul and Altria of Backing Off Plan to Stop Youth Vaping." *The New York Times*, 4 Jan. 2019, https://www.nytimes.com/2019/01/04/health/fda-juul-altria-youth-vaping.html.

KAPLAN, SHEILA. "Vaping Can Be Addictive and May Lure Teenagers to Smoking, Science Panel Concludes." *The New York Times*, 23 Jan. 2018, https://www.nytimes.com/2018/01/23/health/e-cigarettes-smoking-fda-tobacco.html.

KAPLAN, SHEILA, AND JAN HOFFMAN. "Juul Suspends Selling Most E-Cigarette Flavors in Stores." *The New York Times*, 13 Nov. 2018, https://www.nytimes.com/2018/11/13/health/juul-ecigarettes-vaping-teenagers.html.

LIPTON, ERIC. "A Lobbyist Wrote the Bill. Will the Tobacco Industry Win Its E-Cigarette Fight?" *The New York Times*, 2 Sept. 2016, https://www

.nytimes.com/2016/09/03/us/politics/e-cigarettes-vaping-cigars-fda-altria
.html.

MEIER, BARRY. "Race to Deliver Nicotine's Punch, With Less Risk." *The New York Times*, 24 Dec. 2014, https://www.nytimes.com/2014/12/25/business/race-to-deliver-nicotines-punch-with-less-risk.html.

NIR, SARAH MASLIN. "New York State Bans Vaping Anywhere Cigarettes Are Prohibited." *The New York Times*, 23 Oct. 2017, https://www.nytimes.com/2017/10/23/nyregion/new-york-bans-vaping-ecigs-bars-restaurants.html.

NOCERA, JOE. "Can E-Cigarettes Save Lives?" *The New York Times*, 16 Oct. 2015, https://www.nytimes.com/2015/10/17/opinion/can-e-cigarettes-save-lives.html.

NOCERA, JOE. "Is Vaping Worse Than Smoking?" *The New York Times*, 27 Jan. 2015, https://www.nytimes.com/2015/01/27/opinion/joe-nocera-is-vaping-worse-than-smoking.html.

NOCERA, JOE. "Smoking, Vaping, and Nicotine." *The New York Times*, 26 May 2015, https://www.nytimes.com/2015/05/26/opinion/joe-nocera-smoking-vaping-and-nicotine.html.

RICHTEL, MATT. "Dire Warnings by Big Tobacco on E-Smoking." *The New York Times*, 28 Sept. 2014, https://www.nytimes.com/2014/09/29/business/dire-warnings-by-big-tobacco-on-e-smoking-.html.

RICHTEL, MATT. "The E-Cigarette Industry, Waiting to Exhale." *The New York Times*, 26 Oct. 2013, https://www.nytimes.com/2013/10/27/business/the-e-cigarette-industry-waiting-to-exhale.html.

RICHTEL, MATT. "E-Cigarette Makers Are in an Arms Race for Exotic Vapor Flavors." *The New York Times*, 15 July 2014, https://www.nytimes.com/2014/07/16/business/e-cigarette-makers-are-in-an-arms-race-for-exotic-vapor-flavors.html.

RICHTEL, MATT. "E-Cigarettes, by Other Names, Lure Young and Worry Experts." *The New York Times*, 4 Mar. 2014, https://www.nytimes.com/2014/03/05/business/e-cigarettes-under-aliases-elude-the-authorities.html.

RICHTEL, MATT. "Selling a Poison by the Barrel: Liquid Nicotine for E-Cigarettes." *The New York Times*, 23 Mar. 2014, https://www.nytimes.com/2014/03/24/business/selling-a-poison-by-the-barrel-liquid-nicotine-for-e-cigarettes.html.

RICHTEL, MATT. "Some E-Cigarettes Deliver a Puff of Carcinogens." *The New

York Times*, 3 May 2014, https://www.nytimes.com/2014/05/04/business/some-e-cigarettes-deliver-a-puff-of-carcinogens.html.

RICHTEL, MATT. "Where Vapor Comes Sweeping Down the Plain." *The New York Times*, 26 Apr. 2014, https://www.nytimes.com/2014/04/27/business/e-cigarettes-take-hold-in-oklahoma.html.

RICHTEL, MATT, AND SHEILA KAPLAN. "Did Juul Lure Teenagers and Get 'Customers for Life'?" *The New York Times*, 27 Aug. 2018, https://www.nytimes.com/2018/08/27/science/juul-vaping-teen-marketing.html.

RICHTEL, MATT, AND SHEILA KAPLAN. "First Death in a Spate of Vaping Sicknesses Reported by Health Officials." *The New York Times*, 23 Aug. 2019, https://www.nytimes.com/2019/08/23/health/vaping-death-cdc.html.

SPAN, PAULA. "Some Older Smokers Turn to Vaping. That May Not Be a Bad Idea." *The New York Times*, 8 Dec. 2017, https://www.nytimes.com/2017/12/08/health/smokers-vaping-ecigarettes-elderly.html.

TAVERNISE, SABRINA. "E-Cigarette Use by U.S. Teenagers Rose Last Year, Report Says." *The New York Times*, 14 Apr. 2016, https://www.nytimes.com/2016/04/15/health/e-cigarettes-smoking-teenagers.html.

TAVERNISE, SABRINA. "F.D.A. Imposes Rules for E-Cigarettes in a Landmark Move." *The New York Times*, 5 May 2016, https://www.nytimes.com/2016/05/06/science/fda-rules-electronic-cigarettes.html.

TAVERNISE, SABRINA. "A Hot Debate Over E-Cigarettes as a Path to Tobacco, or From It." *The New York Times*, 22 Feb. 2014, https://www.nytimes.com/2014/02/23/health/a-hot-debate-over-e-cigarettes-as-a-path-to-tobacco-or-from-it.html.

TAVERNISE, SABRINA. "Safer to Puff, E-Cigarettes Can't Shake Their Reputation as a Menace." *The New York Times*, 1 Nov. 2016, https://www.nytimes.com/2016/11/02/health/e-cigarette-vape-njoy-bankruptcy.html.

TAVERNISE, SABRINA. "Smokers Urged to Switch to E-Cigarettes by British Medical Group." *The New York Times*, 27 Apr. 2016, https://www.nytimes.com/2016/04/28/health/e-cigarettes-vaping-quitting-smoking-royal-college-of-physicians.html.

THOMAS, KATIE. "Vaping Products That Look Like Juice Boxes and Candy Are Target of Crackdown." *The New York Times*, 1 May 2018, https://www.nytimes.com/2018/05/01/health/fda-crackdown-vaping-children.html.

ZERNIKE, KATE. " 'I Can't Stop': Schools Struggle With Vaping Explosion." *The New York Times*, 2 Apr. 2018, https://www.nytimes.com/2018/04/02/health/vaping-ecigarettes-addiction-teen.html.

Index

A

Abrams, David B., 63, 66, 88, 94
Altria, 8, 14, 16, 50, 51, 54, 69, 71, 112, 113, 115, 126, 184-187, 207-211
American Cancer Society, 30, 65, 91, 144, 181
American Heart Association, 30, 181
American Lung Association, 30, 54, 175, 176, 181
American Vaping Association, 96, 121, 122, 150, 171
Anise, Roy, 14, 16
Arias, Ileana, 129
Arnott, Deborah, 91-92

B

Benowitz, Neal L., 65, 66, 106
Big Tobacco, 8, 11, 20, 31, 32, 62, 66, 67, 68, 72, 78, 80, 81, 96, 112-116, 119, 124-127
Bishop, Sanford D., Jr., 51, 52
Bloomberg, Michael R., 176, 181-182
Blu, 11, 15, 16, 20, 34, 35, 69-70
Bostic, Chris, 209
Bowen, Adam, 156, 158
Brandt, Allan M., 115-116
British American Tobacco, 67, 191
Britton, John, 66, 82
Brown, Blake, 141
Burns, Kevin, 189, 190-191, 210
Burwell, Sylvia Mathews, 171

C

Cabrera, Cynthia, 106, 114-115
Campaign for Tobacco-Free Kids, 52, 68, 80, 121, 159, 172, 182, 187, 189
cancer, 12, 16, 35, 42, 52, 55, 57, 58, 63, 66, 69, 72, 73, 74, 75, 82, 84, 85, 98, 99, 103, 107, 115, 117, 119, 124, 147, 171, 192
cannabis/marijuana, 38, 39, 59, 128, 130, 143-145, 149, 192, 198
Cantrell, Lee, 104, 106
carcinogens, 10, 24, 57, 61, 69, 70, 73, 76, 94, 97, 98, 107-111, 117, 141, 143, 147, 148, 189, 196
Carmona, Richard H., 13, 19-20, 37
Centers for Disease Control and Prevention (C.D.C.), 13, 18, 55, 64, 82, 83, 88, 90, 93, 94, 95, 99, 119, 125, 128, 129, 133-134, 137, 139, 159, 175, 203
Cole, Tom, 50, 51
Compton, Wilson, 143, 144
Conley, Gregory, 96, 121, 122-123, 150
Cordisco, Stephanie, 114
Cuomo, Andrew M., 175

D

David, Matt, 154
Davis, Victoria, 209
D'Elia, Tallmadge, 122
dripping, 109, 140-142
Durbin, Richard J., 36-37

E

Eaton, David, 118
e-cigarettes/vaping
  banning of, 49, 89, 175-176, 180-183
  deaths/illnesses from, 104, 122, 128-131, 178
  as gateway to tobacco, 18, 19, 61, 64, 80, 82-83, 86-87, 117-121, 137, 155
  growth of industry, 11, 55-56, 69, 83, 138, 175
  how they work, 57
  and older smokers, 93-96
  quitting use of, 163-169, 203-206
  regulation of, 17, 19, 20-21, 24-25, 28, 29-30, 31, 44, 49-54, 62, 80, 83, 103, 105, 126, 141, 170-174, 177-179
  safety/dangers of, 25, 28, 35, 49-50, 57-60, 61-66,

222 VAPING

73–75, 79–81, 82–84,
  85–87, 88–92, 103–106,
  107–111
and sales to minors, 17,
  24, 29, 32, 85, 87, 126,
  141, 170, 193
and smoking cessation,
  12, 18, 19–20, 26, 29–30,
  32, 35, 37, 55, 58, 82–84,
  86, 91, 93, 97–102, 118,
  155
and use by teens, 7,
  18, 50, 59–60, 64, 85,
  117–121, 126, 132–136,
  137–139, 140–142,
  143–145, 146–151,
  152–162, 163–169, 181,
  192, 195–196, 203
emphysema, 12, 72

F

Family Smoking Prevention and Tobacco Control Act, 17
flavors, debate over, 33–37, 120, 180–183
formaldehyde, 7, 73, 74, 75, 107, 109
Foundation for a Smoke-Free World, 127
Frieden, Thomas R., 89–90, 91, 139

G

Gardiner, Phil, 182
Gentry, Jeffrey S., 69
Gerking, Nancy, 130
Giovino, Gary A., 173
Glantz, Stanton A., 17, 18, 19, 61, 62, 64, 66, 83, 84
Glynn, Thomas J., 65, 91, 92, 144
Goniewicz, Maciej L., 108, 111

Gore, Sean, 24–26, 27–28, 30, 31, 32
Gottlieb, Scott, 119, 121, 125–126, 127, 155, 162, 178, 179, 186, 190, 191, 207, 208, 209
Gould, Ashley, 147, 161

H

Halpern-Felsher, Bonnie, 167, 169
Healey, Maura, 153, 190
Healy, Jason, 34
heart disease, 12, 57, 96, 107, 112, 124
Herzog, Bonnie, 16, 63, 110–111, 119, 138
Hirsch, Jonathan, 166–167
Holcomb, John, 130
hookahs/hookah pens, 49, 91, 132, 133, 134, 135, 136, 139, 173

I

iQOS, 70–71, 118, 187

J

Jackler, Robert K., 113, 115
Jenson, Desmond, 185
Juul, 8, 59, 97–102, 126–127, 131, 146, 147, 149, 151, 152–162, 163, 164, 177, 181, 184, 185, 188–193, 194–202, 203, 207–211

K

Kessler, David, 76–77
Kessler, Murray S., 15, 16
Kilcoyne, Allison, 145
King, Brian, 93, 95, 129, 134
Kligman, Brittany, 97–98, 99, 100–102
Kovarik, Jennifer, 147
Krishnan-Sarin, Suchitra, 140, 141, 142, 204, 205, 206

L

Landrieu, Mary, 51, 52
Leventhal, Adam, 119–120
Levy, Sharon, 59, 60, 168–169, 206
Lindblom, Eric, 155, 180
liquid nicotine, 7, 14, 24, 42, 50, 57, 63, 73, 89, 103–106, 107–111, 140–141, 147, 172, 177–179
lobbyists for e-cigarette and cigar industries, 49–54
Lorillard, 11, 15, 16, 33, 34, 69
Lowey, Nita M., 51–52
lung cancer, 12, 66, 103

M

MarkTen, 16, 69, 112, 113, 114, 186
McAfee, Tim, 13, 18
McDonald, Emily Anne, 136
Miech, Richard A., 150
Miller, Tom, 156
Monitoring the Future study, 91, 148–149, 150, 163
Monsees, James, 154, 158, 161, 162
Myers, Matthew L., 52, 68, 80, 81, 121, 159, 172, 174, 182

N

National Youth Tobacco Survey, 139, 195, 210
nicotine, 8, 14, 17, 19, 21, 25, 26, 28, 29, 32, 33, 39, 40, 49, 55, 56, 58–59, 60, 61, 63, 64, 65, 66, 74, 76–78, 79, 82, 84, 86, 88, 91, 94, 95, 98, 180, 187, 192

INDEX **223**

addiction to, 33, 62, 85, 113, 114, 115, 117, 163–169, 175, 176, 181, 188, 189, 193, 194–202, 204, 205

liquid nicotine, 7, 10, 14, 22, 24, 27, 42, 50, 57, 63, 73, 89, 93, 103–106, 107–111, 140–141, 147, 172, 177–179

new delivery systems, 67–72

Nitzkin, Joel L., 172

NJOY, 10, 11, 12, 13, 14, 15, 16, 17, 20, 21, 34, 35, 36, 37, 53, 69, 70, 79, 80, 88, 108, 158

O

Ohlhausen, Maureen K., 178
Ownbey, Pat, 28–29, 30, 32

P

Paul, Chip, 23, 105–106
Perraut, Andrew, 53
Peyton, David, 75
Phelps, William, 113, 115
Philip Morris International, 8, 14, 67, 68, 70, 71, 72, 81, 96, 118, 127, 147, 187
Picavet, Patrick, 67–68, 70
Picciotto, Marina, 164–165
Proctor, Robert N., 114

Q

Querbach, Adam, 133, 136

R

Rabinowitz, Josh, 108–109
Reidmohr, Alison, 161
Renzulli, Caroline, 189–190
Reynolds American/R. J. Reynolds Tobacco Company, 16, 20, 33, 34, 50, 54, 68, 69, 70, 71, 72, 112, 113, 114, 121, 161, 180, 181, 182, 183, 191

Rockefeller, Jay, 34
Rodgers, Jameson, 179
Royal College of Physicians, 82, 84, 120, 121
Rubinstein, Mark L., 148

S

Sachnoff, Ira, 163
Saunders, Janine, 134
Schepis, Ty S., 145
Schroeder, Steven, 94, 96
Seyler, Jeff, 176
Shihadeh, Alan, 109, 110, 111
Siegel, Michael, 61, 62, 65, 66, 74
Singh, Aman, 176
Steinberg, Michael B., 62
Sturman, Paul, 79
Sutton, David, 51, 209
Sweanor, David, 89

T

Tanski, Susanne E., 166, 167, 168
tar, 7, 10, 57, 61, 62, 63, 77, 82, 85, 89, 117, 125, 138, 147, 171, 189, 196
Tobacco-Free Kids Action Fund, 181
Tobacco Prevention Toolkit, 169, 203
Trump, Donald/Trump administration, 43, 44, 46, 210

U

U.S. Food and Drug Administration, 17, 18, 20, 24, 28, 29, 34, 44, 49–54, 58, 60, 62, 66, 71, 72, 76–78, 79, 80, 85, 93, 94, 95, 96, 97, 99, 105, 108, 118, 119, 121, 125, 128, 129, 134, 154, 155, 156, 163, 166, 170–174, 177–179, 184, 186–187, 188, 190, 193, 207–211

V

"vape," as Oxford Dictionaries Word of the Year, 38–39
vape shops, 22–23, 25, 44, 173
Vuse, 16, 20, 34, 35, 113, 181, 191

W

Wagener, Theodore L., 26–27
Walker, Natalie, 19
Walsh, Daniel, 23
Walsh, James, 52–53
Warner, Kenneth E., 83, 90, 91, 137, 138
Warrender, Nick, 178
Webb, Ashley, 105
Weiss, Craig, 11, 12, 13, 14, 16–17, 18–19, 20, 21, 34, 35, 36, 37, 158
Weiss, Mark, 17
West, Robert, 65, 84
Wexler, Becky, 187
Whitson, Nick, 22, 24
Wikler, Daniel I., 89, 92
Willard, Howard A., 184, 186, 207
World Health Organization, 114, 127

Z

Zeller, Mitch, 18, 50, 63, 76–78, 118, 121, 129, 172, 173, 178

This book is current up until the time of printing. For the most up-to-date reporting, visit www.nytimes.com.